Tom Paul
Brixton ?

RAD
ACTI\

C000132936

It is the summer of 1986, shortly after Chernobyl, and in a pub in Santon Bridge, Cumbria, within spitting distance of Windscale Nuclear Power Station, they are holding the annual world-famous 'Biggest Liar In The World Competition'. As well as the media and the local farmers, Edward Julius Asbach, local potter and dialect enthusiast, is there with his little tape recorder. And a good job he is, as that night the competition proves to be without parallel. For after three tame performances by three very old Cumbrian liars, the young enigmatic Tommy Little takes to the floor and proceeds to spin a tale lasting over seven hours . . . Little's preposterous story 'Radio Activity' (originally in dialect but helpfully translated and edited by Asbach) concerns the adventures of a roving innocent called William Stapleton. Stapleton, a local college teacher and valve-wireless buff, one evening gets too involved in what he's listening to and finds himself making international, magic carpet journeys at the whim of his defective tuning knob. Time and time over he keeps travelling between Tangiers and Cumbria and at both ends is falsely assumed to be a local radio producer. Trying always for a quiet life and to get himself safely home, he is bullied and abused by celebrities as diverse as producers Si Mohammed, and Geoffrey Beeston, industrial Publicity Officer Wilfred Glenridding and the unparalleled Tangerine poet Moulay Ismail. And for some reason whenever he is 'working for' 'Radio Cumbria' he is perpetually travelling on his way to the same old destination to investigate a mysteriously repetitive industrial 'leak'.

E. J. Asbach has edited the tale into several 'emissions' and interspersed them – it is not known at first, why – with the story of his own relationship with his late father Klaus. The latter, a former Sudeten German P.O.W., had in many ways led an even more preposterous existence than the fictional William Stapleton. West Cumbria's answer to Gulley Jimson, the climax of Klaus's story is seen to be strangely fitting with the substance of his son's remarkable tapes.

E. J. Asbach entrusted John Murray with the manuscript of *Radio Activity*. This is now presented to the outside world as a demonstration of Asbach Jr's thesis that (following Günther Grass who claims the privilege for Berlin) the area around Santon Bridge, Cumbria is most symptomatic of the realities of our age.

1

by the same author:

SAMARKAND

KIN

PLEASURE

RADIO ACTIVITY,

A CUMBRIAN TALE IN FIVE EMISSIONS

BY

JOHN MURRAY.

LINCOLN,
Sunk Island Publishing,
1993.

First published 1993 by
Sunk Island Publishing
P.O. Box 74, Lincoln LN1 1QG, England

Typography by John Wardle
Cover by Geoffrey Mark Matthews

ISBN 1 874778 10 8

Printed by Intype, London

CONTENTS

PROLOGUE. How John Murray got his hands on *Radio Activity.*   9

Asbach observes liars old and new.   17
RADIO ACTIVITY, EMISSION THE FIRST.   33
Asbach replenishes his glass and recalls his deviant father, Klaus.   81
RADIO ACTIVITY, EMISSION THE SECOND.   95
Asbach recalls his Coming of Age and The Great Purge.   122
RADIO ACTIVITY, EMISSION THE THIRD.   134
Klaus has farcical dealings with policemen both honest and corrupt.   152
RADIO ACTIVITY, EMISSION THE FOURTH.   168
Klaus dies of an extremely rare cancer while gasping for a Wee Willem.   175
RADIO ACTIVITY, EMISSION THE FIFTH.   181

EPILOGUE. Asbach revealed as a fantastic liar; John Murray as a colossal dupe. Brief addendum with regard to cataclysmic changes in Eastern Europe since 1989.   187

JOHN MURRAY *was born in West Cumbria in 1950. He read Sanskrit at Oxford and is a full-time writer. His work has appeared widely in magazines and anthologies, and he has published two novels and a collection of short stories. He has recently resumed the editorship of* Panurge *fiction magazine, which he founded in 1984 and edited until 1987. He lives in Brampton, Cumbria.*

for IONE, SAM, TILDA, CRESSIDA and BIG IONE

This engaging trait may perhaps be capped by an anecdote related of another poet, a descendant of many Pre-Raphaelites, of whom it was related that whilst reading his friend's valuable books at that friend's breakfast table he was in the habit of marking his place with a slice of bacon. This excellent and touching anecdote I know to be untrue . . . Such as it is, it goes to show that the habit of anecdote, incisive however wanting in veracity, is still remaining to the surviving connections of this Old Circle.

FORD MADOX FORD: *Ancient Lights*

He was having a lot of trouble with my name. He could not pronounce Tigellinus, and called me either Tigelinius or Tinegillus. Whenever they corrected him he snarled, 'I don't give a damn. What rot. Why should I stuff my brains with trash?' If he came upon a difficult figure of speech or several foreign words in a row he would simply mark it in his book with a 'Z' and say, 'I'm crossing this out.'

ALEXANDER KUPRIN: *I Was An Actor*

8

PROLOGUE.

How John Murray got his hands on RADIO ACTIVITY.

EDWARD Julius Asbach's extraordinary manuscript *Radio Activity* came into my possession in the autumn of 1987, just as I was about to transfer from the industrial west to the rural north of this equally extraordinary county. It arrived unsolicited as a bulky parcel bearing a laughably inadequate postage, so that I was obliged to pay our smiling postman the considerable excess. Put out of temper by that I was hardly mollified to be instructed in Asbach's remarkably terse cover letter that I was to meet him on the 18th of October at exactly 11 a.m. inside the Caramelle Cafe in Workington Bus Station. At this rather singular rendezvous, it was anticipated that I would offer my 'professional' (his quotes) opinion on its merits, and afterwards, he hoped, secure its prompt and profitable publication. Asbach wrote that he had several times heard and seen me interviewed on local radio and TV, and as I was – as far as he knew – the only native locally-living novelist who wrote about local matters, I was the obvious candidate for doing him these 'good offices' (my quotes). He had, furthermore, very good reasons for arranging our meeting at Workington, approximately ten miles from both our homes. Asbach looked forward to seeing me as stated, and if I chose to make some exhaustive notes on his book in advance, that would doubtless aid the two of us as we sat over our coffee in the Caramelle.

I looked at the calendar and saw that today was the 16th of October. I frowned and thought of ringing him at his home and telling him to go and drown himself. Anyone who has ever published anything will be aware of the fearless frankness with which assorted geniuses will turn up on one's doorstep demanding instant assessment of a thousand page block-buster about e.g. pony trekking and provincial adultery. Asbach's brusque cover letter had that feel about it, and I determined as I sat down to take a quick flick through it, that if the first sentence never mind the first page, failed to engage me, I would immediately return *Radio Activity* without any postage at all upon it.

I read it through in two sittings: amused, amazed, disturbed and above all occasionally embarrassed. I was wincing with embarrassment in parts, although for the life of me I can't think what it was that embarrassed me about someone else's book, which was in turn about someone else's invented tall story. This tall story was actually first told at the annual 'Biggest Liar In The World' competition at Santon Bridge near Sellafield in the year of Chernobyl 1986. I had heard of this competition of course, and vaguely remembered reading local newspaper reports about it back in the Seventies. I was amazed to learn from *Radio Activity* that in 1986, someone, a local at that, had taken the opportunity of using this ancient custom to subtly/unsubtly satirise contentious monolithic industries, the attitudes of local people, the nature of local customs. On the other hand, I reflected, as the competition is theoretically intended to be open to the *world*, then surely the standard of entries should occasionally be of the level and proficiency of Tommy Little's. That is, of a seven hour oral fable in the hitherto unknown Moroccan-Cumbrian Magical/Mundane Realistic/Fabular Mode.

More obvious things perplexed me as I read through *Radio Activity*. Firstly, I didn't understand why the Tommy Little fable was being split up into numbered 'emissions', and interleaved with the comical if touching relationship of Asbach with his extraordinary P.O.W. father Klaus. Why, for all the likeable nature of Klaus's wild adventures, was Little's lying fable being meshed with the tale of Asbach's Dad? By the end of the book of course it was crystal clear, and I for one would not have guessed in advance the significant relationship between the two 'absurd' heroes, Stapleton and Asbach Snr.

Secondly, I walk around in a dream much of the time myself, but even I was aware that the Caramelle Cafe closed down a considerable time ago. As a schoolboy back in 1968 I used to drink coffee and smoke *Ariels* there with my girlfriend. Did Asbach intend our rendezvous there as some sort of joke? After reading his book I was prepared for anything in the way of upside down logic, practical jokes, ridiculous anti-climaxes. I, like Asbach Jr., like William Stapleton, like Tommy Little, knew everything about the local tradition of 'gammin' and tomfoolery.

Asbach was standing there outside the dusty frontage of the closed Caramelle when I arrived in on the Border Clipper. The first thing to strike me about him was that the brusqueness of his letter was merely a cover for the complicatedly sensitive, abrasive nature of his temperament. He greeted me quite shyly at first, made a joke about not having been at this particular venue since 1969, and we proceeded the short way up to Tognarelli's milk bar which we both had last patronised in 1972. The second thing to strike me was that he was about a quarter as fat as evidently he imagined himself to be (as disclosed in his *Radio Activity*). His face admittedly was a little puffy around the cheeks and chin, yet in a kind of humorous, attractive, East European way, like some affable fraternal peasant booser in a Hungarian comic film. Asbach had a tubby face but a merely stocky figure. And for all his old-fashioned shyness he had a touching spiky charm about him.

Once ensconced in Tognarelli's, he took a huge gulp of his cappucino and asked me hastily what I thought of his book. I smiled and said I had enjoyed it very much. Asbach beamed and then doubtfully contemplating the word 'enjoy' asked me for a candid assessment of its literary *merit*. I hesitated and then with some hoarseness in my voice said I wasn't sure. I said I thought much of it was funny and that he had done a proficient job in his transcriptions of Little's nonsensical tale. His little bits of dialect gloss were also funny; he had a remarkable ear for the buffoonish flavour of the dialect. Asbach was glad to hear words like 'proficient' and 'remarkable' as what writer is not? For all that, I could see he was wanting me to tell him that his book was a masterpiece of fable-realism-magic-parable, something on the lines of Flann O'Brien's *At Swim-Two-Birds*. Sooner than commit myself to that kind of folly, I said I thought his using Tommy Little's extraordinary oral tale to illuminate his own father's tragicomedy had resulted in an original piece of I supposed documentary-autobiography or some other difficult to place literary category.

Asbach then he looked at me shrewdly and said. 'It's an extraordinary thing. If I were a local novelist, which of course I'm not, I shouldn't be writing limply-disguised autobiography as you do.'

'Oh?' I said, rather startled.

'Not at all,' said Asbach with sudden passion. His face was flaming; in part because he had scalded himself with greedy gulps at the cappucino.

'No,' he went on briskly. 'You must realise that you and I live in one of the most instructive political regions in the entire world. Absolutely everyone in the world has heard of 'Ibn Hafl'. About half the world has heard about our childhood 'lucky mes'. I should say almost everyone in the world by late 1987 has heard of 'Shurnobble's effect on this area.'

'Quite,' I said uneasily.

'So why aren't there any novels, poems, plays about the potentially life and death ironies we experience around here? Why no Maryport Günther Grass; no Workington Milan Kundera; no Whitehaven Mario Vargas Llosa?'

'Quite,' I said shamefacedly.

'Who wants laboured sub-Lawrentian rustic musings in 1987?' he squeaked at me accusingly. 'Who wants straggling *Bildungsromans* about provincial lads struggling away at Oxbridge? Who gives a monkey's fuck,' he asked at the top of his voice, 'about that kind of thing?'

'Do you think so?' I said a little stiffly.

His English was of course as English as English could be. He had not a trace of an accent, even though both his parents were foreigners and he was an only child.

'Günther Grass, you know,' he continued, 'claims that he chooses to live in Berlin because it is the geographical locus closest to the realities of our age. Well I dispute that personally, I really do. I would argue that in fact *Waberthwaite* is closer to the realities of our age than Berlin.'

'Oh?' I said.

'Or Bootle. Or Drigg. Or Seascale. Or Ravenglass. That estuary you know is of such incomparable beauty. I once stood quite alone on Green Road railway station just outside Millom of a summer's evening, and saw the most miraculous marine sunset available on this planet. Once upon a time it can only have been that, an estuary with a scale and a poetry beyond computation. But look at it now, or at least look at its sister estuary further up.'

'Quite,' I said shamefaced. Then clearing my throat I said to Asbach. 'I've tried, believe me, Edward.'

He looked surprised by my use of his formal Christian name. Perhaps he'd have preferred me to call him Ed or 'Ett' as his father had.

'I've tried,' I repeated. 'But good intentions aren't always the best ingredients for writing a decent book.'

'Though they help,' Asbach sniffed, a little patronisingly. 'And let's face it, the world at large might forgive an imperfect satire if the inspiration was sufficiently warm-hearted.'

'I've tried writing a sharp satire,' I said. 'But it was hopeless. It just didn't bite. It was all top heavy with good intentions and deadly bloody boring. It wasn't truly Cumbrian. It wasn't funny. In addition, I've tried writing a straight realistic work with an 'Ibn Hafl' component in the background. That was even more hellish, believe you me! I almost cried with boredom at what I'd written. I'm afraid that the Goddess of Art when it comes to good intentions doesn't really give a monkey's fu . . .'

'Which is where I come in!' said Asbach delighted. 'My chance arrival at last year's competition with a tape recorder and sufficient C90s! My extraordinary racial background! My father ending the way he did! My simultaneous appreciation and scorn for the two-faced way Tommy Little told his 'tyal'! I am the one! I have been in the right place at the right time at the right moment of history and geography! You know, you really must do all you can for me. If you can't do the job yourself, then you must endeavour to aid one like me who can! It's a moral imperative, it's as simple as that.'

I sipped my own cappucino and ate my last finger of Kit Kat which had melted all over my fingers as I listened to Asbach. The melted chocolate felt tacky and outstandingly unpleasant. There is something so heartlessly final about the difference between a firm piece of chocolate and a liquid one.

'What I'd like to know,' I said, to shift my embarrassment, 'is why we are meeting here? I mean why not at your house or at your pottery come to that? It's almost as if we are having some top secret Graham Greeneish confabulation.'

Asbach looked a little shifty and then said what I presumed later must have been a convincing sort of red herring.

'Because I don't want anyone with any partisan affection – i.e. seven-eighths of the county – for Ibn Hafl or 'Martian' come to that, to become aware that I am seeking to publish *Radio Activity*. A Workington milk bar is sufficiently obscure and unthinkable a venue, for no one to be possibly spying or eavesdropping upon us here.'

He was talking so loudly I doubted it. 'You mean you're in some way afraid of publishing Little's tall story?'

'Exactly!'

'That you believe the local industrial giants might decide to take you to court or . . .'

'Worse perhaps,' Asbach said glumly.

'Pah,' I said. 'This isn't Uruguay you know.'

'Isn't it?' he sniffed. 'No, I suppose it's not quite yet.'

'Everything that's conceivably in it is common local knowledge,' I assured him, 'and has been aired in the paper and on the radio and TV at one time or another. The pigeons, the silt, the 'lucky mes', the leaks.'

'Still,' said Asbach, nervously looking about him, 'you never know what might happen.'

'Added to which it is Little's tale, not *yours*,' I said conclusively. 'You are simply reporting what he said at last year's 'Biggest Liar In The World' competition. You aren't embellishing or inventing yourself are you?'

'Not at all,' said E. J. Asbach, with a sudden aggressive determination.

Two minute drill in the dialect

Most of Asbach's home-grown rendering of the dialect snippets can easily be understood by anyone with a little effort. The main stumbling blocks are the changes in the vowels and in particular of the long ones.

Long 'a' as in 'face' and 'naked' usually becomes 'ya' as in 'fyass' and 'nyakt' (pronounced as in Yamaha).

Long 'i' as in 'lie' and 'liar' often becomes 'ee' as in 'lee' and 'lee-er' or 'lear'.

Sometimes by false analogy long 'o' behaves like long 'a', e.g. 'smoke' becomes 'smyeuk' or variant 'smook' (Asbach in one sentence has both variants; a transcription which shows the remarkable fidelity of his ear).

Otherwise it is a case of eccentric vocabulary; most of it do with Viking loan words and archaic Elizabethan usage (as in 'marra').

marra – friend, chap

gadger – chap

lake – play

ter lake wit yersel – to masturbate

flate – afraid (hence *flate-fyasst* is 'with fear-filled visage')

gay – very

va'neah (or *vanya*) – is 'varra neah' meaning nearly, almost

asser – I say

lookster – (look ye!) look!

sister – (see ye!) see!

ya or *yah* – (a variant on 'yan') means one

buck – fuck

laal – little

poick – spit

late – bear, fetch, carry, bring

body – woman

lig – lie (positional)

yakker – rustic labourer

ear – 'ear meaning year

Asbach observes liars old and new.

IT was a brilliant summer's evening in 1986 when I drove down to the pub in the pretty hamlet just below Seascale to watch 'The Biggest Liar In The World' competition. In previous years the Danes and Swedes and Finns had televised this international competition, but in 1986 for some reason, the media coverage was strictly local. The little beck which ran under the bridge adjacent to the public house was gently golden in the sunlight; the sloping bank very lush and inviting; the nearby fells rugged and pungent and pure. Idly I wished I had brought a late afternoon picnic, a half bottle of alcohol-free wine and some chicken sandwiches say, as I knew there would be an hour or so before the competition got properly started. Two young men were drinking outside, standing on the sunlit gravel with upraised pints and squinting with a rather witless complacence at the glorious evening, as if somehow they were partly responsible for it. A couple of well-shaped gimmer hoggs, first class stock even I could see, were leaning by the fence of the field opposite and staring at the two young drinkers with remarkable serene tranquillity.

I took out my expensive cassette recorder and a couple of tapes and staggered over to the pub. I have very few hobbies besides collecting ceramic art books and a passion for fish cookery, but anything to do with the local dialect always intrigues me. I subscribe to the Lakeland Dialect Society booklets and forage through the Cumbrian libraries for anything in the way of genuine humour. Though much of it, especially recent works and especially the doggerel poetry, is most unendearing material.

17

Sentimental and otiose in a manner only possible in a remote and uncritical province whose native tongue at its richest is genuinely imposs- ible to translate. Yet now and again, particularly in the older works, I would come across a gem of a comic story and would photocopy and place it in my file. In periods of gloom or after wrestling with my business anxieties I would fish out my pile of 'Cummerlan Tyals' and proceed to cackle very loudly over a glass or two of Clausthaler. Though from time to time, self-conscious at my simple mirthfulness and rubbing my very ample belly, I ask myself just *what* it is that I am laughing at?

On one level the answer is easy. I am laughing at the unique essence of the old 'tyals'; that is, at pure buffoonery. The adventures of 'idiots', of Jobby and Mary (bravo! Rita Derwent and all her ecstatic columns in The West Cumberland Times and Star), the standard simple farming couple from the hinterland of the fells. Should they for example traipse down to 'Lunnon' to see the sights, wherever they go and whatever they do, they cannot but express their impossible naivety, their rustic artlessness. Appreciable ultimately, alas, only in our musical dialect. In that hiccough- ing assonance of rasping consonants and bizarre deformation of vowels and diphthongs. Cumbrian vowels, like so many meandering hound trails, could stretch for miles (mayyyyyyystly dyuuuuuuuuuh) and with them the winsome expression of the tale-teller, as his cracked fancy extends parallel with the drop of his jaw and the straining of his tongue.

Looking forward to some entertaining foolishness tonight, I was also periodically lost in thought. My name incredibly is Edward Julius Asbach and I live in a country area near the port of Whitehaven. I am the only son of the late Klaus Asbach, a Sudetan German P.O.W who decided to stay and settle on enemy soil, here in West Cumbria, after 1946. I am a self-employed potter, and as well as running a barely profitable gift shop of interest mainly to moneyed tourists, especially wealthy French and Germans, I also teach pottery night classes in a local school. Last night at the class, a big stout woman in her late fifties called Jessie Twentyman, an unmarried hairdresser who drives up all the way from Millom, told a curious and most disturbing tale. Jessie is not exactly a 'tyal-teller' though her way of speaking is humorously emphatic and some would say she is a natural comedienne. She was explaining to us why she had missed last week's class and by the end of her story about a half of us were aghast, the other half entirely sceptical. She had, she told us, two weekends previous, gone walking up by the fells near Ulpha in the region of Devoke Water. The ramble had lasted some three or four hours, it had been from early morning until she drove off for lunch at a pub in the adjoining valley. The only significant memory she had of that particular morning was that there was an exceptionally heavy dew all around. The following night, or rather in the small hours of the Sunday, she had awoken feeling extremely bilious. As if perhaps she had contracted an acute food poisoning, in that little pub possibly, where the deep fried scampi might have been so copious on her plate to compensate for the fact it tasted rather stale.

Jessie had raced into her Millom bathroom, to begin gagging over her doubtless rose-coloured lavatory bowl. Of the scampi, completely metabolised about eight hours earlier, there was not a sign. Instead Jessie found herself retching pure liquid, noteworthy for the fact that it was a violent almost technicolor hue of orange.

'Technicolor orange?' started Mrs Peach, a good-looking junior school teacher from Distington. She is, in addition, a gifted amateur potter.

'Bright orange,' said Jessie, with earnest pursing of her pale and chubby lips. 'Like pent. Like the kind of pent you might spray on your car or your bike if you were wantin folk to sit up and tek a look at it.'

Jessie had vomited the orange paint several times that night. In the morning in great distress she had the young doctor come out to examine herself and her paint, a sizeable sample of which she had kept in the bathroom in a plastic jug. The doctor claimed he was thirty-three but in Jessie's opinion looked no more than a raw teenager. New to the area he had no anxieties about pinning causes upon local culprits. He'd scratched his head and after hearing her story of the walk up by Devoke had looked at first illuminated. Then very dubious. Then again illuminated. Then fleetingly dubious. Then finally quite assured.

'Of course the first thing I thought of was you-know-where,' he'd explained, as he held up her vomit to the sunlight.

'What?' said Jessie, dropping the toothbrush she'd been using to remove the smell from her mouth.

'And then,' said the thin little medical man, fingering his sporty blazer, 'I thought of Chernobyl. And then I thought no, no. Outlandish. So I thought of Sellafield again. And then finally, weighing up all the probabilities, I . . .'

'Shurnobble?' squeaked Jessie, lapsing by regression into pure dialect.

'Yes. And in the end I think it's almost certainly Chernobyl. You can set your mind at rest. It was the very heavy dew that convinced me.'

Jessie nodded speechless.

'I'll have to have it tested at the labs. Still, this looks very much like radioactive poisoning to me.'

'Oh my Christ!'

'It's very interesting,' the teenage doctor had ruminated. 'I wonder how many more this has happened to round here? Lord it *is* interesting!' – he looked as if he wanted to kiss Jessie's jug with proprietorial affection – 'You know that they won't let the South Cumbrian farmers send their lambs to the market any more. Weeks after they should have told them, it transpires.'

'A lamb to the slaughter,' Jessie relayed obscurely to William Todd, a retired Whitehaven miner who was gawping at her with hostile scepticism. Todd by the way is a hopelessly clumsy artist with his clay.

'Scampi!' he said with an unkind leer. 'Ower many balls of Eskdale scampi, Jessie!'

'Chernobyl!' she snorted. 'He sent it away for tests to Newcastle. The tests came back and they said it was radioactive poisoning.'

'So why,' asked Todd with terse logic, 'isn't thoo dead, lass? Or thee fyass all covered in scabs?'

'Because,' said Jessie reddening, 'I only had a limited dose.'

'Thoo,' he said, 'or mebbe thee laal doctor should gah till 'T' Biggest Liar in t' Wurld Competition' that's on at Santon Brigg tomorrow. Thoo'd win it hands doon wit thee orange pent up at Devoke Watter.'

'I'm going to that,' I interrupted hastily, anxious to stop a fight breaking out in a class in a studio not mine. I envisaged all the surrounding pots being smashed to shards, old Todd a nasty mess of blood and liquid clay, Jessie happily garrotting his scrawny old neck just to punish his scepticism conclusively.

'Oh are you?' said Mrs Peach helpfully, as she saw my dilemma. 'As a participant, Mr Asbach?'

'Lord no!' I said with weak mirth, as I saw Jessie conjure with the consequences of doing violence to a frail pensioner. 'No, just as an enthusiast for tall stories. I love funny stories set round here. I like them best of all when they're in good thick dialect. The thicker it is the better.'

Jessie looked derisively at Todd as I said the word 'thicker'. She gave a not very mellifluous laugh.

The tension was gradually deflected as the group at large began a noisy discussion about the recent accident at Chernobyl. All except myself, Jessie and Mrs Peach were most emphatic that such a thing could not happen here in England in 1986. It was quite a biblical certainty which showed in these six West Cumbrians as they confirmed that such a thing was impossible for example at Sellafield or nearby Chapel Cross in Dumfriesshire. It was self-evident that the Russians were primitive in their science; negligent and cheeseparing in their safety procedures; careless of their population; and of course totalitarian in their government and media. The truth about Chernobyl, they all agreed, would never come out because the Russians knew nothing of truth. This is not how William Todd expressed it precisely but certainly what he meant when he said: 'They'll click hold of thee, Missus Peach, and fling thee in jail just for opening thee gob over *theer*. Especially if thoo's aunty-nookler!'

Aunty-nookler? I was visualising Jessie's technicolor paint as I noted a bright orange cigarette packet near the bar door. There were about twenty or thirty people, mostly locals, in the bar, and I peeped and saw a similar number in the lounge. I saw the man from the Whitehaven News, a reporter from Radio Cumbria, a woman from Border Television, three or four familiar faces from the Dialect Society. I bought myself twelve bottles of non-alcoholic Clausthaler lager as I had no intention of spending half the night fighting to get to the bar. In any case I needed to stick to my seat to attend to my expensive little cassette player.

Various of the media people waved and through the throng of farmers

21

and shepherds indicated by mime and dumb speech that they would chat with me later. Because of a dearth of local potters I am invited into Border TV about once a year to demonstrate jug-making; onto Radio Cumbria likewise to talk about say the therapeutic and socialising effects for the mentally-handicapped of using the potter's wheel. Last year the Whitehaven News displayed a curiously leering mugshot of me when I did a sponsored-potting on behalf of Christian Aid. I looked to put it squarely mentally-handicapped myself. I am a podgy, shy, sardonic, halting, jesting kind of chap who can never conclusively resolve whether I'm happier in company or on my own. In my mid-thirties people often assume I'm ten years older and once I remember with acute chagrin one of my father's customers assuming I was his stout kid brother. Klaus laughed very hard at that and pointing at me said that, 'he hess an old-feshiont heed on him, hess Edward!'

Klaus my father was a linguistic monstrosity, regardless of his other extreme eccentricities. It is a dire thing to be embarrassed by one's own father, but certainly even as a little boy I resented the fact that my father's Germano-Cumbrian speech encouraged my schoolmates not only to laugh at him as if he were some expectorating clown, but to turn on me whose English and Cumbrian dialect were as faultless as theirs and call me – God help us! – a Nazi!

Yes, in the early Fifties, through till the early Sixties, both Klaus and his son Edward were hallooed at by small Cumbrian children as Natsis or Nasties. This made Klaus laugh very hard. What after all were the taunts of eight-year-old balaclavaed kids to him after the 999 Korps, or the French P.O.W. camp where the defeated Germans had fought for the luxury of a stone to sit upon? In my own case though, neither to exaggerate nor minimise, the taunting had its effect. It made me, how can I put it? less than a hundred per cent sure of myself, to feel that in some manner I was marked by heredity or contiguity or . . . name . . . or no, more exactly *language*. I was called Asbach, not Twentyman nor Minto nor Little nor Minshaw nor Farrell nor Renney nor all the quintessentially Cumbrian names. Despite the fact I spoke unbroken English and for my first ten years a pungently thick local dialect, that I was Cumbrian to the bone and knew next to no German much less the

22

Czech that Sudetner Klaus occasionally lapsed into, I always felt the foreigner; either that or the in-between, the neither one nor the other.

However I won't make a meal of it. No more than Klaus made a meal of his own history of hardships. They had been colossal, mythical, epic. Despite which Klaus contained a profound quantity of comedy by which I mean he created it, he was funny, monstrously funny, mostly without intention. Some people even thought he was simply an idiot and I blush now myself to think that often I was deeply embarrassed by his deeds as well as his speech. He drank like a Balkan Gargantua, which is to say he was *ein echt Mitteleuropäischer*. His spitladen enthusiasm; his maniac's energy; his larger-than-lifeness: all these were his continental, his Central European heritage. I, by some compensatory tide, took after my mother Ilse, a refugee from Austria whom Klaus married in 1947 in a registry office in Carlisle. Ilse, now in her seventies, is quiet, tender, nervous, steadfast, sober. She and I often get drunk together over a dozen bottles of non-alcoholic lager and reminisce fondly about the departed monster.

I was feeling a little melancholy there in Santon Bridge at the thought of my dead father and the image of Jessie Twentyman vomiting up what might have been the gift of an exploded Ukrainian power station. The two seemed connected, understandably enough. It was impossible to keep Eastern Europe out of Cumbria and always had been. For example in the part of town where I grew up there was a refugee Ukrainian family called Petrovic. The little boy James who was two or three years younger than I, was also called a Natsi/Nasty by his peers. For it was Cumbria and it was the Fifties and those little children assumed Ukraine and 'Jurmanee' must be the same (and more than likely their parents did not differ . . .)

This summer's evening in 1986 in Santon Bridge there was no prior warning of the forthcoming fiasco. There were only four competitors for the prize of 'Biggest Liar in the World' and they were all seated calmly at the same table in the corner next to the window. Three of them, all in their late seventies, were instantly recognisable from previous competitions and the fourth, the man of mystery, the oral wonder, was scarcely

23

outlandish in his appearance; merely moderately odd. His name, *Tommy Little,* was as excessively local as local could be. It was like being called Abdul Haq if you were a Pakistani or Joe Murphy if you were a Dubliner or Murdo MacLeod if you lived in the Gaidhealtacht. His tyal which lasted all the way through from nine-thirty until four-twenty a.m., was related in an unexceptional if melodiously dulcet North Cumbrian dialect. He told the judges when they asked for his name and address that he worked on a farm called Ridgerstown up by Bewcastle of the famous eighth-century cross. He even gave them a fictitious post code, CA6 6QZ. The judges nodded companionably and swapped anecdotes with Little about hound trails at Spadeadam Farm, the ones next to the strategic R.A.F station which is barred to the general public. Little spoke apparently knowledgeably about trails at Walton Moss, Smithfield, Bailey and all those other godforsaken hamlets around Brampton and Longtown. The judges and his co-competitors then mentioned names of specific North Cumbrian celebrities, mad old farmers and madder old shepherds they knew from the trails, and Little nodded serenely as if he well knew those celebrities too. But after finishing his tale of course Little vanished from Santon Bridge, abandoning his prize, and no one saw hide nor hair of him after. Much later the judges, the reporter from Radio Cumbria and myself, got out every map we had in our various cars and scoured the Bewcastle area for a farm called Ridgerstown. The nearest thing we could find was Dodgsonstown down by a ford between Roadhead and Sleetbeck. Two days later I bought a small scale O.S map of the Bewcastle area and for good measure the ones for Kershopefoot and Scaleby. I spent a good hour examining them all for a farm called Ridgerstown. Up that way every hamlet, farm and telegraph pole is called Somethingtown. There were Oldtown, Newtown, Howtown, Roweltown, Justicetown, Selbystown, Dodgsonstown, Chapeltown, Uppertown and Grahamstown. Not a hint of a Ridgerstown – a subtly credible fabrication if ever there was!

In any other context, certainly had it been related in orthodox English, Tommy Little's tale would have been hailed as quite artistically refined. Critics, professors, pundits of all hues, would most likely have praised it as a piece of fabular, mythopoeic *Kunstmärchen.* Employing choice inscrutably penetrating literary measurements, they might well have decided it was diurnal and cataphatic. It was this sophisticated if unyielding artistry which at an early stage in his recital led me to think, God Almighty, if I do not tape, edit, translate, publish Tommy Little's tale then the world at large will be deprived of something utterly extraordinary! The locals (i.e. the genuinely *local* locals) who effortlessly understood his dialect, were sure enough surprised by the grotesque convolutions of his tale; the multi-layered craziness of his 'plot'; the trans-global travel via a valve wireless; his hero's hopeless search for the phosphate boat from Tangiers to Whitehaven (the quest always to be going home to one's roots, it could scarcely be anything else); the timeless theme of exile from the provinces wrapped about in a surreal confection involving the respective features producers of Radio Cumbria and Radio Tangiers. Then most damningly there was the not very subtle satire about British Nuclear Fuels Ltd and its unfortunate leaks. The locals, uneasy and critical at first, eventually laughed at this and applauded Little's fantastic impertinence. His was after all a 'tall tyal', mad from start to finish, and therefore his oblique sarcasms about monolithic philanthropy and the equivocations of its Publicity and P.R. men were all taken as being just a bit of 'lakin (fooling, playing) nowt mare'.

Meanwhile the assembled professionals, the media folk, to a man and woman outsiders with a very limited knowledge of the local dialect, made as much sense of the tale as they could. They sought frequent translations from bilinguals the likes of me. And they were of course riveted, glued for the whole seven hours in an understandably egotistical manner as one of the principal characters in *Radio Activity* was an imaginary Whitehaven studio producer called Geoff Beeston. The *actual* Whitehaven producer, a thin, curly, blonde, lively man of about twenty-six, Tim Boston, kept turning round to his newspaper and TV colleagues and grinning with a mixture of light-headed pride and tremulous self-doubt. Tommy Little in his seven hour recital slipped effortlessly back and forth between dialect and proper English. Most of the time Geoff Beeston's dialogue with William Stapleton the global voyager was rendered in a perceptively accurate perversion of media tyro's English. So that even fresh-faced Boston had little trouble in discerning the constant insinuations of media smoothness, deference, disingenuousness etc.

25

Impertinently depicted within the unusual framework of a humorous rustic tyal, Boston, I could see, was assailed by a sense of painful vulnerability. I could see his brain demanding of itself: how come this piece of nonsensical folk entertainment, the standard fodder of local radio outside broadcasts (I'm standing here, Tim Boston, at Santon Bridge near Sellafield, waiting to hear from, yes, that's right, The *Biggest* Liar in the World!) was threatening to turn on Tim himself and his good-natured simulation of hectic mirth. It was the first time in his five years with Radio Cumbria that he had ever felt the barbs of a local satirist. He was hurt and stunned, as well as uneasy and perplexed. Cumberland and satire, why they just didn't mix, they were perfect strangers to each other. Cumbrians typically played the ponderous fool and kept their heads down; they liked lots of the same thing over and over again. They were not interested in political dissent, anguish, art, exotica, God. They were interested primarily in anything local, that is, in each other. They liked gossip, clan history, genealogy, drink, whist, dogs, trails, fox hunting, pigeons, employment, BNFL, Marchon, martial arts and videos. I could see all this spinning furiously through Tim Boston's youthful, curly, harmless head just as I asked myself the related question, who the hell *is* this bloody Tommy Little?

Item: (I reasoned to myself) his dialect is faultless, obviously learnt at the teat, therefore he must have been born and bred in Cumbria. Moreover it is genuine *North* Cumbrian, he probably does originate from Roadhead or Bailey or Bewcastle or some other back-end-of-buggery.

Item: Little imaginatively creates a rather original fable about a radio fanatic William Stapleton who travels the airways literally and ends up wandering around the docklands of Tangiers. In a vain wish to return to the more comforting backstreets of Whitehaven, via the boat he assumes in reality does in 1986 ply between the two ports with phosphate rock. His knowledge of Tangiers also seems definitive. This implies a history of travel or perhaps substantial prior reading or research. Was Little maybe a merchant sailor in his youth? Surely not one in a hundred North Cumbrian farmworkers has ever been to backstreet North Africa. Nor could they simulate a credible conversation between Tangiers media men and the artless English college teacher William Stapleton could they?

Item: Tommy Little claims he is thirty-five but he could feasibly be forty-five or fifty-five. His hair which is lightly greying is short and shaved at the back. He could be a ruggedly-barbered fell-farm yakker but — look at his collarless collier shirt; his dowdy black waistcoat; his immaculate white galoshes! — he could just as easily be some wandering relic of the Sixties or Seventies. Morocco; cut-price global travel; hashish, fabulism; even his weird fairy tale of the airwaves, makes me think of the swinging Sixties and the dangling Seventies. See how Little slips from the mention of hound trails rendered densely and musically in dialect to a defence in articulate English (by Wilfred Glenridding) of BNFL's subsidy of cultural artefacts at Maryport's maritime museum. Little's string of references, his cultural résumés, his imagined discourses between Third World professionals, all these point to some years spent as a student or amateur scholar of some kind outside the purlieus of wind-blasted Bewcastle!

The first 'tall tyal' came from Tucker Hodgon (Tukker Hodgin) from Ulverston, and was from any point of view a lame affair. Tucker in his youth, when he was just a lad of sixty say in 1970, could improvise all sorts of fertile nonsense about Barrow boggles (ghosts) and Conishead monks and could lead a pub crowd on with red herrings and pointless mile-long divagations up to some lunatic anti-climax where at last the stupefied audience well and truly realised it had been had.Now at seventy-six he was hanging on obtusely to his flagging reputation and with a good gallon or so more beer inside him than would have inspired a compensatory pity in the likes of me. The audience was kindly to the erstwhile genius, but bored. His tyal was a thinly disguised version of something I had heard in the school cloakrooms in 1960. The world peregrinations of the iggly-wiggly worm, the insect which in a miraculous manner passed through the water pipes, sewers, lakes, streams etc. from Ulverston (hee hee!) to Paris (ho ho!) via Moscow, Delhi, Bangkok etc to come to rest at last in the Yangtse region of China.

'An wat does ter think came out o't' tap in Shiner when laal Hung Kung the railway wukker turrnt it on in Shan-high?' Tucker quizzed us all in the bar at the end of the twenty minute rigmarole.

'The Ulverston iggly-wiggly worm!' roared back producer Tim

Boston who had his tape recorder two feet from Tucker's puce and bulbous nose.

'Naw! It was *watter!*' bellowed Tucker who coughed and collapsed into a hellish fit of whinnying mirth. I sighed from my distant chair as I saw the old fool was so addled by Hartley's Special that he really did think he'd told a corker! Boston threw himself into similar fits and wheezingly informed his mike that they were a gay(very) queer lot down at Ulverston. Then turning to a trio of young labourers sitting noisily at the front he made a *sotto voce* jest about his unintentional pun 'gay queer' to which the spry chaps loudly wahooed. I sighed once more and kept my finger on the pause button of my own tape recorder. I looked expectantly to Fidler Armstrong and Harrison Beatty (male Christian names in these parts are often the maternal maiden name). As I've said the fourth contestant Tommy Little, with his rather bland serenity of expression (like a gimmer hogg after a leisurely feed) gave no promise of being better than drunken old Tucker.

Fidler and Harrison were thankfully in a different league from Hodgin. They were both aged seventy-nine and both had remained deliberately sober and alert for the serious business of improvisation, raconteurial rhythm, pause, false climax, interrogation of the audience and so on. Despite this – I had read variations in several privately-printed booklets over the years – both their tales were derivative and also quite similar. They both employed those comic elements favoured the world over by all ages and classes as they both concerned the area of the back passage and the backside. Likewise both treated of the mistaken application of inappropriate medicine to these comically afflicted areas. Fidler wove his tale around a fictitious aunt and uncle and I noted Harrison's face drop at first as he was obliged mentally to recast his tale as the adventures of a female second cousin. Doubtless Harrison also saw the similarity of the cloacal themes but at this stage of the game was unable to furnish an alternative.

Fidler's story of which I taped the first half, was about his Uncle Boffer and his Aunty Madge; in the days before the First War when they farmed up by Orthwaite, by the top side of Bassenthwaite Lake. Old Boffer, alas, was becoming crippled by backache (*so he'd gurrn an gripe up*

28

his puzzent fyass wid the muddrous attacks of pyan) and was proof against any half-hearted ministrations of the Keswick practitioner. That rough old charlatan frequently rattled up there by pony and trap to their remote hillstead in order to relieve them of four plump chickens in return 'fer dyeuhin bugger aw guid till Uncle Boffer's back!' Finally, wearied to distraction by her husband's self-pitying complaints and ill temper, Fidler's Aunty Madge acquired a tube of the notorious patent analgesic cream 'Fiery Jack'. Potent alike for rheumatic ewes, cows with bruised teats, horses with staggers or bicycles crippled by rusted cogs. Sixty-year-old Boffer was forced by his wife to strip 'bollick nyakt' by the roaring fireside while old Madge standing some foot behind him unscrewed the tube top and gave vent to an enormous squirt of the blistering balm. The Fiery Jack shot out like hissing vitriol and plopped moistly and obligingly on to the small of Boffer's back. Unfortunately though it was of such plangency and near liquidity (*t'tin was aboot foteen 'ear owd, an hed been liggin in t' back of Minnie Renney's laal sweet shop doon at Bassthwat, till puir owd Madge had thowt ter pucchass it!*) that the generous plop immediately started to sear and froth its hellish way down between the cleft of Boffer's backside (*reet atween Boffer's buddick chicks!*) and from there like a bouncing rubber ball it slowly settled and began to fizz and smoke like burning spittle around his withered old testicles (*ter smyeuk aroon t'owd lad's dangelan bollicks!*).

Boffer, roaring obscenely, had capered yelling into the freezing night, cursing his negligent idiot of a wife! And there under the gentle stars on the top of the deserted fellside, he'd dipped his blazing balls and behind into the old shit-spattered horsetrough. Xenophobically denouncing the 'Lunnon manifacters' of 'Feery Jack' and threatening to drown Madge in the trough as soon as his balls had stopped melting . . .

I had heard and read it all before, and yet I laughed considerably. Bollicks, back passages, Fiery Jack, backsides, buddick cheeks, flaming ointments, yes I loudly heed and hawed like all the rest at Santon Bridge. Tim Boston had edited out the references on his tape to 'bollicks' though he left in 'buddick chicks', I noticed, when I listened to next day's relay from Radio Cumbria. The youthful producer was just as sensitive to the delicacy of local listeners when he played some (a very little) of Harrison's story about his second cousin Winnie, a martyr to would you believe it? her painful haemmorhoids . . .

A plump farming lass of about thirty-five, Winnie worked before the Second War alongside the missus in the kitchen of a farm at Whelpo near Caldbeck. She was married to skinny Joe Roe the farm labourer and the pair of them dwelt in a tied cottage overlooking a little beck and a footbridge. Like Boffer to his rheumatics, so Winnie was a martyr to her chronic piles, and often had to get grumbling Joe to push the nasty little things back up into her back passage. After years of meagre relief from various suppositories, creams, gels and emunctories advertised in the small columns of the *Keswick Reminder* or the *Penrith Observer* Winnie Roe had all but given up hope of ever relieving her tormented anus. Like Boffer, her trials made her peevish and fractious, and in the days before TV, the Open University or Marriage Guidance, inevitably drove her husband down to the poky little pub at Hesket Newmarket.

Then one night in the autumn of 1939, a ten hour power cut (they'd had electric in the beckside cottage from as early as 1937). Winnie scorning the fuss of a dripping candle, simply bathed and undressed herself in the dark, in the little back kitchen where the sink stood. In the same darkness too she took out her teeth, swilled them, plopped them awkwardly into the glass, picked up her useless tube of pile cream, and without any hope whatever squeezed a small handful up her unhappy bum.

Half way through the night she turned to Joe Roe, beerily exhaling after a night in Hesket and a joyous exercise in blind acrobatics as he'd tried to wash himself and get quickly into bed in a power cut.

'Bye,' she'd cooed with some of the attractive winsomeness of her pre-haemmorhoidal days, 'bye but yon new pile cream frae t'pyaper has impreuvt the itchin up me behint, Joe!'

'Pfah!' Joe snored. 'Pfuh!'

'It's luvly an cyeul up me back passidge, like a laal watter fa', like Spoot Force say dribbling doon! It's seah cyeul an comfy, Joe! Tomorrer ah is ganna write off till t'manifacters an ask them ter send me a hunnert mare tyoobs, an they can stick me fyass on t'packit if they like an say.

Winnie Roe reckermends 'Paternoster Pile Cream' cos it's done her back passage neah end of guid up at Scar Cottidge, Whelpo, Cowdbeck, Cummerlan!'

Joe murmured that they might prefer to stick a picture of her behind on the packet and Winnie grunted and fell asleep. However, next morning when she'd gone to check on the spelling of Paternoster, Winnie discovered the tube of pile cream tucked away safely in its box in the medicine cupboard. Reeling at her cackhandedness in the dark, she observed that the tube she'd squirted up her buttocks bore the unsatisfactory brand name of *Euthymol*.

'And ivver after,' Harrison concluded, as the generous roars went up in Santon Bridge, 'it wass mental tyeuthpyasst she squatted up her itchy back passidge. Coss it wass only a guid dollop ev Yoothymmel ivver giv me seckent cussin Winnie any relief frae them bliddy owd hemmrides!'

It looked as if Fidler would sweep away the trophy for 1986, especially as his guttural improvisations about the acridity of Fiery Jack and his vivid similes about burning spittle etc had visibly impressed the four judges. Then Tommy Little stood up at twenty five past nine, and there was a hush that signified not so much reverence as a swelling ocean of muffled titters. That cosy smile of his was from some angles astoundingly gormless. His ahistoric, austere garments – by and large the collier's gear of the Thirties – seemed rather too subtly affected. There was a loud whispering from the gargling young labourers at the front making hilarious reference to 'yon comical stripey laal gadger'. This ridicule made Tommy Little smirk even more cutely. I flicked on my cassette player without much hope. An hour and a half later of course I was racing to my old car to get hold of another pair of C90s. When all four tapes were full (after six hours, by half past three in the morning!) I had to bowl back bleary-eyed for my last remaining tape. By that stage I was so exhausted I thought I might be hallucinating both the vision of fresh-faced Little whose voice had turned barely a fraction huskier, and the sixty or so purple-faced and bloodshot audience not one of whom had fallen asleep during his marathon narration.

I have translated and edited the seven hours of tape which constitute Tommy Little's *Radio Activity*. The translation consisted of rendering much of it from idiomatic dialect into a reasonably equivalent but above all readable English. Where some of the dialect humour or artistic exagger-ation would have been lost in a literal translation I have given an imaginative equivalent in proper English. I have not, I solemnly swear, embroidered or distorted the truth of Tommy Little's lies. I have rendered his mendacity with veracity. I have put his 'tyal' into I hope tolerable English and tried at all times to retain the flavour and the humour of his tropes, conceits, hyperboles. This has not been easy, but then neither can Tommy Little's four hundred and twenty minute narration have been a matter of leisure. Perhaps he vanished without trace from Santon Bridge, simply too exhausted by his feat of continuous creation to accept the acclaim, trophy and cheque indubitably his.

Throughout my translation I have occasionally put in snippets of the original dialect just to remind the world at large of the source from which the story came. Also sometimes at those points where the subject matter must have seemed impossible ever to have expressed in rustic dialect in the first place. Naturally these examples become less and less* in his tyal, as the world is obliged to acknowledge that nothing – not even nuclear physics nor for that matter the *Entfremdung* of the Moroccan *Gastarbeiter* – is beyond comprehensive expression in 'the guid owd Cummerlan twang'.

---

* Not as far as I can see. J.M.

RADIO ACTIVITY,
EMISSION THE FIRST.

TOMMY LITTLE RELATES

WILLIAM Stapleton was a tall, ruddy, cautious, obstinate, querulous but indecisive man of almost thirty-six. He had small blue eyes, very wide cheekbones, stiff black hair, and a large pair of slightly asymmetrical ears (*yah great lyeug was juss a laal bit powkin oot further till t'left than t'yan on t'reet*), and a bulbous lower lip that in his childhood had won him the unpleasant nickname of 'Loglip'. His dog was called Papcastle and his wife Rhoda was originally a Sharp. Rhoda's grandfather Thompson Sharp had initially farmed in Copshaw Holm/Newcastleton, Roxburghshire on the Scotland-England border, but had raised his son, Rhoda's Dad, Wilson Sharp, in industrial West Cumbria, the country area near Whitehaven to which he had transferred in the early years of this century. Rhoda Stapleton taught all subjects including P.E. and the flageolet, in a primary school near Whitehaven, and William taught just one in a nearby Technical College. His subject was General Studies, and the majority of his young students were teenage male technical apprentices employed either as instrument mechanics or process workers at Windscale Nuclear Power Station.

Most of William's students thought that his subject was idiotic and by extension thought Stapleton himself a complicated sort of buffoon. Stapleton's syllabus brief for the education of the sixteen-old apprentices ran to three dozen pages and was subtitled, believe it or not, 'A Taxonomy of Educational Objectives'. Primarily he was hired to teach them 'Life and Social Skills' (thirty-five pages) which comprehended everything from self-awareness via question-naires of a highly personal nature; to the accurate use of and transcription of messages from the telephone; to an accurate verbal description of how to screw and unscrew a hinge from a door; to an awareness of the advantages of a wide knowledge of all types of contraception; to an indication of the disadvantages of contracting syphilis, AIDS or genital crabs. In between he was also encouraged to 'promote a tolerance of the diversity of means of artistic expression' (one page); meaning to play them gusty recorded excerpts from classic operas; to read to them with drama and gesture from James Joyce or Gerald Durrell depending how he and they felt; to subject them to American audio-visual slide-packages of the stunning accomplishments of Degas, Manet or the Pollulaio Bros; to have them doing hour-long table readings of *Ubu Roi* or *Billy Liar* or *The Two Gentlemen of Verona*, depending on which way William and they found themselves out.

Class EMOE1A thought that Shakespeare was 'piss', that Jarry was 'shite', but that Keith Waterhouse was 'only alf shite'. Class EMOE2A thought Waterhouse, Shakespeare and Jarry were all extravagant and inseparable shite. Class EMOE3A responded to his overture of reading parallel adventure passages from Sven Hassel and Ernest Hemingway by insisting in raucous unison that the prose and imaginative powers of Mr Hassel were in every respect superior to the dead Yank's. Class EPOE3B thought that Salvador Dali should have been strangled in his septic cot; that Velazquez knew how to draw a lass's (Venus's) bum nicely, but *that was all*; that the only good thing about 'Flobber' was the hunting scene in Julian the Hospitator and even that got suffocatingly dull as the old French master went on and on and on . . .

Rhoda was very happy in her job but William was complicatedly dismayed by his. Idealistic in his probationary years, he had initially bent over backwards to encourage attitudes of social and individual tolerance, liberalism, independence and originality among his young lads. After seven uphill years he had become sour, cynical and occasionally vindictive towards these indifferent apprentices (*vinegar-fyasst, a septic, an noo an than he'd ratch up aw makk ev gamm an scheme ter git his own back on t' lads frae Sellerfeld*).

Wm. Stapleton sometimes lay awake at nights hatching up intricate schemes to dismay his unbending students. To a man they all wanted homosexuals castrated, in addition to being impounded in rigorous laagers on Bowes or Alston Moor as a fitting reward for the unforgettable scourge of AIDS. They desired that all Blacks and Pakistanis be barred from competing for work with white Englishmen and in the long view wanted them all to be returned compulsorily to Africa (sic). When Wm. Stapleton mocked them with the undeniable truth that there were less than a dozen Blacks in the whole of West Cumbria and that their cheerful racism was so to speak all theoretical and redundant, the lads responded by saying that yes, in line with Botha, Vorster etc. they were intent on defending Cumbrian racial purity to the hilt.

'Duss thoo *reelly* like niggers, William?' asked Terry Montague from the back of room B1. He was an effeminately beautiful sixteen year-old who spent seventy-five per cent of his wages on designer fashions from Newcastle boutiques. His keep to his mother was almost a half of a biblical tithe; a full three pounds per week.

Observe Wm. Stapleton doggedly speaking first principles to a child only just becoming a man. That he, Stapleton, liked some people and not others irrespective of their pigmentation. Stapleton at thirty-six was becoming exceedingly pig sick of arguing first principles with these smug provincial youths who never encountered a genuine bogeyman from one year to the next.

One day in a mood of surly vengeance Wm. Stapleton paid over-zealous attention to the thin handbook accompanying the American audio-visual package on 'European Surrealism'. Having the previous week shown Terry and friends some slides on the work of Dali, Duchamp, Ernst etc. and elicited their scornful ridicule at such infantile derangement (*'aw heeds twisted upside doon,'* scoffs *laal Terry, 'an eyes where t'mooth should be, an t'wimmins' tits glued on till t' crack atween t'backside an . . .'*) this week William conducted his own nasty exercise in *practical* Surrealism.

He commanded EMOE1A each to take a pristine sheet of paper from their files. To fold that sheet in such and such an impressively complicated manner, exactly two inches along one margin, twenty

three centimetres along this bottom edge, observe me most carefully will you, boys? Now open it up, unfold, and repeat the
identical procedure along the opposite edge but with a slight but
vital adjustment of those previous parameters to one and a half
inches and twenty one centimetres. Then take a sharp pencil,
preferably a 3B, and draw a small circle along one folded edge, of
approximately three centimetres radius (*do I need me cumpass,
William? Wat's it aw in aid of Will? Are we makkin kites, Mister
Styapleton?*). No, no need for compasses, freehand will do, provided
the circle is perfect! Yes, they might be kites, yes indeed, Mousy!
No no, let's be honest, it's a surprise, lads, what we're doing here
in this General Studies exercise. Now then, unfold completely and
then reshape it into a thin one inch strip by successive tight foldings.
So that you have in effect a little paper fan when you open it out.
Yes, that's right Montague, excellent, you have it to a tee! Now
then . . .

This scholarship level origami went on another twenty minutes,
with several more freehand circles, a few hypotenused triangles, a
half dozen squares, a dozen more foldings, a tear or two, and finally
an extremely finicky insertion of a loose edge into a tear. Just as
they were all busy with the last master-craftsmanly operation,
William picked up the class litter bin and went around the hot faced
sixteen year-olds one by one. With a smirk he picked up each of
their little enigmatic artworks, screwed them up tight, and flung
them disdainfully into the bin!

'*Satori*!' he beamed at them victoriously. 'Do you *get* it, all of
you? That'll teach you little bastards to expect one and one always
to equal two! Have you ever been led up the garden path, lads?
Have you ever been had?'

His students all went mad! Montague and Fergie wanted to kill
their General Studies teacher. Timson called him a bastard and a
shagger and refused to apologise even under threat of being sent to
the principal. Mousy burst into tears and said he had wanted
to make a *kite*; in fact he *had* made a kite, and Mr Styapleton had
gone and destroyed it! Montague shrugged the padded shoulders of
his £125 jacket and loudly demanded to know what the hell all that
rubbish had been in aid of. William responded by telling Monty he
was adhering to 'a taxonomy of educational objectives' and that

he was in addition trying 'to encourage a tolerance of the diversity of artistic means of expression'. Montague curled his handsome lips and said Stapleton was 'a big soft twat' and a 'bliddy wanker'. Wm. Stapleton went purple and bellowed back that if ever he called him anything like that again he'd have him bounced out of college by the main steps until Montague's nasty little teeth rattled. Montague went as white as some of the white specks of his designer jacket. The whole class went very white as Stapleton's temper when it came was colossal and terrifying.

Away from the Technical College, Mr Stapleton pursued a modest collection of outside interests. Rhoda attended many a night class in subjects such as Italian, Hatha Yoga, Public Speaking, Car Maintenance and Computer Programming. They were a compatible, sympathetic couple despite or because of the fact they spent much of their free time independently. William gardened; read; went walking the lower hills with Papcastle on summer nights; while Rhoda studied the *utthitaparsvakonasana*! (my exclamation: E. J. Asbach) or word processing or voice projection or *Il Signor Smith e un commerciante*. Especially during the winter but at all times of the year William's favourite leisure was those hours he spent alone in the company of his vast valve wireless. The Stapletons had their separate furnished dens; an attic in William's case and a converted bedroom in Rhoda's. In William's attic he kept an old mono record player which in some respects was brother to the valve wireless as with its squatness and simplicity it had a face and a character (*a way ev lyeukin at Willum an t'wurld*) all its own. Once he entered his attic Stapleton became in some respects his truer self, and by a defiant process of self-hypnosis never allowed himself even to think of the college nor his apprentices. Secure in his hermetic den Stapleton was not a humdrum teacher . . . he was a free soul, a man recreating himself in a unique fashion.

The attic had prints and posters of Samuel Palmer, Paul Klee, Miro, a Mughal miniature and an ink drawing by Hokusai. The light was from a table lamp adjacent to the valve wireless which sat in some obese splendour on an old-fashioned bedroom locker, its personal podium. The wireless was about thirty years old and possessed five wave bands: long, medium, two short waves and a VHF. Sited high in the attic and with an aerial dangling out of the skylight Stapleton's radio received its high frequency transmissions with a brilliant clarity. He twiddled along VHF for Radio 3, Radio 4, Whitehaven police and ambulance calls. He disdained the long wave which consisted almost exclusively of tedious French news and current affairs stations (bah!). The short wave bands were as if recondite, mystical (*frae t'back ev behint, gowstly, gay queer*) unfathomable progressions of hissings, fizzings, splutters interrupted by waxing and waning babels of Slavonic, Hamitic, Latin, Semitic, Finno-Ugrian, Germanic, Baltic imprecation. Their messages were nearly always shouted, hurled at the listener in an offensive minatory tone (*aw groolin an bellerin an slaverin!*) as if perhaps a gun were being pointed at the announcer's head and that he in turn was pointing some sort of oral weapon at the listener!

The short waves made Wm. Stapleton ponder diffusely on totalitarianism, torture and untruth. He knew no Czech nor Albanian nor Arabic nor Rumanian but he could tell by the bluster and curious tonelessness of those broadcasts in 1986 that whatever they were saying, with whatever vehemence and defiance in their voices, it was all *absolute untruth*. Occasionally of course he received English language broadcasts from Tirana, Sofia, The Voice of America, Bucharest, and the richness of mendacity (*aw bliddy twaddle aboot coonterrevolooshnary, bushwa aunty soshlist, bushwa aunty sofia propgander an aw makk ev clart like yon!*) in these cases was also stunning. There was no truth anywhere in these uninformative soap operas and he gasped for a moment like a fish hoicked out of water as he reeled at the sheer cumulative weight of untruth in this world (*aw the bliddy lees an aw the bliddy lears in aw the bliddy wurld!*). Furthermore, had he allowed himself, he would have brooded by association on the manifold prejudices and absolute fantasies of his young BNFL instrument mechanics and process workers whose received opinions about everything from radioactivity to social democracy partook of the same mindlessly craven wish for personal security and private and fiscal superiority.

William Stapleton hovered, like most of us, on the medium wave, though in his case not for the refreshment of 'Any Questions' nor even of 'Any Answers'. Stapleton enjoyed jazz and ethnic folk music and was a devotee of African, Oriental and Balkan vocal music. Which explains why more often than not he found himself for one hour of most nights of the year listening to *Radio Tangiers* on which between eight and nine Greenwich mean time from Sunday to Thursday were broadcast some traditional songs of lamentation (*Morkan wimmin gurnin an yowlin aboot missin their chaps an their puir laal arts brekken an snappen*). Of course he also period- ically tuned in to Radios Sarajevo, Sofia, Ankara, Budapest and anywhere else where the Islamic 'artistic mode' of dolorous yearn- ing manifested itself in the folk music. Yes, William hovered over those formerly Turkish dominions where the Ottoman music had taken root, even among the hostile Greeks who howled and keened on Radio Thessalonika. But Radio Tangiers was Stapleton's favour- ite; partly because it seemed to have the same lady singer on every broadcast going through the same familiar repertoire of about forty traditional songs. Indeed William who had been born and raised in Waberthwaite near Sellafield was more Cumbrian than he cared to acknowledge. *For at the end of the day he enjoyed an infinite amount of identical repetition of the same little pleasures!* (My italics, E. J. Asbach). (*Like maist Cummerlan fellers he liked dyurn t'syam thing time an time ower; even doon ter squarkin an gurnin alang wit t'Morkan wumman Fatto Mah, woh kept cryin and bawlin fer Mehmoot woh cared mare fer his dogs an his awks an his bores an his untin than fer his wumman . . .*)

Sadly there was an idiotic hindrance to Stapleton's unhampered enjoyment of Fatoma's songs. By a curious idiosyncratic defect in his thirty year-old receiver, the focusing knob at the side seemed to have difficulty in staying tuned to Radio Tangiers for the full hour that William intended. Instead between nil and three times an hour on average, it might 'slip' along the waveband a tiny fraction of a centimetre (that is, in global terms, a continent or three) and nine times out of ten, by a peculiar irony, it always slipped to the same station adjacent to Tangiers' internationally allotted fre- quency. (And almost as disconcerting it would with the same caprice decide to 'slip back' to Radio Tangiers when it had had enough of the unwanted station . . .)

Just as William with eyes gently closed was earnestly warbling along with Fatoma her unutterable sorrow at the inconstancy of men and the insuperable emotional distance between herself and the dog-daft Mehmet; just as William was buried up to his neck in an aching poignancy of love-in-separation . . . the tuning knob would go **BLIP BLIP BLIP!** and slip along and drag him against his wish to – of all stations on the entire bloody globe – *Radio bloody Cumbria*!

'I'm standing here outside the brand new Asda that's just been built outside Aspatria,' bawled Geoff Beeston to swooning Stapleton, 'and I'm going to have a few words now with some of the first customers who've just been inside. Uppermost in my own mind at any rate are the things which I imagine concern all of us Cumbrian consumers. Is the day of the old fashioned Cumbrian corner shop completely at an end? Are convenience and of course cheapness the only values that matter to us in 1986? I'm confident that the shrewd citizens of 'Spyatri'! will have some fierce opinions about what means so . . .'

'Ball *off* and *bounce!*' shrieked Stapleton at Geoff Beeston as he furiously seized on the tuning knob and whistled it back to Fatoma and her snapping heart. It hardly needs to be underlined, the unutterable bitterness of heart of the lone romantic who had been briefly transported to another world; to a second religion; to a different continent; a wholly separate set of aesthetic and spiritual constants (*t'awryentals, yer see, hev a queer owld way of lukkin at luv. They like ter yawl on aboot fwoak pinin an pinin fer wat they carn't hev*); the supreme bitterness of Stapleton at being wrenched so rudely from intense musical emotion to the numb inconsequence of a hypermarket opening up outside 'Spyatri'.

'I hope,' spat Stapleton as he returned to the lament, 'that it crumbles overnight! I hope some bankrupt corner shop proprietor has the sense to go and gelignite it!'

A philosopher might have talked about 'a hormic drift'* (*an ormic drift*) on the part of the valve wireless which as we've stressed looked as if it had a face and a personality all its own. Expressed in other ways, just as Stapleton could not other than by self-hypnosis and Radio Tangiers, get away from the aftertaste of his job, nor from his students who in turn could not, even if they'd wished to, get away from BNFL, nor BNFL from Cumbria, nor Cumbria

---

* What on earth is 'hormic drift'? J.M.

from the larger suzerainty of England, nor the UKAEA from its international parent body, so Wm. Stapleton could not escape from Cumbria completely, even on his five-band wireless. A teleological drift (*gah back, gah back, gah back till bliddy Cummerlan!*), a kink in the tuning knob corresponding to a kink in the medium wave band, had him between nil and three times an hour bolting back from exotic Tangiers to an outside broadcast in Workington, Maryport, Wigton or . . . Sellafield . . . or a studio session in Whitehaven or Carlisle.

It was about a month ago, just after the tragedy where the Chernobyl nuclear station blew up in the Ukrainian's faces, that Stapleton's extraordinary global journey began. Previously he had travelled the airwaves to Tangiers, Sarajevo, Istanbul, Algiers, but this night he traversed the globe literally through the medium of his quaint old wireless! Some of you as children might have thrilled to tales like 'Bedknobs and Broomsticks' or Aladdin or the Wizard of Oz, and think that this bone true story of mine, Tommy Little's, is just a variation on a fairy tale. Some of you might think that William Stapleton merely went into some sort of entranced hypnotic state that deluded him into believing he actually walked round Tangiers with the radio producer Si Mohammed and other Moroccans when in fact he'd never left his comfy Cumbrian armchair. It needs to be stressed incidentally that William always *sat by* his radio, clocked intently on a chair immediately in front of it, hands ready to retune away from Geoff Beeston if need be, back to Radio Tangiers. Stapleton did not lounge six feet away as if politely watching a television. He was seated there on the job in intimate communion with his receiver. Of course all serious radio lovers are the same in this respect. For instance if they take their transistor to bed with them they rest it on their chest or stomach or bosom or chin rather than place it democratically on the chest of drawers three feet away. Listening to a radio for a true listener is a thoroughly private experience, it is not for crude sharing. It is a kind of ritual communion with a Commanding Voice, far closer to the concentrated reading of a book than it is to the lackadaisical scrutiny of television.

So imagine Stapleton sitting there, the light just fading outside one evening in early summer, squat and stocky in front of his booming valve wireless. Everything is solid, stolid, rectangular, steady, a parody of northernness. Imagine it as a sentimental picture by some overlauded northern artist. There is a feeling of resistance, slowness, *heaviness*, tranquillity, hypnosis. Think by analogy of the diesel from Carlisle to Barrow-in-Furness. You have alighted from your hi-speed, fussy, cosmopolitan, loudspeakered train from London to Carlisle and are now on the branch line to the comical west. You have dropped several units of skin resistivity as you find yourself as relaxed and droopy and dreamy as a treacle pudding. Everyone on the diesel you observe is similarly low, slow, squat, dozy, serene *(ivvrybody's eeds is wagglin slow an cosy like them laal puppit imitashun boxer dogs thoo sticks in t'back ev thee car)*. You might even be travelling in some obscure foreign peasant province like the Ukraine were you not impressed by the determined attempts in these your fellow travellers at contemporary London fashion. They have come from the vagrant west coast to shop up in Carlisle which these days beckons all comers – including continental Europe in whose railway stations the city council has placed tourist advertisements booming e.g. *Fahren Sie nach Carlisle!* – to see the castle, Hadrian's Wall, the nearby lakes, the wonderful land of the lakes! A sentimental drawing of you and your Cumbrian diesel travellers would have precisely the same sympathetic feel as a charcoal sketch of Wm. Stapleton and his dog and his wireless and mono record player out there in the countryside near Whitehaven in 1986.

William today is feeling exceptionally fatigued by the obduracy, stolidity etc. of his Sellafield students. He comes to his old wireless with something of a sick man's appetite for strong medicine. Today he has had to argue his lungs away with young Montague who had over lunch been imbibing some propaganda from his elder brother Sid. Sid, a radioactivity monitor, had just been reading a ten year-old theoretical work by Sir Fred Hoyle which boldly insisted that anti-nuclear sentiment in the west was deliberately stirred up by the unscrupulous Russians. An intelligent examination of the relevant geological maps apparently showed that there was a perilous depletion of radioactive deposits in the Soviet Union. The west, therefore argued Sir Fred, had the geological advantage when it came to uranium and so on, which explained why the specious

Russky was so busy covertly supporting Friends of the Earth and
C.N.D. in the U.K., France and U.S.A.

'Horseshit,' said Stapleton contemptuously to Montague. 'A
classic case of paranoid projection. The man's own mind is totalitarian if nothing else. His intellect and spirit are on a par with Stalin's.
They have to be for him to dream up such drivel.'

'Oor Sid says thoo's a communist, Will,' Montague answered
slyly. 'He knew what *thy* reaction would be!'

'But I'm not a communist, Monty,' said Stapleton tersely. 'I'm
a lapsed Primitive Methodist and an enthusiast for Buchmanism.'

'Bollicks,' sniffed Montague walking away in a pair of gorgeous
fawn trousers that had cost his mother eighty-five pounds from
Carlisle's *Next*.

Stapleton desperately twiddled to Radio Tangiers. He breathed
a little more calmly as Fatoma burst out into a raging fever of
miserable yearning.

My heart is torn; my stomach is particularly heavy
My eyes are sunset-red with ceaseless weeping
For Mehmet is out and leaping with his hawk
And my soul is in a terrible hell
For he sports with Lahcen his young hound
Lahcen has my Mehmet; this is the cruel truth
But whom do I have? Have I, in fact, got aught at all?

Just as William had Papcastle who sat panting underneath the
Hokusai, so Mehmet had Lahcen who sat panting by the pond after
a hard day's hunt. Thank God, conceded Stapleton, that Rhoda is
not as possessive as Fatoma, not violently jealous of old Papcastle
(*Styapleton kent wat this partickler song meant cos he hed t'syam tyeun on
a reckerd and it tellt him wat it aw meant on t'back ev t'sleeve. He didn't
unnerstan Arrapick, ev course, cos they'd nivver towt im that at colleage.*)
Intensely romantic only with regard to musical appreciation,
William sat there crooning his heartfelt drone along with the
Tangiers singer, his thoughts pleasingly wisplike and inconsequen-
tial. He pictured happily a bottle of retsina Rhoda and he would
have as a late night aperitif along with some first class olives his
wife had purchased in a Cockermouth delicatessen. It was still
impossible to buy olives in *Whitehaven* unfortunately. Not even the

BNFL magnox expansion had brought olives nor even capers to Whitehaven, though it had brought a wine bar, two kebab houses and a wholefood cafe. While he mused in this sympathetically meandering way, Fatoma's beautiful song came to its tragic climax. Her hour of singing was up. Stapleton scratched his ill-shaven cheek and picked ruminatively and ingeniously up his nose.

Then William almost died of a heart attack! As within an instant he seemed to be bodily catapulted *somewhere else*! To be victim of a sudden gush of amnesia and violent locomotion! He shuddered convulsively at the extreme strangeness of the cataclysmic sensation, then blinked again as the Tangiers announcer promptly addressed him in perfectly *intelligible* Arabic.

'William? William Stapleton? Si Mohammed! Absolutely *enchanted*!'

'Are you?' gasped Wm. in Arabic, to a suddenly materialising background and a young human figure in the foreground.

'But please please will you excuse this awful mess in the studio here? I've been far too busy to get things tidied up in here at the last minute.'

William choked. For it was about ninety nine degrees and he was sweating like a hothouse geranium! The hair was standing up on the top of his large head and the back of his small neck. Stapleton did not know a single word of standard Cairo Arabic, never mind colloquial Moroccan Arabic. He did not. Yet apparently now he *did*.

He was standing there dazedly blinking in the sleek expensive new studios of Radio Tangiers, shaking hands with Mr Si Mohammed, producer of *Classical Love Songs from Fatoma*. Si Mohammed, an immaculate and very good-looking young man of twenty-four was jauntily smoking an imported Gauloise, offering his pack with an absurdly confident expression to Stapleton. William who did not smoke took one with trembling hands, and inhaled a huge gulp as his heart began to hammer . . .

'As I say I'm sorry about the outrageous shambles in here! Fatoma you see just drops her shopping down on the floor. My wife who's having her hair done just now is no better. That's her ghastly bloody clutter scattered over there by the news desk.'

'Think nothing of it, I beg of you,' stammered William in

perfect Arabic, rubbing his nose and cheeks which were unpleasantly sweaty. It was the intense evening heat of midsummer and William felt his armpits all but melting.

'Remarkable,' whistled Si Mohammed. 'Your Arabic pronunciation is quite faultless!'

'I . . .'

'Moroccan Arabic no less! The real thing! Did you have some training, William?'

'Eh?'

'No, scarcely likely I suppose. No, but you must have lived in Morocco to get such a fine accent?'

Abruptly he left William to his own devices for a few minutes and exchanged humorous, energetic banter with another young man who had entered Fatoma's now empty studio. Si Mohammed then strutted back loftily and gushed to Stapleton that *that* was Moulay Ali, the highly renowed presenter of Morocco's very favourite pop programme.

Then:

'Where exactly was it you've come from, William?' he asked through fantastically over-hasty puffs of his Gauloise.

'Whitehaven,' said Stapleton, in Moroccan Arabic.

Si Mohammed looked grave. 'In England?'

'Oh yes.'

'Of course! But do you know it's the first time we've had any international contacts here not Francophone?'

He gazed at blank-faced William for an acknowledgement of the uniqueness of his visit. William pursed his lips and replied:

'Actually I was sitting with Papcastle in my place near Whitehaven . . .'

'Near London?' interrupted Si Mohammed hopefully.

'Not at all,' Stapleton clarified. 'It's in Cum . . .'

'Qom?' interrupted the producer amazed.

'It's near Scotland,' William blushed. He always blushed when he explained to outsiders where Cumbria was. Less than two per cent of the British knew where it was, or indeed anything at all about it. 'It's in England but right at the very top. In the far north western corner in fact.'

'Really your Arabic is exceptional,' Si Mohammed beamed,

taking his arm affectionately. 'Fancy them teaching it in Whitehaven.'

'Perhaps they do in the A streams of the comprehensive,' Stapleton murmured dazedly. 'No, I was . . .'

'At any rate your station *is* Whitehaven?'

'What?'

'Your radio station! The circular we had last month from our National Network Public Relations Department in Rabat said that you were a chief station manager from England.'

'I . . .'

'No, I thought not!' Si Mohammed smirked. 'You have far too much intelligence for *that*. No you could only be a producer like myself. They've got it all wrong at Rabat, upside down obviously. I don't remember anything in the circular about your working near Scotland so they've obviously passed the telex on to some minor clerk in personnel who's copied it down with his eyes closed. Would you like some mint tea by the way?'

'I'd love some,' said Stapleton dizzily. 'I feel incredibly hot. It's incredibly hot here isn't it?'

At this point Fatoma emerged from the studio. She had been standing talking impassionedly to Moulay Ali who was now leerily gazing after her. Fatoma was even more beautiful than William had fantasised. She had wide, vivid brown eyes, a full and candid gaze, a certain set expression of nascent irritation. (*She hed an owld-feshiont squint on her an a fyass that says I divn't mind argy-bargy wit a feller that makks bliddy gamm of me*). Though she looked rather weary as she gave the guest from England a frank stare of curiosity.

'It went *brilliantly*,' purred Si Mohammed. 'Flawlessly my dear.'

'Thank you,' said Fatoma expressionlessly. 'It damn well ought to after fifteen hundred performances.' She flung herself down on a stool and then picked a packet of halva out of her shopping bag. She began to munch it dolefully. 'I'm as tired as Mehmet of her incessant bloody yearning.'

Stapleton flinched with surprise and disappointment. Timid if not terrified by these incredible circumstances, he couldn't help saying mournfully to her nonetheless. 'Don't you identify with the part then, madame?'

'You're kidding,' snorted Fatoma incredulously. 'I think she needs a sky rocket up her silly behind, the idiot! She should have poisoned the dog and throttled the blasted hawk long ago. Or better still throttled Mehmet. That would have been a lasting solution to her pathetic problems,' she ended with a sly grin at Si Mohammed.

Si Mohammed grinned a naive little grin at her cynicism. He pointed at William in his yellow Marks and Spencer's cardigan and said. 'This is Mr William Stapleton, Fatoma! He's the chief producer at Radio Whitehaven.'

'Cum . . .', began William.

'Qom?' interrupted Fatoma amazed.

'Radio Cumbria,' explained Stapleton, who had never been inside a radio studio in his life. 'They do have a Whitehaven producer but it's called Radio Cumbria. The main studio is in Carlisle.' He stared at them staring at his rapid explanation and stammered. 'Have you heard of Carlisle? There's a slogan on all the British railway stations says "Come to Carlisle". I believe they have them on some foreign stations too.'

Si Mohammed mumbled importantly that he might have seen a 'Come to Carlisle' poster down at Casablanca. Fatoma glanced at him very sceptically, then asked Stapleton:

'What do they say about Whitehaven? Do they say "Wend to Whitehaven"?'

'Why do they ask people to "Come to Carlisle"?' asked Si Mohammed, handing William a large glass mug of mint tea. There was about a quarter of a pound of what looked like watercress stewing in hot water. There were six sugar cubes on the saucer and six more busy dissolving in among the watercress.

'They want tourists I suppose,' said William, reeling, almost gagging at what tasted like the spearmint toffee of his infancy liquidised and steeped in honey.

'For pilgrimage?' asked Fatoma. 'Is it a spiritual centre? Like Qom?'

'For money,' answered William. 'They want tourists for money I suppose.'

He blushed at the general motliness of mind he felt despite his incredible facility with Arabic. 'Ah, they don't actually say "Wend to Whitehaven." '

'At any rate, he *is* a brilliant producer,' Si Mohammed said, and then smirking at Stapleton's obvious bafflement added. 'With Arabic like that! Have you ever heard such a faultless accent, Fatoma? You'd think he was born and bred in Tangiers. It's incredible. I feel I could almost pinpoint the street where he learnt those inflections, those rhythms, those little nuances. It was definitely somewhere in the medina wasn't it? Or overlooking the sea?'

'I was born in Waberthwaite,' Stapleton conceded.

'*Waa b'th wa'at?*' echoed Fatoma. 'Is that in the Yemen?'

'Nonsense. Tangiers medina,' insisted Si Mohammed. 'Is it the name of a house in . . .' he screwed up his perfect eyes and flawless nose, '. . . in Rue Zaltouri, Maimuni, Oued Has, somewhere like that?'

'It's near BNFL,' stuttered William.

'*Ibn Hafl?*' asked the producer cupping his ears incredulously.

'No, BNFL,' William muttered once again, suddenly deciding that all he wanted to do was to come clean on all fronts. But as soon as he made this decision he was struck by a really horrible thought. If he started talking about being transubstantiated from Whitehaven to Tangiers on a magic carpet whose threads were so to speak rather subtly invisible, they might decide to put him in a Moroccan madhouse. Or even give him over to the police as some dubious Moroccan impersonating an English radio producer with the suspiciously flawless accent of a native Tangerine.

'Ibn Hafl,' chuckled Fatoma sceptically. 'I think William's playing a game or two with us.' She smiled approvingly. 'Anyway, stop grilling him so ruthlessly, Si Mohammed. Who says he has to tell you everything about himself?' She narrowed her eyes playfully as she went on. 'Where was Si Mohammed born come to that? Where was his father born? Where was his old grandad born?'

Si Mohammed whose grandfather had been a water carrier but whose father was the manager of a three star hotel in Tetouan, turned suddenly remarkably inquisitive about Radio Cumbria. He wanted to know all about its programme schedules; the names of its producers; its budgets; the fees paid to performers; its sponsors; William's precise salary; the head of station's salary and the salary of the tea boys.

William Stapleton who never listened to local radio from one year to the next (other than forcibly, in response to his tuning knob's homing instinct) still read his *Radio Times* from cover to cover and had a phenomenal memory for things not worth remembering. Thus without pausing for breath he was able to sketch for Fatoma and Si Mohammed an informative synopsis of the Radio Cumbria schedule.

'Saturday dawns on "Cumbria Countryside",' he explained, as he gingerly gargled his spearmint tea, 'with Tony Gust as its regular presenter. Which is followed by "Saturday Scene" with Harry Harrison, as he sets you up for the weekend with what's on: the market prices for fat lambs at Cockermouth, Lazonby, Wigton, Penrith etc., plus a comprehensive sports preview. This is followed as far as I can recall by "Saturday Roadshow" which is promptly succeeded by "Go Country" . . .'

'A natural history programme?' asked Si Mohammed with tense fascination.

'Cowboy songs,' corrected Stapleton (*coopoy tyeuns and do-si-doh by fellers wearin chaps an stitsuns*). 'Followed by Beeston's Pot-Pourri.'

'What the hell is that?' asked Fatoma, startled.

'Music intended to relax the audience into a benign weekend mood . . . interspersed with local sports reports.'

'It all sounds a bit old fashioned,' said Si Mohammed with disappointment.

'Sunday sees Harry Harrison back again with "Sunday Scene". Full, I believe, of nice relaxing music. Followed by the "Sunday Breakfast Show" which consists by and large of music that is soothing. This in turn is followed by "Countywide" which is just before "Sunday Requests" (for some tranquil music intended to relax the Cumbrian nerves). Which is just prior to Harry Harrison saying "That's Entertainment" (easy listening is the name of the game) followed immediately by an education magazine called "Across the Board".'

'Thank God for that,' gasped Si Mohammed fervently.

'This is succeeded by "Sportstalk Sunday".'

Fatoma looked dazed, not to say disbelieving.

'During the week,' Stapleton went on with unstoppable hysterical fluency, 'there are a great many three hour relaxing music shows with special guests: Cumbrian notables; local politicians; visiting celebrities from the great world beyond. Many of the weekend programmes are repeated once if not more during the week. There are also of course phone-ins which are immensely popular so I'm told.'

Si Mohammed disappointedly gulped his mint tea and inquired. 'What do they phone in about?'

'If they wish to exchange a hat rack for a video cassette. If they are looking for some tea-urns for a chapel hall.' (*An Styapleton thowt till issel, Isn't it wunnerful that ah know the bliddy Arrapick fer 'at-rack' and 'cha-urran' and 'shappel'!*)

Fatoma scratched her pretty ear and grinned at him as if he were some becardiganned jester subtly mixing fable and fact.

'What are your best programmes, William?' asked Si Mohammed anxiously. 'From a professional's point of view?'

'The news,' said Stapleton after long pondering. 'Give them . . . I mean give *us* our due, we do some very good news bulletins often syndicated to the national BBC.'

'The BBC!' snorted Si Mohammed reverentially.

'Yes, it is . . . I mean we are *BBC* Radio Cumbria. So it . . . so we have no advertisers nor sponsors, none of that. We also have a very low budget for all our programmes and pay our freelance contributors next to nothing. The producers . . . like myself . . . are on salaries and by dint of hard work and ambition hope to leave Radio Cumbria, having taken what we can from it, and then go and work for commercial television and become very rich.'

Si Mohammed stared with even greater admiring scrutiny as he heard him talk about using local radio as a springboard to national television. Fatoma noted his eager appreciation and sneered. She was not sneering at William though whom she still believed to be cleverly leading Si Mohammed along with a playfully embroidered story.

'What is,' began Si Mohammed, uneasy at Fatoma's pitiless glare, 'what *are* the principal news issues, William, at your Radio Cumbria?'

William shrugged and scratched his sweating nose again. 'Ah unemployment. Ah employment also. New industries I suppose. You see we have had an economic recession for about seventy years in industrial Cumbria whereas Britain overall has only had it for a decade. So if a new factory employing six people opens up we make a loud celebration on the radio and elsewhere. Otherwise the news is usually about our controversial industries, the ones that effect the British nation at large.'

'Controversy?' asked Si Mohammed bemusedly.

'BNFL.'

'*Ibn Hafl*,' laughed Fatoma slapping her arm approvingly.

'Windscale; Sellafield; BNFL. They are all the same. It is all the same thing you see, Si Mohammed.'

Si Mohammed looked uncomfortable at William's curiously coded speech.

'They are all a nuclear power station, Si Mohammed. This huge nuclear power station is built at a scattered hamlet called Sellafield and the specific part of the hamlet where it resides is called Windscale. BNFL means British Nuclear Fuels Ltd. But they are all one and the same and indivisible, like the world famous Christian trinity.'

'A source of controversy,' Si Mohammed agreed. 'The Christian trinity is rather fantastic in my opinion.'

'It employs about half of industrial Cumbria,' William explained, relinquishing the dregs of his tea. 'Thousands and thousand of workers, plus cartloads of contractors from Glasgow, Newcastle and elsewhere. If it were to close tomorrow the county would be in a dreadful state. The country at large is moderately afraid of it, especially after Chernobyl, and they are very glad that the West Cumbrians are not afraid of it at all. Some of them think the Cumbrians are possibly staring mad not to be afraid of it, and the government thinks likewise, but is extremely pleased also as the country has to have nuclear power, it is the law. The Cumbrians' staunchness and reckless courage is therefore absolutely indispensable to the welfare of my nation at large.'

'But where,' demanded Si Mohammed, 'does such remarkable courage come from?'

'I haven't a clue,' said Stapleton. Then wincing at the memory he added. 'I actually teach young BNFL men who deny all possibility of danger, either locally, nationally or internationally.'

Si Mohammed whistled approvingly. 'You are a teacher as well?

51

That's surprising. I thought it was only in countries like Morocco one needed two jobs to survive. By the way, what is your exact salary at Radio Cumbria.'

Stapleton grimaced as he blurted from the top of his head. 'Twelve thousand pounds per annum.'

'Two hundred thousand dirhams,' gasped Fatoma after two seconds computation. 'Would you like to take us out on the town to celebrate the fact of your salary?'

Stapleton looked terribly awkward as he fished inside his trousers to unearth what he suspected was about two pounds in silver. Instead, to his gaping astonishment, he came out with a bulging fistful of hundred dirham notes . . .

'Where should we go?' he said hoarsely to Fatoma. 'I honestly don't know the town at all. It really is my very first time here!'

'Nonsense,' said Si Mohammed sharply. 'She was joking, the silly sarcastic bitch! I will take us all out for a meal, William! Including you Fatoma, even with your constant sulks and boring complaints. Just let me pick up my wife's things and we'll catch her at the hairdresser's. It's right at the bottom of Boulevard Pasteur so we can cut across and eat at Rue Sanlucar.'

'Where your brother-in-law always eats?' said Fatoma disdainfully.

'At Lahcen's,' said Si Mohammed with a frosty look.

The singer pulled a face of ineffable disaffection. Her beauty, William re-remarked, really was of the order of mythology or scripture.

'Do you want a free meal or not? What's wrong with Lahcen's anyway? His tagines are brilliant.'

'It's not Lahcen, it's your brother-in-law.'

'You tell that to my wife,' said Si Mohammed curtly.

'Habiba never speaks to me,' she answered. Then she turned to Stapleton and said. 'She suspects me of infidelity with Si Mohammed because of our professional proximity. Tell me, William, can you think of anything more ridiculous?'

'I . . .'

'Si Mohammed is only a boy of twenty-four,' she went on scornfully. 'Though it's not for want of trying on his part. Nor of that other precocious juvenile Moulay Ali, the disco king of

Tangiers. Look at him there, babbling away into his mike as if he was Bob Geldof's little brother.'

'William – what do you think about Moroccan pop music?' babbled Si Mohammed, keen to avert the heat of Fatoma's scorn.

'It's outstanding,' lied William, as he tried not to listen to Moulay Ali's latest choice. It was like a surreal travesty of Fatoma's beautiful lament.

'It is certainly not tranquil nor relaxing,' the producer said portentously. 'Our Tangerine listeners do not want to relax! They want to be invigorated, diverted, entranced.'

The three of them stepped out into the Place de France, Tangiers's most illustrious square, the centre piece of the *ville nouvelle*. It was all white gleaming concrete, hallucinatingly hygienic, and reminded William of some rebuilt German town like Köln or Aachen. It made Whitehaven look like the Gorbals. Si Mohammed noticed his impressedness and nudged him playfully.

'You still insist you've never lived here, William! Never mind! I like people who have secrets and play the part, who don't give too much away.'

'Pah,' said Fatoma, and then chased away a ragged boy who was about to fall upon and clean Stapleton's shoes. As they passed down the Boulevard Pasteur Stapleton was even more impressed. Fine emporium after fine emporium, each as glamorously exclusive as in München or Bath, selling in the main costly-looking souvenirs and antiques. There were bejewelled daggars, Berber carpets, painted pots, carved musical instruments, touching little make-up pots and applicators carved out of wood. There were gorgeous silken chelims hanging by the dozen above aloof and beautifully dressed proprietors. Most of the Moroccans promenading down the boulevard were dressed like his companions in very smart western attire, but now and again he saw a wealthy-looking male in a clean, immaculate *djellaba*.

'How does this compare with Whitehaven?' inquired Si Mohammed through his reverie.

'It's more like Carlisle,' William temporised. 'The very smartest bits of it, that is.'

'*Come to Carlisle*,' chuckled Fatoma, using her hand as a megaphone. 'Come and listen to Beeston's Pot-Pourri.'

'Hah! said William with queasy cheerfulness. By which we mean he was in a complicated state of amnesic shock, as he simply could not acknowledge how it was he had switched continents by listening to his old valve wireless. In part, in a very small part, he was exalted by his adventuring around a smart African city with these two illustrious radio personalities, colloguing with them in choicest Moroccan Arabic. The other part was of course terrified, and wanted to be back safe at home in Whitehaven with Papcastle and Rhoda, sipping retsina and munching olives, which was as much as he wanted to have to do with the Middle East *from now on* thank you very much . . .

All of a sudden William Stapleton felt as if he were being wound up by clockwork and forced to make a pointed sort of speech. (*Styapleton felt as if sum laal invisble gadger wuss winin im up like a clockwukk moose an makkin im say aw makk ev set speech an daft propgander.*)

'From one point of view,' he began with this sudden frantic gust of eloquence and hand gestures that apparently came from nowhere. 'From one point of view I come from the Third World myself.'

'Eh?' said Fatoma amazed, as if she recognised the artificial nature of this speech.

'Yes,' chuckled Si Mohammed, thumping him vigorously across his cardigan. 'The Tangiers medina, you old rogue!'

'No,' William smiled, at Fatoma rather than the producer. She was listening as if riveted to his mechanical oratory. 'No from Whitehaven. Or from West Cumbria, it amounts to the same. I come from Britain's Third World and I don't see that as too whimsical, not at all. Let me explain straight away that the splendour of this part of your city makes my little home town look like the back streets of Lahore. You see, what I'm trying to convey is . . .'

But by now they had reached a French coiffure house *Madamoiselle*, and there waiting at the door for them was Habiba. Habiba was short, plump, attractive, sulky, frowning and fleetingly aloof. Seeing Stapleton she looked quizzical; seeing Fatoma critical. She then looked back to Stapleton quizzically critical. Finally she glowered at her sleek young husband and snarled that he was over half an hour late. Si Mohammed shrugged rather fearlessly and said that he'd been entertaining an outstandingly distinguished radio producer from England, Mr W. Stapleton. Habiba looked baffled by William's yellow Marks and Spencer's cardigan and its contrast with her husband's beautiful French suit. She gave the Cumbrian a stiff nod. William held out his hand and then embarrassedly withdrew it. Then to his shy amazement he rallied and in decorous most felicitous Arabic loudly declared himself absolutely delighted to meet the remarkable wife of a remarkable Moroccan media man!

Habiba looked most suspicious but snorted that she too was undoubtedly charmed.

'William is a man of mystery,' Fatoma addressed the air rather than Habiba. 'He speaks perfect Arabic, like a back street Tangerine, yet claims the only Third World he knows is Whitehaven in Cum . . .'

'Qom?' broke in Habiba, addressing Si Mohammed. 'Qom in Iran?'

'Yes, Cumbria,' her husband agreed with a possessive grin. 'Yes, he discourses in sly paradoxes like a poet. In fact all considered William has the looks of an English poet. You'll be fascinated to meet Habiba's brother, William.'

'He is a brilliant artist,' said Habiba aggressively to Stapleton. 'Moulay Ismail is second to none.'

'Yes,' said Fatoma. 'Isn't he just.'

'As I was saying,' Stapleton impulsively pursued, as if driven by that same invisible hand as they passed down into Rue Sanlucar, 'I know what it is to come from the Third World myself!'

'But of course,' said Fatoma poker-faced. 'A hat rack for a video cassette. But of course!'

'I come from one of England's poorest provinces,' Wm. insisted. 'As I told your husband, Habiba, we have had an economic recession for about seventy years. Until ten years ago we had hopeless road connections with the world beyond our confining mountains. Then the expansion of Sellafield was mooted and it was considered appropriate to have a capacious dual carriageway from Penrith to the West.'

'Sellafield?' asked Habiba, mystified.

'Ibn Hafl,' laughed Fatoma. 'A nuclear power plant like the Ukrainian Chernobyl.'

'Heavens,' sighed Habiba.

'Before it was a nuclear power station,' William explained to Habiba, 'it was used to prepare fissile material for nuclear weapons. It was called in those days Calder Hall. This was the fourth aspect of the tripartite monolith (*like yan ev them Intoo gods wid three fyasses an an extra yan fer luck!*): Windscale/Sellafield/BNFL. It thus goes beyond the Christian trinity in its quantity. You'll probably be unaware of this but in 1957 there was a major nuclear accident, a smaller version of Chernobyl at C.H/W/S/BNFL.'

Fatoma grinned widely at his acronymic eloquence.

'There was a radioactive fire at "Ibn Hafl" in 1957. Substantial quantities of flaming radio-iodine were emitted into the West Cumbrian air and ultimately into the milk of the cows in the adjacent pasture.'

'Heavens,' said Si Mohammed.

'The government at the recommendation of the scientists, had all the local farmers throw their milk away, and furthermore told the West Cumbrians that there was nothing at all to worry about. It is an impressive anecdote that when the works and local fire brigades turned up on the scene neither of them had the faintest idea how to extinguish a radioactive blaze. In fact at first they poured on enormous volumes of water, as if it was just an extra large bonfire.'

'William's fairy stories,' said Fatoma, 'really are first class.'

'My point is,' said William, still in his very assumed voice, 'is that these hazardous industries are always built in the Third World. If not in the true Third World then substitute Third Worlds. Great British Third Worlds: West Cumbria; Dumfriesshire; Caithness; Wales etc. They do not build them on the outskirts of Bournemouth, though there are ample reserves of freshwater thereabout. They do not customarily build them in Chelsea, even though the Thames is bursting with water and London has a few dozen unemployed as far as I know.'

Stapleton found his odd clockwork voice petering out as they reached Lahcen's. Indeed he coughed, as if to signal the end of his tongue having been invaded and possessed. The party took an outside table on a noisy side street and Si Mohammed ordered beer all round and recommended William try the lamb tagine with prunes. The Englishman was starving by this hour and hungrily wolfed it all down, prune stones included. Habiba was still energetically sulking and steadfastly refused to countenance never mind converse with Fatoma. Fatoma was in a diffusely cheerful, mischievous frame of mind, largely caused by her contemplation of the extraordinary Englishman. William was one of the craziest radio producers she'd ever met, a foolish if harmless Nazarene who apparently had none of her own colleagues' boastfulness nor banter nor that exhausting sexual innuendo.

'Where is your brother?' Stapleton thought to ask Habiba, to break an embarrassing silence between Si Mohammed and her.

As if in rehearsed response a powerful Peugeot came roaring round the corner and halted with a deafening scream of brakes. It drew up about six inches from their white plastic table and Stapleton rose and ran to save his life. His glass of beer was wobbling liquid onto the saffron stains of his plate. Fatoma seated next to him merely shrugged and mouthed the name 'Moulay Ismail' as if it were a pitiable joke or curse. The car door flew open and a grinning, swaggering extravagance of about thirty-five lurched whimsically out of his vehicle. His sunny grin was outstandingly all-inclusive; not so much complacent as that of an artless little boy or youth. Indeed on the surface Moulay Ismail seemed an affable, warm individual and Stapleton smiled in response as he accepted his large hand.

Moulay Ismail held the Englishman's paw for about ten seconds, crushing it painfully and grinning the while. William started then laughed as heartily as he could, but finally gave in and winced. In response Moulay himself pulled a face of exaggerated pain, removed and shook his huge hand as if puny Wm. Stapleton had been the he-man! William laughed with tortured amusement at this subtle circus comedy. Fatoma gave a bored shrug to indicate that this was how Moulay Ismail always behaved towards new masculine acquaintances (*an thoo can aw predict oo he carrit on wit gut-lyeukin Morkan bodies fust time he clappt eyes on em*). Habiba and the hand-crusher then kissed and after that Si Mohammed embraced his brother-in-law. Fatoma stared obstinately at the ground when Moulay Ismail attempted to approach her.

'She's in the sulks,' chimed Si Mohammed over-critically, as if to appease Habiba.

'She's afraid of the bear,' chuckled Moulay Ismail like an outsize suction pipe. He rattled himself approvingly on his great chest and then said in a rather wheedling apologetic tone. 'Your broadcast tonight was sheer magic, Fatoma. It was pure nectar; white moonlight; it was lovely honey!'

Fatoma continued to stare vacantly at a discarded carton on the ground. Waving a disdainful hand at her silence, Si Mohammed introduced the chief features producer of Radio Cum . . .

'Qom?' grunted Moulay Ismail disbelievingly.

'No, England, though half of it's in Scotland apparently. He lives right next door to a nuclear power station that set on fire thirty years ago. They had to throw all the farmers' milk away.'

'Shame,' said Moulay Ismail cheerfully. 'Tell me. How much do you make as an English radio producer?'

'Two hundred thousand dirhams a year,' Si Mohammed supplied and went on to elaborate proudly on this special educational visit by a foreign producer organised by the big wheels at Rabat. Moulay Ismail nodded importantly with attentive eyes of hurried calculation. William thought it might be to do with their respective salaries but Fatoma murmured *sotto voce* that he was simply feeling jealous of his limelight and foreign status.

'Tell me what you think of my car,' Moulay Ismail commanded Stapleton. He was briefly interrupted by the proprietor Lahcen who was seemingly used to acting the meek footstool to the discriminating poet. They went through severe and tortuous exegetical analysis of Lahcen's menu until the poet with an appropriately grave finality ordered special kebabs and a double portion of tomato salad.

'It's a beauty,' said Wm. politely in his faultless slum Arabic.

'It cost me a hundred thousand dirhams,' Moulay Ismail hissed wetly in his ear. He had moved his chair immediately adjacent to the Nazarene so that Fatoma had risen and shifted next to Si Mohammed. As they discussed her next broadcast together, Habiba stared disdainfully into space. Moulay Ismail continued a highly confidential conversation with a forcibly riveted William.

'A hundred thousand!' he whistled impressed. 'You must be a millionaire, a sheikh, an Ali Baba.'

'I am simply a success,' Moulay Ismail spat into his ear. 'Nothing more. I am simply a great, an enormous success.'

Stapleton blinked then smiled with flattery. He was always glad to appease those who thrived on it. It cost him nothing after all.

'Si Mohammed tells me that you are a talented poet.'

'Yes I am. I am an exceedingly highly successful poet.'

'Quite,' smiled ingenuous Stapleton. 'But I don't expect you making a living out of it, do you?'

'What on *earth* do you mean?' thundered Moulay Ismail with real poetic bellicosity.

William flinched then blushed as he stated his cautious doubts. 'What I mean is, surely you don't support yourself as a poet? Here in Morocco I mean.'

'And why on earth not?' snorted Moulay Ismail with a cavalier flick of his vast head.

'You bought a hundred thousand dirham car with your poetry earnings?' persisted William numbly. For some reason he still felt as if he had his hand being crushed by the Peugeot owner.

'But of course!'

'Christ Almighty!'

'What?' coughed Moulay Ismail through a ton of dripping tomato salad. Wm. saw three black olives in place of six front teeth. 'Oh the way Nazarenes swear! Tell me, Stapleton, how many children have you got?'

'None,' counter-coughed William, looking remarkably put on the spot by such frank interrogation. 'We will have before long, *hamdullah*. But we have none precisely at the moment.'

The poet smiled at his nervously garrulous explanation. 'And how old are you, William? Tell me exactly how old you are!'

'I'm thirty-six.'

'And how old is your wife?'

'Rhoda's just turned thirty.'

Moulay Ismail stared at Stapleton as if he were a withered, ludicrous eunuch. 'You are thirty-six and you have *no* children! Why is that? Explain yourself!'

'But we have a dog,' tittered Stapleton weakly. 'He's called Pap – '

'Gah!' muttered Moulay Ismail. 'I am only thirty-four and I have five children! Five very vigorous boys, Stapleton!'

'Oh?' said William stickily. 'You'll need to write a lot of poems to feed them. A dozen a day. Don't you find?'

'Eh?' growled Moulay Ismail, clattering his glass of beer violently on the table.

'You have a lot of dependent dependents,' Stapleton flattered the highly fertile poet.

'Gah,' laughed Moulay Ismail with brittle generosity. He thumped Stapleton on the back with an excess of his virile vigour. 'I think in my case it is a question of *race*.'

William frowned expectantly, terrified out of his wits.

'Africa!' Moulay extolled, pointing to an imaginary blazing sun above their heads. 'The heat! Eh? Yes! The sun creates the heat! The heat creates virility, power. . . . fertility in my case. Both physiological and artistic! Over in England it's always cold and raining, isn't that true? As a result of which the males there are not half so sturdy. I believe that is a sufficient explanation.' (*Mooly Ismel says wit Inglish chaps gitting drensht an pisht on day in day oot, the fellers nivver git enuf eat frae't sun ter mek their pitifel ballocks dangel strang an lusty! But in Morko with rowstin eat aw t'time, t'laal Morkan lads ev lazy lob-ons frae dawn till bliddy dusk!*)

Instantly sapless sexless Stapleton felt an overwhelming wish to be back in the countryside near Whitehaven! At home with Rhoda, perhaps doing something about what Moulay Ismail regarded as a risible lack of physiological brio. William who always felt constrained and reduced by the shortcomings of his queer little home county, felt intensely this old wish to be back there safely hampered, safely reduced and happily constrained! He craved his old bondage like a runaway slave in delirium. He wanted to go home. (*He wantit ter gah yam, ter gah back till Whitehebben!*)

Spontaneously in broadest dialect he cried aloud. 'Ah want ter gah yam!'

'Eh?' laughed Fatoma. 'What the hell is that gibberish? Has the beer made you sing?'

'Ah want ter gah yam!' repeated Wm. dolefully.

'Turkish? Coptic? Armenian? Naughty William – you aren't just a damn Jew from the Mellah after all are you?'

BIP BLIP BLIP VLIP!

Geoffrey Beeston climbed energetically into the driver side of his C registered Fiesta while passenger William dazedly adjusted his seat belt and stared about him at a recently built car park. They were on a slight hill elevation, it was a sunny day, and looking to the side of him Stapleton could see the backstreets of a very grubby part of a red brick city which he did not at first recognise.

'*Hamdullah!*' he said loudly to Beeston whom again he did not at first recognise. 'Thank God to be back here in what looks very much like the north of grubby old England to me.'

He spoke in English of course, other than his initial interjection. As did Beeston who seemed wholly unsurprised by this recent arrival in the front of his car.

'Rightio, Billy boy,' he said cheerfully. 'Sellafield cooling towers here we spurtieth.'

Spurtieth?

Sellafield! What? Stapleton had never felt so relieved to hear that familiar name, that ineffable statement of time and place and definition! *Ibn Hafl* indeed! He placed his hand affectionately on Boston's tweed-jacketed shoulder and said. 'You are really going across to Windscale?'

'At this bloody rate once a week,' grumbled Beeston, a little awkward at the passion in that shoulder clasp. 'Still, I enjoy the undeniably scenic drive. We'll cut through to Cleator Moor via Swallow Hill and Moresby Parks and then towards Ennerdale and then over the tops into Calder Bridge. You get an absolutely gorgeous view of Calder Hall from up there.'

Stapleton almost wept to hear those familiar names of those mostly dirty little villages! Home! Away from that poisonous fantasy, that horribly unreal interlude of being whisked to bloody Morocco – of all places! – on a magic airwave. (How exactly he had fortuitously arrived in the front of Beeston's car when he was last seen in England in his own attic, he decided for the moment not to worry his head about.)

'Drop me off at – ' and William named the hamlet just outside Whitehaven where he lived with Rhoda and Papcastle.

Beeston dealt him a glance of comic censure. 'You lazy bloody beggar! You're coming with me all the way to Sellafield! Whether you like it or no!'

After a second or so of cold calculation, Stapleton smiled queasily. With a glassy premonition. That he was not after all properly corporeally back in England, back home in Cumbria . . .

No, he was still radio-controlled, he sadly hazarded, as he gazed anxiously about him, trying to make sense of this new location. The premonition was of course that his valve wireless tuning knob had just gone and slipped and whisked him back to Radio Cumbria! Oh Christ, he thought horrified, at this vision of himself being catapulted at the whim of omnipotent physics from one half of the globe to the other. *Oh Christ, oh Christ, oh Christ!*

'You must be that local producer chap,' he mumbled. 'You're Jack Brighton aren't you?'

'Ha!' responded Geoff Beeston as he pulled past a modern block of offices which proclaimed itself to be simultaneously a tax office, a driving test centre and finally the studios of BBC Radio Cumbria.

'Aren't you Jack Brighton?' Wm. said miserably. 'You certainly correspond to his likeness in the Radio Times North West edition.'

Beeston shrugged long-sufferingly. 'I'm like Shiva, I get called everything. Dave Bristow; Tom Baistow, Ted Bursough; Tod Brisket. You might think Geoff Beeston is a simple enough formula to remember. I'm sure I should remember it if I were someone else. If I were called for example William Stapleton. Beeston. The double vowel is distinctive enough to help commit it to memory. It's a town in Nottinghamshire as well, come to that, like Mansfield or Sandiacre. And I come from Staffordshire which isn't that far off. Perhaps,' he concluded ruefully, 'I should have called myself Reginald Rugeley, after our local coal-fired power station.'

Stapleton squeaked unheedingly. '*Where* in hell are we? This isn't Whitehaven as far I can see. It's horribly familiar but this isn't Lowther Street or Duke Street.'

'For a Cumbrian,' said Beeston, turning up a very long,

straight, two-laned road which stretched past umpteen cheap shops and cafes and dirty-looking fronts, 'you have a peculiarly subtle sense of playfulness.'

'Oh Christ I know where this is,' said Stapleton aghast. 'This is bloody Botchergate. This is bloody downtown Carlisle, isn't it!'

'*Come to Carlisle,*' warbled Beeston unmelodiously as he deftly overtook a parked potato lorry.

'Wend to Whitehaven,' corrected Stapleton. 'And drop me off at my house at — , will you?'

Beeston shrugged impatiently, with a little less of that inflexible ease which was his only possible means of proving an accomplished media tyro in the provinces. 'Give it a rest, will you. You're learning how to operate a tape recorder and how to conduct a live interview! You've got to do it sooner or later, or they won't take you on as a freelance presenter. Which is your solid gold bloody ambition, isn't it? You have to have some first hand experience, Bill, no way round that one. And these jobs I can assure you, signor, are like gold dust, even if they do pay in fools' gold, in brass buttons that is. It's like being a solicitor to some extent; you have to pay to get your blasted articles. They're all queuing up for this kind of experience, so they can end up one day like yours emphatically, a bona fide producer.'

'A *Whitehaven* producer?' Stapleton confirmed, feeling rather like Si Mohammed.

'Geoff Beeston, prima facie! Preema fassya, marra, in Cumbrianese. The world's expert on Windscale, that's what I be! The man forever on the job like Henry Miller or Casanova.'

'Tell me,' gulped William unamused. 'Who is it that I'm interviewing?'

'You really are a dozy Cumbrian, aren't you?' said Beeston looking at him with baffled irritation. 'You're talking to Wilfred *Glenridding*, Bill.'

'Glenridding? That's a blasted street in Keswick,' protested Stapleton. 'Or rather no, no it isn't, it's the name of a fell.'

'BNFL Publicity Officer,' Beeston snapped. 'For Christ's sake don't you go and mix him up with little Cumcatch.'

'You're joking,' snorted Stapleton, looking genuinely outraged. 'A man called Cumcatch!'

'A man called Horse, tatumtata. Cumcatch is the nice short nervous one. He's the Windscale P.R., as you well know.'

Stapleton put both fingers in his ears, breathed fiercely through his nose, then pulled the fingers out again.

'And what's the difference?' he begged, stunned.

'Eh?' sighed Geoff wearily.

'Between Publicity and P.R.?'

'Well that one's simple enough, even for a simple Cumbrian. Or rather especially, appropriately for a simple Cumbrian! Publicity means explaining, clarifying, justifying, expatiating on: dangers, worries, anxieties and, I suppose, leaks. P.R. on the other hand is giving out grants, disbursements, funds, pump primings, argent, lucres etc as a reward to the hospitable local community. Cumcatch puts precious lifeblood into the veins of athletes, Maryport museums, Whitehaven housing associations, more or less anyone who wants a bit of spoiling and isn't actually affiliated to Greenpeace or the Kremlin. Glenridding is the tall, testy, burly, assertive one before whom Cumcatch bows with tremulous reverence.'

'Does he really?' said Stapleton, afraid of Glenridding already.

'Because Glenridding is fearless and unflappable. He's amazing. Don't you think so, as a concerned local? I mentioned it to Candy the other day, that if something like Chernobyl were to happen here tomorrow Wilfred Glenridding would be ready with a press release on best Croxley script to the effect that *by and large* the local population need have nothing at all to worry about. Most tellingly of all, staunch Glenridding himself would undoubtedly believe it. Ken Cumcatch would also certainly believe it. All the locals like yourself would most certainly believe him.'

'Would I/they?' snorted William, indignant among many indignations at being taken for a nondescript local. 'But what about when – just let me throw this in the air as a wild possibility – they started to perish and puke from gamma radiation in Egremont and Gosforth?' (*Will sez ter Beeston gadger, wat aboot when t'marrers in Egmont and Gosfer starts ter pyook up their rings and fry like best back byacon when Sellerfield starts makkin a melt-doon comoshun like Shurnobble?*)

'Wilf'd tell them they have *nothing to worry about*. To go to

64

bed for the afternoon with a Paracetamol and a back copy of Tit-Bits.'

Annoyed above all by Beeston's remorseless media cheeriness, Wm. protested. 'And what about when – just let me fling this in the air as a mad hypothesis – they were *dead*?'

'They would have *nothing* to worry about then. Would they? Glenridding would issue a press release to say the corpses *by and large* need have nothing to worry about. I mentioned that to Candy. I said at no point along the line would anyone panic. Least of all the dead, God bless them. Glenridding is capable of mass hypnosis, I'm sure of that. He's a very brilliant man, undoubtedly.'

Stapleton snapped. 'I can see that you admire him, Jack.'

'Geoff,' corrected Geoff. 'Of course I do. If his job came up tomorrow I'd love to have it.'

'Eh?' said William confusedly. 'You wouldn't really, would you?'

'Because for one, his salary's an absolute crore of rupees.'

'A million dirhams a week?' mumbled William.

'A fair whack,' agreed Beeston. 'But it's his biblical certainty, Bill, that impresses in a faithless, uncertain age like this. I mentioned it to Candy that if I had unquenchable faith like Wilf I could rule the world by Tuesday. Anyone could. Personally I think old Glenridding copies our premier's jaunty style. He just doesn't see obstacles; they don't exist in the philosophical sense. He has true biblical certainty and the world bows down before him.'

'Like an *Übermensch*,' said Stapleton. 'Do you know,' he added, 'that I personally see doubts and obstacles everywhere?'

'Do you?' asked Beeston in a consolatory voice. 'Then you'll like Ken Cumcatch. What a very nervous, but very nice old chap he is.'

As Beeston took the Cockermouth turn off at Thursby he explained to his apprentice interviewer that he had two other events to cover between here and Sellafield. Late afternoon there was a worm-charming competition at Kirkland to raise funds for the Ennerdale Young Farmers. They'd have to do that after the BNFL interview but the all-day hound trail at Low Cock How Tarn (*Low Cock Hoo Tarn*) might be covered before or after. It all depended on how fast the traffic was between Cockermouth and Whitehaven.

There were, he fretted irritably, bloody roadworks in Cockermouth town centre, which might delay matters. Stapleton nodded then asked him numbly why he had met Beeston in Carlisle when he was actually a Whitehaven producer. Beeston at this smirked with an absurd complacence and explained that he'd been for an advance planning and policy discussion with the station manager at Carlisle. Where he had indubitably taught the very old boy a compelling thing or two about ideas, innovation and even cost effectiveness under new budgetary strictures . . .

'Of course this damn hound trail *has* to be done,' the boy producer went on testily, 'because it's part of the Fellside league table knockout. It's actually the semi-final of the Senior Maidens.'

Looking at Stapleton's loose-mouthed stupefaction he said. 'Some local you are! You really don't know what a Senior Maiden is?'

'I haven't a clue!'

'It's an old bitch,' chuckled Beeston throatily. 'It's a category of hound in a hound trail. The red hot favourite is Blissful Lass from Skirrlywarble. Won't there be some pile of farmers and woollybacks losing packets at Low Cock How! And I'll also be interviewing her proud owner Jakie Hodgson some time this afternoon.'

Not unpatronisingly he informed Stapleton that Skirrlywarble was the euphonious name of Jakie's farm in North Cumbria, in that spectacular wilderness between Longtown and Bewcastle. Equally officiously he educated him in the fact that up in barren North Cumbria they were all dog-daft, hound-mad, trail-crazy. Presumably, he smirked, with nothing but fields and pine forests and the subterranean Roman Wall and next to no tourists and odd little market towns like Longtown and Brampton, there was nothing to do but gamble all your life-savings on the Senior Maidens.

'No doubt,' said Stapleton curtly. Who was incredibly irritated with Beeston and not just on account of this interview. For it was one thing cheerfully to mock one's sad little home county oneself; quite another to have it so derided by a twenty-four year old media man from Rugeley.

Just as they were passing through the outskirts of Bothel, it occurred to him to ask Beeston what this BNFL interview was actually *about*.

'Eh?' said Beeston deafly. 'Oh, there's been a radioactive leak.'

Stapleton's hair immediately stood on end. 'You what!'

'Yap, but only a dribble. Damn all Bill, absolutely nothing, you have it from me. Nothing compared with the newsworthy one a fortnight ago where they shut down a part of the plant. Not that that was anything to worry about particularly, from a mature perspective. As Wilf clarified, there was no mensurable *harm* to the public then, and the six process workers themselves were all as right as sausages afterwards.'

'After what?' gasped William.

'After a hose down with titrated carbolic or Rightguard or whatever they use. I forget exactly how they decontaminate 'em but it's basically like spraying with lots of soapy water. At any rate, this icky baba one that happened yesterday morning was very opportune for you! You have something to get your teeth into when you roast old Glenridding about it. Remember to ask him how many millisieverts and picobecquerels and nanoREMs and all that megabaloney yesterday's leak emitted.'

'But I don't know anything about sieverts and becquerels and REMs,' said Stapleton aghast. 'Nor picos, nanos, micros, millis . . .'

'Nor does the Whitehaven bruiser nor the Maryport marra nor the Workington wank-ah,' interrupted Beeston boredly. 'Nor does Glenridding. He has an aggregate – if that's the right collective noun – of physicists write down all that data for his Croxley script press releases.'

William continued to look aghast and insisted on knowing how he could be certain that this leak was nothing worse than a dribble (*Styapleton went aw flate-fyasst, he wantit ter pish issel wit nurfs, and he clicks hod ev Beeston gadger an sez till him (wurds till t'effect) – oo the buck does thoo know that this leak of thine is juss like a laal babby's piddle?*) The producer looked temporarily pensive and finally answered that Glenridding would hardly be sitting there himself day after day at BNFL giving out all these spurious assurances if the place *really* was buzzing with lethal radiation. Biblical certainty maybe; but the Information Officer was not in the literal sense, a martyr.

'Anyway it's all rather beside the point,' he added disappointedly, 'as the local paper has beaten us to it.'

From his lap he handed him that day's Whitehaven News (*Whitehebben Nyoose*) in which on the centre of p. 18 in 36pt. bold ulc (*thutty six point bowld uppranloer cyass*) underlined, it said: *A-Plant Leakage 'Not a Hazard'*. On the same page in 18pt boxed ulc it read: *Early Birds Will Charm The Worms at Kirkland Young Farmers.* Also in 12pt italicised bold with a wave underneath it: *Distington Man Commits a Nuisance*. Fascinated by the last item, Wm. learnt only that the man had been fined twenty pounds for committing his nuisance at 11.15 pm on St Valentine's Day 1986.

'Committing a nuisance?' he said, looking at Beeston. 'I used to know what that meant, but I've forgotten.'

'Some Cumbrian you are,' laughed Beeston. 'It means taking a piss in public.'

'You mean an unauthorised leak?' asked Stapleton.

'That,' chuckled Beeston, 'is rather a subtle use of punning metaphor for a simple Cumbrian.'

'Tell me,' snapped Stapleton at last rounding on him in fierce irritation. 'Are they all master satirists and latter day Arnold Bennetts in Rugeley still? They were the last time I was down there for a dirty weekend in the Black Country.'

Beeston had taken over three years – the mental equivalent of three decades if you are only a youth of twenty-four – to develop his hardy professional carapace. Accordingly he was these days unassailable when it came to things like coarse verbal aggression. He laughed uncomprehendingly at William's sarcasm and then demanded to know exactly how many 'nuisances' had been reported in this week's paper. They were spread all over the thing to act as useful paragraph fillers he explained with amusement. Bemused by such a wild request, Stapleton swiftly riffled through its cluttered pages until he came to his final tally.

'Twenty four,' he announced. 'Twenty four men in the White-haven area have been fined for unauthorised leaks.'

'And do you know if human urine is a health hazard?' Beeston quizzed him in something of a factitious interviewer's voice. They had just turned onto Bellevue roundabout and then down the narrow road to the Cockermouth roadworks. 'Or does it blind the little kiddiwinks like dog muck?'

William Stapleton didn't know but he scratched himself and began to feel itchy as they talked about all this urine. He felt much the same as when he'd had a pee himself and then needed to wash his hands. There they stayed stationary at the roadworks for about ten minutes and Beeston drummed his many-ringed hands with a deep irritation. At this rate, he grumbled, the Ennerdale YF worm charming would have to be put on ice. Blissful Lassa of Skirrlywarble would have to wait until after Stapleton's inaugural interview at BNFL.

'Still, what I really admire about you Cumbrians,' Beeston suddenly carolled with a kind of rosy gurgle, 'is the sheer bloody daftness of your entertainments, Bill! I think it's won- won- won-wonderful I really do, I think it unique. I ask you where else in the whole world would you get half the population hypnotised by these lop-lugged animals chasing over the fell-sides a trail left by a blasted *aniseed rag*? When all's said and done the poor buggers never actually *get* any aniseed, they're only tantalised by it, they pursue the mere illusion of the stuff. And if you're not going mad over hounds you crazy Cumbrians are sticking your heads through framed canvas and pulling ugly faces!' He snapped his fingers impatiently. 'What's the word for it, Bill?'

'Gurning,' Wm. supplied, restless at this liquid eulogy which sounded like Beeston's prepared valedictory broadcast to West Cumbria before he hived off to London ITN and a colossal salary.

'*Grimacing!*' Beeston gurgled. 'As a national sport! Or shinning up greasy poles at Egremont Crab Fair! Or telling "tall tyals" down at Santon Bridge! You'd wonder I suppose – unless you just assume that you *are* all constitutionally idiotic – why you Cumbrians of all the counties in this country would choose to play the idiots.'

'Wouldn't you,' Stapleton concurred stiffly.

Wm. stared warily about him and rested his gaze at last on the back of the Trout Hotel. This was the place where Mr Bing Crosby had stayed to make a lucrative promotional film about trout fishing. Alas Bing had failed to catch any sort of fish, so they'd had to secure one from a local shop and bind it on the end of his rod. William stared at Cockermouth's grandest hotel and wondered briefly how this airwave version of the building varied from the real version, The Trout he would have observed if he'd driven down himself in his normal corporeal body on a normal Saturday morning to buy olives unobtainable from Whitehaven. Instead of in this sonic if not ultrasonic dream body! For a dream was the nearest thing he could conceive to this radio experience, though he knew chillingly enough that this wasn't really like a dream. Dreams rarely made any sort of sense and even if they did it was a serendipity sense, certainly without pointed logical sequences of dialogue etc. Sequence, causation and so forth were entirely in the air in dreams. Nevertheless William *had* staunchly remained himself in this 'dream'. Even if Beeston, Si Mohammed, Moulay Ismail etc. were all behaving so theatrically aggressive, attitudinising, and self-seeking like the laughing stocks of fairy tales or knockabout satire.

'Oh no I haven't!' he whispered to himself, suddenly crestfallen. 'No I haven't, have I?'

Beeston stared at him but eschewed any rejoinder. The traffic lights stayed firmly on the red. William gasped noisily to recall that no, he had not remained himself on this airwave bargain break for one! Back there in the Place de France in Tangiers he had begun making tendentious impertinent speeches about Cumbria being Britain's Third World. When look at them! a few sample West Cumbrians rolling down the road here with their carrier bags full of pot noodles, filter coffee, twelve tins of Pedigree Chum and a pair of first class videos for the weekend!

At long last the two media men were on the impressive arterial A66, steaming along parallel with the River Derwent which looked remarkably swollen and vigorous and vital today. They passed signs for Brigham and Great and Little Broughton and a lone hot dog van called Luxury Eats which looked as if it had been closed for decades instead of in accordance with the Gone To Lunch sign. Wm. looked down at the faded yellow buttons on his faded yellow cardigan and reflected that his wife Rhoda and dog Papcastle probably *existed* in this airwave dimension too. But how, in what fashion? Would the new Papcastle be barking at him in a hectoring, convergent manner, like a canine Moulay Ismail? (*Would laal Papcassel be yelpin an snurtin at his maister instead of likkin an slabberin aw over Willum's fyass? Barin his greet fanks like a Hunt ev Basker Fell?*) Would Rhoda Stapleton be

70

tolerating his old slack, random, passive attitude to life, or instead
be uttering every sentence with a threat, answering every question
with a bark, posing every response with the mechanical assurance
of a sage in a mystery play?

The neat country-style villas of Swallow Hill (*yon bit ev Dissinton
where t'lads oot ev t'pubs nivver powk their cocks agyan t'woes and pish aw
ower em ter commit a 'Public Nuisance'*) gave way to the steep ascent
to Moresby Parks, the forlorn signs to poor old windblown Pica.
Up on the heights with the vast immensity of the Solway and two
dreaming ships at anchor below, they looked down to the sprawls
of Lowca and Parton and both media men blanched at the two
ugliest villages in the world! (*My exclamation. E. J. Asbach.* Two
collier lads near the front vociferously born and bred in Parton,
were ready to lynch Tommy Little at this point.)

'Lowca,' Beeston mused with all the innocent severity of a man
who makes his income via *the word*. 'Lowca and Pica, Bill. Low-ca
and Pi-ca. Some obvious connection there, don't you think?'

'They're both horrible little rows of pit terraces,' Wm. agreed.

'No! I mean waddyacallit, etymologically. That-where-the- Ca-
is -Low and That-where-the-Ca-is-Pi.'

'Too many variables,' sneered Stapleton impatiently. 'We don't
know what "ca" means and we don't know what "pi" means.'

'A corruption of "high",' said Beeston combatively. 'High Ca
and Low Ca obviously. That's what an intelligent amateur like me
thinks at any rate.'

'Well what is "ca"?' snorted Stapleton with very bald annoy-
ance. 'Unless it's "cack" which is local childhood argot for "excrement". Upper and Lower Excrement, is that what you're saying,
Jack?'

'Geoff!' corrected Geoff, wounded almost to the surface of his
carapace. 'And I genuinely thought you wanted to succeed in the
media, to get your voice across the airwaves at all costs! Don't you
realise that it's an elementary qualification to be fascinated by your
mother tongue? Aren't you fascinated by *words*, for their own sake,
Bill?'

Stapleton retorted bluffly. 'No! Only by what they lead to, not
by words themselves. That would be a spurious idolatry, Geoff.'
(*An yance mare, owd Styapleton felt as if sum gadger wuss tekkin ower his*

pooers ev speeach an mekkin him cum oot wit aw mak ev formla an cocksure opinon.) 'Don't you acknowledge,' he went on, 'that some of the dreariest life-hating pests in the world are mad about philology and ety-bloody-mology? That even shire Tories like verb roots and *mus-muris*, Geoff?'

'Do they?' gasped Beeston astonished.

'To be sure,' Stapleton insisted. 'They don't give a damn about politics; sociology; fiction; history; current affairs; their wives; their husbands . . . but they *do* know and it gives them incommensurate joy, that the words for mother, father, sister, brother, cat, dog and fart are all cognate in Attic Greek, Old Irish, Vedic Sanskrit, Old Persian, Hittite, Elamite, Ossetic, Old Church Slavonic, Gothic *and* Vandalic.'

'Well I didn't know that!' Beeston admitted with enormous fascination. 'I really didn't know that.'

So engrossed were they in their disputatiousness (*Beeston gadger an Willum wuss that hot-fyasst with linwistick dispoot an argy-bargy*) that they entirely omitted to take in Moresby Parks. Beeston who had intended to buy a snack from the shop there which advertised Hot Pie's (sic) swore at his forgetfulness. Before they knew it they were heading down the little brow at Keekle and staring at the caterpillar township of Cleator Moor nestling like some Peloponnese village in the lap of the glistening mountains.

'It always reminds me,' said William,' of Areopoli. Always. You see Rhoda and I honeymooned in Kithira. Which we reached via the length of the Mani.'

'Diss ev course is little Oirland,' quipped Beeston, as if he were the first to know as much. 'Pica and Lowca glued together and multiplied by ten.'

'Kithira was full of Greek Australians,' reminisced Stapleton, 'coming back to their roots for their annual holidays.'

Cleator Moor had grown in the latter half of the nineteenth century from two or three farms to a boom town of mile long poky terraces. The boom had been in iron ore and, crying out for labour, the pit proprietors had imported whole villages from Sligo and Mayo, plus a smaller number from Cornwall, so that today the now severely-depressed little community was as much Irish as Cumbrian. Nearly a half of it was fervent Roman Catholic. Impetuously Geoff Beeston pulled up outside Farrell's bakers for a hot pie and Stapleton noticed inside the shop that there was an enormous handwritten tally where the price of a pie (36p) was listed in separate units from one to fifty. He observed for example that forty seven of Farrell's hot pies would cost a pie-enthusiast £16.92.

'I'll get you a hot pie,' clucked Beeston as he disappeared into the shop.

'I'm a vegetarian,' lied Stapleton.

'Well I'll get you meat and potato then.'

Wm. sighed impatiently for the producer to return. Meanwhile two late middle-aged women stopped next to Beeston's car and conversed.

William and Beeston were munching their hot pies as they drove down over Cold Fell. Rising up in the distance they saw Low Cock How Tarn and the milling crowds, vans, chip stalls. It was a sharp fine afternoon with a bracing chill of a breeze to it. They passed a great swathe of pine forest and after that a perfectly preserved stone circle. At once the relics of ancient magic and fertility ritual made Stapleton blink, for he too was presently powered by a kind of magic. Half a dozen feral fell ponies skeltered among the megaliths. Then as they passed an even vaster pine wood they looked down onto a fell-circled valley whose immensity made Stapleton quiver. For the terribleness of Nature in its unembarrassed fullness made him feel small and weak and . . . guilty for some impalpable reason.

'That view of that valley is quite impossible,' he said to Beeston with sincere confusion. 'Isn't that impossible beauty incalculable?'

'Splendid,' Beeston assented, staring at nothing but his worries about Radio Cumbria. Then rousing himself briefly he added. 'But talking of beauty, Bill, just look at that view down there.'

Stapleton looked straight ahead and as well as the still, blue Solway he saw not an ancient megalith but a contemporary monolith. It was Ibn Hafl! Undeniably in the vault of the sea and sky and the sheaths of pine and pasture in the foreground, Sellafield nuclear power station looked beautiful! The cooling towers looked like fetching childrens' toys, like elements of some imaginative Bayko or Lego set. Even the ugly remnants of Calder Hall, the two spindly buildings closed since the fire of 1957, had a pleasing tender look of rickety decrepitude. The sun glittered all over the huge world-famous gleaming apparatus of Sellafield and it looked a bonny heartening sight from up here in the fells.

They turned down the sharp descent into Calderbridge and there on the left were the ruins of Calder Abbey, barred to the public by their present owners.

'Immense age,' William mused to Beeston. 'Abbeys; stone circles; ancient worship. Even I can sense the devotion and the awe, Geoff, I swear I can. I can feel the religion, the spiritual quantities. It feels queasy but it feels godly. It's all very big and very great.' (*He shufft his fingers inter t'lyeugs and snortit through his beak, then latit them oot agyan.*) 'Am I being wound up by clockwork when I say this? No, I don't think so. What am I trying to convey? I'm trying to say that the powerful sacred element around us over there in the beautiful abbey and back there at the beautiful stone circle and even that beautiful valley we looked at . . . that all that is in the immediate vicinity of another but as it were *secular* immensity'

'Getting back to Highca and Lowca,' Beeston countered seriously, 'I'm convinced my guess was the right one.'

Stapleton said firmly, 'I must check you of this cheeseparing habit of caring more for the anatomy of words than for their physiology. Words do not exist independent of mouths and human beings and vocal organs. Now then, pay close attention. Look first at those cooling towers and then look deep into my mouth.'

'You have some recent fillings,' said Beeston uneasily. 'And I can't look too closely or I'll drive into the Golden Fleece's front door.'

'What,' demanded Stapleton, 'is the terror of atomic energy unbridled, but the acknowledgement of the *inconceivable* immensity of energy generated by the fission of matter itself? I know only a soupçon of physics but even I am aware that e equals mc^2 (*ee eekels messy squares*), Geoff. The energy liberated either for peaceful purposes of electricity or the peaceful destruction of Japanese cities, is the minute mass which is fissiled times the speed of light times the speed of light (*t'spid ev leet times t'spid ev bliddy leet!*). And we all know what sort of a big boy the speed of light is, don't we?'

'It's not my medium,' grunted Beeston, as he turned right at Calderbridge and then sharp left for 'Ibn Hafl' itself. 'The speed of sound isn't very big at all, Bill. Why even an old crock of a supersonic jet can break through it.'

William glowered at his colleague. 'I once knew someone who referred to Radio Cumbria as Radio Valium.'

'Come again!' said Beeston amazed.

'It was a sour conclusion but an element of it was passing accurate. Do you happen to know why so much of its music is *so* relaxing? Even in your own delightful Pot-Pourri show? This cynic of an acquaintance by the way was of a rigid Marxist hue. He believed that our elected cabinet urged Radio Cumbria deliberately to play soothing music to stop its populace fretting about this hazardous monolith in front of us. He was crazy of course. Nearly as crazy as Sir F. Hoyle in my opinion.'

Beeston braked sharply and with great relief. 'Here we are at the main gates. Just you stop chattering so randomly and start rehearsing your first questions to Glenridding and Cumcatch.'

'Beware of nobles with diminutive Christian names,' Stapleton jabbered in a hellish fit of nerves. 'Sir Tom, Sir Dick, Sir Harry. They're all unmitigated crooks; bankrupts; tax dodgers.' He found himself shaking as he picked up his tape recorder and as Beeston acquired their pass from the security guards. 'And apropos abbeys; stone circles and Windscale, what I'm saying is that playing – howbeit so judiciously! – with the structure of matter itself, should have been left to the gods. Those ancestors of ours used stones and abbeys to house the gods/God. Only *they* are big enough to handle it. Look at Einstein (*lookster Yan Styan!*) The man shit a building brick at the realisation of what he'd done . . . Don't play with fire, Geoff. You're not Zeus or Indra or Prajapati or Ormuzd or Yahveh. I'm saying all this just in case this harmless leak you refer to happens to be more than either of us can comprehend. Where do they give out the titrated carbolic by the way? Do we have to go into some sort of shower and take off our watches? Don't you see,' he gulped hysterically. 'We can't see it, we can't taste it, we can't smell it. It's like a verse out of the *Shvetashvatara Upanishad*! (My exclamation; E. J. Asbach) (*Like a vuss oot ev t'Shwet Ash Wattery Panny Shad*) It's not this, not that (*nut sek an sek, an nut sek an sek summat else!*) but whatever it is it's beyond our powers. Ayee! Ayuh! Ayuh!,' he began to splutter helplessly. 'I'm starting to panic and sweat. I think I'm going to piss myself and become a public nuisance! Agh! Agh. Save me Daddy, Mummy, Daddy!'

Beeston grinned at his apprentice's extravagant first night nerves. He prodded him affably in the ribs and assured him that this sort of terror was standard for a first interview and especially an interview with someone important. Perhaps, he added, they should have started Stapleton off on worm charming. Still, it was too late now to cancel the interview.

'Glenridding and Cumcatch have adjacent offices,' he explained as he led his apprentice confidently along a limitless maze of corridors and reception areas. From a hundred quarters typewriters were clacking, word processors bleeping, light banter flowing between local women secretaries and masculine managers in tidy suits, none of which gentlemen were strictly local. Wm. heard voices of technical and managerial rank from the North East, from Lancashire, from Suffolk, from Glasgow, even from Northern Ireland, the Outer Hebrides and the Isle of Man. He could not at all substantiate why he felt as if these incomers possessed the place imperially, and that the locals really were like 'natives'. These secretaries were not of course dark-skinned nor grovelling but they had that indefinably Cumbrian *physiognomy*! (My ital. and exclamation, E. J. Asbach) (*T'Cummerlan eeds wuss aw mare er less square, t' fashul bwoans square, their voisis, their jwoaks an gammin aw as squatt an square as a laal telly scrin frae t' fifties!*) Just to confirm himself in this apparently nonsensical observation, Wm. Stapleton took his fingers delicately round the perimeter of his own fizzog and confirmed that, yes indeed, his own head was thoroughly and typically rectangular. He took a quick glance at Beeston's bobbing jocular young scope, and confirmed that his was certainly a lot more oval with a slight ellipsis at his perfectly tapered chin. Beeston's ice cream cornet of a beard seemed indeed to have been painted on by silk screen printing.

'Jean, Doris, Debbie, Sharon, Tricia, Leslie, Margie, Nanette!' Beeston carolled. 'No? Tired? Really! Busy — you don't look it! Some of us *are* busy. Who's this I've got with me? This is Billy Stapleton, a brand new man on outside features. A freelance. And guess what else? He's actually one of you! He's a local. A truly *local* Cumbrian local. Hi Mimsie, Mary, Myrtle, Madgie, Maisie, Ken!

Sandy! Sidney! How's our new baby? Superbly grandiloquent! Justin's two years old now. In fact Candy's just started to wean him and . . .'

He stopped talking about weaning as a bespectacled pin-striped hugeness of a man in his early fifties, energetic, dauntless and grinning, descended upon him and his protégé. Immediately this vast newcomer paused to size up Stapleton. To compute perhaps the half-life of this yellow-cardiganned chap's persistence, curiosity, obduracy, literal mindedness and other kernel quantities. Then he turned back briskly to his old chum Beeston and warmly pumped his hand.

'A local?' he echoed incredulously but with hoarse, brisk warmth. 'Accompanying you in what capacity?'

'Bill's a trainee producer, Wilf,' grinned Beeston. 'Who's come along to roast you about yesterday's leak.'

'Oh?' Glenridding ruminated, extremely ponderously, as if he were dimly recalling some meaningless memory from childhood. 'Good God, I'd entirely forgotten about *that* bagatelle. I've been so taxed today by humdrum but essential business that I'd entirely forgotten about that little bit of howdyedo!'

Beeston waved a copy of the local paper disappointedly before Glenridding's glasses. 'You got a clean bill of health from our rivals.'

'I tried to get you,' Wilf strenuously apologised. 'But you were out when I rang 5156.'

'Detained unavoidably,' Beeston smiled, 'up at Carlisle, teaching our very old boss some very new tricks.'

'Good man! You're such an ambitious young bastard and bollicks to the also-rans! And hell's bells, the young chap there at the News is very keen. Personally I've never understood why there has to be such desperate competition between you and them. Do you really think the marras who buy the local paper fling a brick at their radios every time they come across your station and vice versa?'

Beeston looked at him disbelievingly. He scratched his painted-on beard for a sharp analogy. 'You know Wilfred, how you sometimes privately point your finger at Marchon chemicals down the road?'

77

'Do I?' said Glenridding with insouciant numbness.

'When the public fails to respond to competitive terrors like background radiation from the rocks of Ennerdale fells; cigarette induced lung cancer; AIDS etc.'

Glenridding looked ruminative, uncomprehending, unreachable and immensely deep.

'Well,' concluded young Beeston like the precocious young inquisitor he was. 'It's the same principle. BNFL is to Marchon detergents as Radio Cumbria is to local journalism.'

'I really don't follow that comparison,' the P.R man sniffed. 'But I do notice that Allbright and Wilson aka Marchon detergents are cleaning up their cabaret acts.' He turned confidentially to Stapleton. 'Between you and me, they've been getting away with horseshit for donkeys, Bill! Any fool knows you can't produce immense quantities of sulphuric acid and release vatloads of SO_2 into the atmosphere as if it were fairy dust . . . and not cause all sorts of . . . adventitious phenomena. It took a visiting manager's car, a brand new C reg. for Christ's sake, to suffer unwanted paint stripping after some particularly generous emissions, before they finally acknowledged that perhaps acid doesn't always have to be rain to be acidic! The bloody imbeciles! A C reg. Volvo blistered like after a bloody nuclear attack. Ahahaha!!' (My exclamation upon an exclamation, E. J. Asbach).

Cackling throatily he led the two young men into his office where seated was a nervous, thin, sympathetic little man, balding, restless and immeasurably deferential. He hastened humbly to introduce himself to the yellow-woollened trainee as Kenneth Cumcatch and immediately Wm. Stapleton thought, aha, this one ought to have been thirty-year manager of the drapery department at the nearest Coop.

'Here is little Sister Charity,' Glenridding declared with apparent affection, hammering Cumcatch vigorously on the back. (*Like Eric Morkam might ev clattert laal Urnie Wise when they were lakin aboot on 1966 Christmas Specktackler.*) 'He and I are a truly symbiotic duo. An inseparable pair like William and Ginger or . . .'

'Sherlock and Watson,' Cumcatch offered bashfully.

'I don't follow that analogy,' Glenridding rejoined. 'Holmes was remarkably eccentric wasn't he? I'm damned if I'm at all odd! No but you and I are a strategic team, Ken. We are an ineffable combination, like the Royal Couple say. You give of our bounty, of BNFL's bounty that is, to supplement and in some respects to add to the poetic finish to my honest brokering. Honest brokering, Bill,' he added scathingly to the new media man, 'isn't enough for a deviant proportion of the population. The average veganite protester who knows no physics, maths, biology, nothing of economics, ergonomics, energy statistics, damn all of the real sanguine carnivorous bloody world! will still quibble away with the experts as if it's his divine bloody right. Whereas the well-tempered *ordinary* Cumbrians bless their hearts – I say that admiringly to a truly Cumbrian Cumbrian like yourself! – are content to let the experts exercise their expertise as the best experts have been doing since time immemorial! Ken's bran tub, the BNFL purse, is simply an eloquent expression of our gratitude to the local community for their unflagging trust in us, in the experts' expert expertise that is. And there's nothing cynical or sophistic or chicaning about *that*.'

'I thin . . .' objected Stapleton.

'Of course not! Good man! You're a genuine 110% Cumbrian and you're as sanguine and unshakeable as they come! You are aware that our brethren down the road Allbright and Beautiful (*Marshan's new posh nyam, mare er less*) don't dish out grants and cheques like we do even though the adjacent council houses get pitch blacker and pitch filthier by the year . . .'

'I thin . . .'

'You're quick to spot the rank hypocrisy, Bill! We at BNFL acknowledge that we raise certain inchoate childish anxieties, unjustifiable as they be. We therefore pay out a sort of symbolic compen., a sort of anxiety payment to the community in acknowledgement of their pitiful but pitiably human inability to set their empirically baseless doubts completely at rest!'

'This morning,' chipped in Mr Cumcatch, clearing his throat very modestly. 'I had the tremendous pleasure of meeting the secretary of the Hensingham Pigeon Fanciers. A very nice friendly old chap called Tommy Leatherhead. He and his pigeon group . . . is that the right wo . . . pigeon society? . . . league, orga . . . he and his friends and his birds are delighted he claims by our little gesture of the twenty thousand pounds . . .'

END OF EMISSION THE FIRST

Asbach replenishes his glass and recalls his deviant father Klaus.

TOMMY Little paused for exactly four minutes, finishing his recital with a teasingly self-deprecatory smile. Then he walked slowly across to the bar and quietly requested a bottle of Mackeson with a dash of lime juice. The audience cleared its parched throat, murmured loudly, exclaimed softly, scratched its ruddy weather-tanned face, pale jaws, beery calm. There was an unusual concentration of silent embarrassment in the air, perhaps at such a perverse display of virtuosity. Of course Harrison and Fidler were terribly dumbfounded, grinning as awkwardly as a pair of schoolboys promoted overnight to play for England's football team. It was as if they had delivered nothing better than a pair of Christmas cracker mottos while this shepherd from Bewcastle had casually decided to recite the Kathasaritsagara plus the Mabinogion, the Kalevala and the Mahabharata. Only old Tucker of the iggly-wiggly worm was sufficiently drunk to assume that Tommy was imported cabaret, a male stripper from Burnley or Blackburn, and the old man was quick to assure everyone he passed on his way to the Gents that 'yon Lancashire comick hess a gay lang tung on him, asser! But when is he ganna tek his clarse off an dyeuh a bare-arse dance?'

I of course was tremendously excited to witness the first dialect *epic* ever recorded. Though my excitement was not quite the same as the restive stir I saw among the locals. Quite a few of its younger end was employed at one or other of 'Ibn Hafl' or 'Allbright and Beautiful' and their amusement at his radio story was initially shrill. Whereas the old South Cumbrian farmers, some of whom were presently reeling from the fact that their hilltop lamb, thanks to Chernobyl and the hyperadioactivity of their felltop cud, was no longer fit to go for slaughter, laughed with malicious glee at those references to the Third World and Ibn Hafl. Many of them had long worried impotently about the unknown quantities from the stinkhorns visible from their felltops. By now, by the late summer of 1986, they had both local and international radioactivities to fret about. But in any case, the tenor of Little's delivery was subtle, mellifluous, understated. Even when he played the blustering Moulay Ismail or the hectoring Glenridding, he allowed the passions of his actors to be played impersonally. The satire was almost someone else's, Little seemed to be saying. He was merely the conduit, the mouthpiece. Just as his hero Wm. (pronounced Wum, by the way, in Little's mouth) felt himself at times to be wound up by a clockwork mechanism and forced to make doctrinaire statements about the 'tragic' sociology of Cumbria, so enigmatically grinning Little seemed to be saying to us, I am simply the innocent vehicle for a tale to be spun.

I switched off my tape recorder for that four minute interval and looked carefully about me. I need not dwell overmuch on the puzzled reactions of the media folk present: Tim Boston's baffled response to a possible send-up in a difficult dialect, his resort at an early stage to repeated glasses of strong rum, his switching off his fancy audio apparatus once The Tale of the Tangerine was seen to subtend The Saga of Sellafield. I looked about me and suddenly I started. In fact I start with emotion approximately once a month, in all sorts of Cumbrian public houses and hotels. To earn a living I have to travel fairly extensively over the entire county, placing my pots in numerous Lakeland craft shops as well as in my own. On these jaunts I always prefer a toasted sandwich in a quiet corner of an empty pub to sitting in a poky cafe, invidiously sharing a table perhaps. Approximately a third of the pubs in the county cause me to stop in my tracks and the reason is that they force me to remember my father Klaus in his most enduring and highly visual aspect. For assuming Cumbria has about a thousand pubs between Barrow and Kershopefoot, between Anthorn and Appleby, then three hundred and thirty of them contain my father's pictures!

As a rule pub landlords go in for his vast yard-square framings in their pubs and sitting-rooms. And where the Turks never tire of Atatürk's face, seemingly the Cumbrians never tire of their much-loved lakes. Klaus in those thirty years he dwelt in Cumbria (formerly Cumberland, Westmorland and Furness-Lancashire) must have painted at least two thousand representations of our romantic heritage. Derwentwater, Windermere, Bassenthwaite and Ullswater were in most pressing demand, say approximately twelve hundred between them, or three hundred per head. Wastwater, Ennerdale, Crummock, Loweswater and Buttermere he probably reproduced only a hundred times each. Of out of the way tarns-with-knobs-on like Elterwater, Rydalwater and Haweswater, he executed no more than twenty or thirty likenesses. Klaus generously allowed his patrons to believe that each representation of each lake had been done *in situ*, skew-if-beret and battered easel could be imagined too if liked. In reality one summer's week in 1948 Klaus and Ilse had sped round the county on his AJS and side car and captured all the principal and lesser lakes and a dozen or so tarns with Klaus's twenty seven shilling camera. Klaus had had sense enough in 1983 not to paint in a squat Forties Humber or a Riley or Ford Popular in the Loweswater foreground. Yet equally sensibly he acknowledged that whatever subtle geological erosion had occurred in the last thirty years on the shores of Ennerdale or Wastwater 'neah bukker in T'Plack Cuck in Aspee will notice neah diffrence, Ilse!'

Yes, two dozen old photographs provided the templates for some two thousand pictures of the Lakes, of which three hundred were mural size and correspondingly costly. Or at least they should have been, as my mother bitterly complained, for we were never anything but badly off in my childhood. Perhaps in deference to the rock bottom economics of the village peasant life he had known in the Egerland (German Czechoslovakia) and elsewhere, Klaus was not averse to spirited bartering. And if in a euphoric or delirious mood, which he usually was six nights out of seven, might well sell his latest painting, the fruit of twelve hours feverish hard work, for drinks all round the crowded bar, two bottles of Jennings rum to take home and 'oh a Beppsham an a paket off saltit peenoots for Ilse!' In any event not all his paintings were enormous in size. He did little cameos, large cameos, little portrait sizes, large portrait sizes. He also perfected a technique of painting lakes and tarns on lacquered silk, which he claimed was his own invention. The result was a quite refined and touching old fashioned curio effect, the kind of thing you might rumble across in a dusty backstreet antique shop. Of these 'patents' of his Klaus was exceptionally proud and fantastically boastful.

'Lukk at thiss yan,' he would complacently purr to some interested customer in our Whitehaven council house, the place where I spent most of my childhood. By about 1949 Klaus had learnt to speak quite intelligible German-Cumbrian, having disposed of Czech entirely and speaking German with Ilse only in my absence. 'Lukk at thiss yan! Isn't she a byüty? It's byütiful eh? It's so luffly the careful wukk I did theer. Painstekly done on silk and I inventit the teknik meself.'

'Really?' politely from the customer who might have driven forty miles from Carlisle or Ulverston, so wide was Klaus's growing renown.

My father would continue to assure the customer that all his work was as beautiful and that he had severe problems in making private preferences. On some days he was convinced that his great big canvases were the most outstanding; other mornings he was literally moved to tears at the sight of his own little cameo silks.

'It teks patience,' he croaked earnestly as if the visitor were possibly some trifling sceptic.

'Oh I'm sure,' the innocent chap would hasten to apologise.

'An lotsa dedcashun of coss!'

'Of course! By golly I see that, Mr Asbach.'

By his spontaneous series of boasts and hypothetical rejoinders of dissent; of laughably laymanish contradictions which Klaus would pooh pooh out of the room as the mystified visitor was heckled into owning and then disavowing these oppositions . . . my father would embarrass the dazed customer into outdoing even Klaus's powers of admiration.

'It's very very beautiful. It really is excellent, Mr Asbach. I've never seen such a remarkably vivid depiction of Coniston.'

'Ollsswatter,' corrected Klaus.

'Ullswater, of course! The patience, the dedication must have been stupendous.'

'Fotty-five pund,' Klaus concluded with a boyish finality. 'And it's wuth iffry penny! I cunt let it gah for less. I really cunt.'

My father was the only flesh and blood example I have ever seen of a truly impassioned artist, the cliché of literary fantasy, the very image of Joyce Cary's Gulley Jimson. Until 1975 when he retired from his very last manual job, he rose at five every weekday to spend a couple of hours on his painting. At weekends and on retirement, he allowed himself a lie in until seven unless his hangover were particularly cruel when he would crawl out of his bed at half past eight. He would make himself and Ilse a strong cup of tea, bear hers carefully and solemnly to their bedside, and would then go and lock himself in his workroom and proceed to paint for the entire morning without break or refreshment of any kind.

Klaus was a full-time artist for a mere nine years, until his death aged seventy-four in 1984. Thus what might have galled him more than anything about Edward his only child, was his unparalleled decision to make a *career* out of his art; to become an apprentice potter employed at some twenty-three pounds a week on a Work Experience Programme at Charlie Timson's pottery in backstreet Maryport . . .

'Pots!' he swore at me disgustedly, as if I'd said 'pets' or 'piss'. 'Pot in Merrypot? You must be bliddy crazy, Eddie!'

'What the hell do you mean?' I replied defiantly. 'You're an artist yourself! One of the most dedicated I've ever met!'

'Juss as hoppy, son!' he exclaimed, the spit flying liberally as his ingenuous emphasis showered both me and Ilse who was watching calmly from her favourite armchair. 'I allus heff a bliddy chop, eh, an niffer bin oot from bliddy wukk since I fust left prisner war camp in 1946!'

His speech in moments of heat became more and more like vaudeville Kraut with a Whitehaven bias. Yes, he went on with a violent punch of his fist against the settee upon which he and I were seated and whereon I was being sideways interrogated as on a fairground swing. Klaus through an old friend of one of his customers had managed to secure me a start in graphic design in a set of cramped and cluttered offices down near Whitehaven harbour. I was taken on at eighteen with one and a half A levels and offered block release studies at a special craft college down in Lincoln. I stuck this treadmill of glorified workshop technology, of school

T.D. with knobs on, for a good four years, of which about six months were spent in quite wholesome digs in Lincoln. In that lovely city I fell in love with an unhappily married woman called Elsie, ten years my senior, and broke my heart for the first and only time. She would neither leave her town planner husband nor make a final break with me, which painful latter course in retrospect was surely *her* responsibility. I was after all a mere boy and Elsie was a very experienced woman. After leaving Lincoln in a quivering heap of remorse and with hopelessly diffuse proliferations of impossible schemes (e.g. to get Elsie to move up with her two little girls and live in sunny proximity – the same council house – with Klaus, Ilse and me, until we married and got ourselves our own little nest) I returned to Tempo Graphics for precisely one month.

I had known the pottery owner Charlie Timson for years. He was bald, unkempt, energetic, about thirty, and scratched an impossible income as a potter cum photographic developer cum sign painter down near Maryport docks. He had let me play around on his wheel since I was a boy, whenever Klaus and I used to go through to his shop to buy some artist materials which he also stocked in small quantities. He had often remarked to a smug paternal Klaus on my visible originality and nascent flair. Without saying anything to anyone but Timson I arranged a meeting with Manpower Services at the Employment Office and within two weeks was there in the back room with Charlie, commuting by diesel between Whitehaven and Maryport, my rail fare consuming over fifty per cent of my income. Klaus happened to be drunk (he'd just sold two miniatures of Talkin and Floutern Tarns at the Black Eagle) when he found out what I'd done. He started off with a lot of filthy bluster, then some maundering threats of violence. Ilse reproved him sharply so that he shook his old fist dramatically at her and offered her the back of his hand as well. She was just about to laugh out loud at his nonsense when seized by a quite overpowering anger I struck my father smartly on the chin and sent him flying in a heap before the television set! Ilse looked at me aghast, clearly anxious to condemn me for such completely out of character pugnacity. Then she changed her mind, raised herself arthritically from her chair, and went over to lift her foolish husband from his comically spreadeagled posture. I expected him to continue to bombard me with his favourite drunken triplicate obscenities ('laal bastakuntafugga') but instead my blow to the chin seemed to produce an immediate amnesia, for shooing Ilse away Klaus shot to his feet and instantly offered to make coffee for the three of us! My mother and I sat speechless and mystified while he pottered about in the kitchen tipsily whistling. Finally, as well as the coffee, he beamingly re-emerged with a huge platter of salami and würstel *Butterbrot* . . .

The next day he was sour, he kept stroking his wounded chin, and was very unforgiving. I was, he growled, a fool who had thrown up all chance of a decent career in pursuit of some whimsical 'attankraft shite'. Over the breakfast table Klaus muttered to us that only idiots tried to make a living out of 'Kunst'; fools and, he conceded, geniuses. And I, he glintingly assured me, was no genius whatever that lackadaisy baldie Timson told me! I could pot reasonably but not brilliantly and the most I could hope for was to end up a feeble Jack-of-all-trades with a dusty little craft shop in a hole like *Maryport* whose houseprices and consequently shop rents were about the cheapest in the land for very good reason!

'Ed, they dunt buy pot in bliddy Merrypot,' my father beseeched me, in a memorable last ditch effort to reverse my plans. 'They buy peer an ship and fish an ot pie in all they pie.'

'It's developing as a tourist town,' I countered defiantly. 'They're pouring money into it to make it a national holiday attraction.'

'Merrypot,' guffawed Klaus, rising from the table with finality. 'Merrypot is dutty laal Cummerlan toon wit neah chops, neah money, neah future, Ed! It's a pot but the pot dunt wukk, it's kaput, like your bliddy pottry . . .'

'They call it the Gem of the Solway,' I countered. 'They're going to make a big marina; a little miniature railway; an art gallery-cum-cafe-cum-craft shop.'

'Merrypot,' Klaus insisted haughtily, as if he knew this county better than any expert, 'will allus be Merrypot! Merrypot will niffer be Torky.'

That very night to my embarrassed incredulity, Klaus and I both happened to be watching a television programme, a film biography in the form of clips plus interview with the former pop star Adam Faith. Would anyone believe it? but at one point Adam's interviewer asked him what the roughest place was he'd ever played in those tumultuous years in the early Sixties, when he was the country's number one star. And without hesitation Faith smilingly returned:

'Ah a little place ap in wossname Kamlan, cowd Mairpo. I fowt we was gowin to get *murdered*!'

My father almost burst an artery in his glee! Moreover his antipathy towards Merrypot and Timson grew and grew as he saw how much happier I was as a penniless potter. To confound him totally I actually succeeded in saving two or three pounds a week out of my government pittance. No, I informed him tersely, it did not bother me that I couldn't afford a Honda 50, much less a little car. I pushbiked everywhere or hitchhiked to visit friends in Manchester or Newcastle. No, I protested firmly, it did not worry me that I couldn't go out for a drink more than once a week. Aha, Ed! So what about a woman, a girlfriend, Klaus taunted, wouldn't it be nice to have enough pocket money to take a woman out for a meal at the Briery House or to the pictures on Tangier Street? Didn't I have a 'sechs drife' he demanded cheerily, the very image of a sensitive counsellor. Or did I prefer to 'lek wit yerself!' he chortled in ribald dialect.

'You're the lake man,' I said obscurely, assuming it would go over his smirking head.

He stared at me very curiously. 'Wat thoo mean, Ed?'

'You have the corner in lakes,' I said, weary of his constant jibing. 'You lake with yourself artistically when you paint all those bloody lakes.'

Downmarket tourist ephemera; pub lounge decor, I was hinting in my young superiority. Charlie and I made artistic pots for sensitive people who appreciated style and distinction. Klaus smiled at me sarcastically and then pointed out the shameful obvious. Which was that his churning out Derwentwaters by the dozen had been the only way of supplementing the lowly income from the various factories where he and Ilse had toiled when I was little. It was *Lake* Derwentwater had paid for my school uniforms; *Lake* Loweswater had got me a new Dawes bicycle when I was ten; even 'bliddy laal Ilterwatter' had allowed him to buy me some decent frames for my childhood glasses when I was sick of other children laughing at my National Health monstrosities.

Blushing guiltily, I told him I was actually saving up to start my own business. Klaus chortled and exploded as if I'd talked of aiming to be an overnight rock star. During our argument, incidentally, I happened to be taping some costly imported jazz guitar records loaned me by Charlie Timson. I could not afford such luxuries myself, but I could afford to tape over old cassettes I was tired of. For no reason but plain perversity, Klaus suddenly demanded:

'Hoo lang you been teppin, Eddie, that rubbich! It seem like bliddy ours to me!'

I answered calmly. 'Oh since about six o'clock.'

He sniffed disdainfully, with a martyrish air. 'You know – it's aw elektrik! It all cost *money*, yon teppin, Ed!'

I nearly told my own father to go and fuck himself.

'What?' I said in cold fury. 'Can't I even tape now? *Where*,' I went on, confused as I always am when angry, '*where* do you get all those bloody moods from, these *whims* and and . . .'

He cackled victoriously and went out to the Black Eagle, his favourite local. I could clearly envisage him telling all his old cronies that his son couldn't be bothered with women, he much preferred to *lake* with himself. I snorted and again without enlightening either of my parents, I made arrangements to rent the room above Timson's shop as a bedsit. I rang up Charlie and offered to let him dock my wages of a fiver a week. Charlie generously let me off with three and said I might have problems with mice, but not as far as he knew, cockroaches or rats. At twenty-two I left home decisively and with quite a sheepish Klaus moving my stuff across in multiple journeys with his three-wheeler Reliant. After which our relationship improved exponentially with time, if only because of the fifteen miles that now lay between us . . .

Klaus Asbach had been born in the Sudetenland in 1910, the eldest son of Joachim and Alena, poor German- and Czech-speaking peasants. Starved out of the wasted countryside by 1918, they moved to Prague and my grandfather began a relatively prosperous period in a formerly German-run steelworks. On the afternoon of Klaus's ninth birthday Joachim was hideously burnt to death in the old coking plant in the centre of the works. The old Bessemer converter (first developed of course in

Workington, Cumbria) had tipped and leaked some molten ore onto him as he'd been standing directing some younger men on overdue cleaning operations. Watching his screaming the petrified operator had followed the sensible course and promptly emptied the lot across him, to put him quickest out of his agony. Shortly after that tragedy my grandmother died of puerperal fever after giving birth to the baby of the family, Reinhard. He and the three little ones were taken into a Prague orphanage and Klaus was reluctantly taken in by country relatives who kept a small farm near Asch. They found him employment as a village cobbler's apprentice and like something out of Gorky, or so he related it with relative dispassion, he slept under a table on a palliase, as a kind of live-in watchdog as well as wageless apprentice. They did not beat him true enough; they did not starve him. Neither did they feed him on anything more robust than cabbage soup and copious potato puffkes. Neither did they 'luff' him in any tangible, memorable form. By the age of seventeen, in 1927, he was a skilful young cobbler who had moved into Asch itself, where he set up in trade with a Slovak who apparently embezzled both of them out a living in their first two years. Meanwhile, Klaus made monthly visits to his two remaining orphanage brothers, and began doing little sketches, at first just for private diversion, on the lengthy train journeys. He set up in business twice more as a cobbler and bankrupted himself both times. In 1935 aged twenty-five, he joined the Czech army where at least he could hope to be fed and clothed in amongst countrywide depression. By now the Fascist Konrad Henlein was gaining a vast following in the Sudetenland with his *Sudentendeutsche Heimatfront*, hinting at secession to the Vaterland and an end to 'racist' Czech hegemony. In joining the Slav army my father was of course something of a fifth columnist for he was pledged now to defend the new Czechoslovakia against the wolfish designs of Germany.

My hungry father was determined to serve whoever would feed him and would have fought either for or against Genghis Khan to achieve that end. Once the Nazis did invade, as a Sudetner he was automatically transferred to the German army, and thence to combat and adventure in various parts of France. At first he was a corporal attached to a minor police station in suburban Paris but was later transferred to a forest area near Metz. Here he was given the crucially important job of guarding a German arms line believed to be the foremost target of local saboteurs. Curiously Klaus and his four comrades guarded it from horseback – so he insisted to my questioning glance – and after six months of nothing happening, not a squeak nor murmur, grew vociferously bored with the task. The Metz maquis were either bluffing or non-existent, Klaus and friends all sneered and concurred. On the 25th of November 1944 Klaus Asbach was comfortably snoring in his hut when he should have been on his horse some hundred yards from the bridge which was competently blown to smithereens just as a train carrying several tausend-millionen Deutschmarks of arms and explosives tootled hopefully across it. Within an hour my terrified father was put under armed escort and transferred to a military prison on the outskirts of the town. Within a week he was taken by train all the way to München for a special tribunal, court martial whose outcome would surely be either death or something worse.

It was worse. They transferred him to the *999 Command*, a remarkable body of motley felons, assorted common psychopaths, and soldierly deviants like himself. The Reich used them as cannon fodder for they were sent to all the hot spots, front lines, suicide areas, without, of course, the protection of arms. Instead they were provided with picks and shovels and adjured to get digging. Dig trenches, redoubts, erect barriers while under fire. Dig or die, scum! Dig for still possible victory, like they force them to do over in England . . .

My father and his 999 colleagues marched with their rustic, musical implements the whole way from Freiburg up the length of the country to Aachen and then deep into Belgium to meet the invading allies. Speedily defeated and on the run they proceeded to march the whole way back again, digging their redoubts as they went. On their retreat, still in Belgium, Klaus and a child molestor Büttmann escaped and remained on the run for about a week before being caught by a shambling envious-looking foot patrol led by a dauntless young Leutnant Tischbein, twenty-seven and fanatically incredulous that the tide at last could be turning against him. Monocular Tischbein apparently insisted on supervising these riffraff deserters himself and was about to take them in person, once again *nach München*. He and his loaded pistol and Büttmann and

Asbach were all together on the Munich train, all three contrapuntally snoring, when Klaus rose stealthily, hesitated before deciding to leave the child molestor with his boyish captor, stole Tischbein's monocle and excellent calf-leather boots which he had taken off while he snoozed, and leapt as far as he could as the train slowed down at a bend.

Finally Klaus was caught by some Canadians, the first he'd ever met. A trio of tanks entered the deserted Alsatian hamlet where he was pensively strutting in Tischbein's gorgeous boots, and the accompanying soldiers seized upon this quaking enemy with glee. The Canadians decided to put him up on one of their tank barrels and to rumble along with the crumpled-looking Kraut dangling there like Donald Duck, cowardly clinging on for his life. The soldiers marching below laughed their heads off at such perfect comedy. Klaus hung on with a weak grin, gazing down imploringly at the foreigners, terrified out of his wits. Of course if he'd fallen he'd have been mashed underfoot by the trundling tank. The Canadians laughed at his twenty minutes of terror, then quickly handed him over to the French.

He was in the French camp for about a month, the horriblest of his life. A precious possession in that camp was a *stone* (a bliddy stown Ed, wuss like a luffly chool!) something to sit on and fix yourself upon among a desert of bare earth and bleak weeds. The French (bliddy kunz, Ed, bliddy furmin!) characteristically treated them worse than beasts (wuss than bliddy shite, the kunz). An unbelievable stroke of fortune took a number of these captives across the Atlantic to Iowa at the request of the American H.Q. They were set to work in the fields under relatively affable supervision, and were given gluttonous quantities of cream, eggs, butter, ham, chicken, bread, to sustain their moderate labours. From nightmare to euphoria, from death to life. But Klaus was miserably apprehensive when after three months he was shipped back over at the request of the British to England, and after some hanging about in Berkshire, to a P.O.W. camp at Bassenthwaite in far-flung Cumberland. His unique predicament was particularly ironical. He was not in any true sense a *German* (certainly not ideologically nor sentimentally); he was a Czech who had happened to speak the German language. He did not desire to return to a decimated country where he had neither relatives nor friends in 1946. Unquestionably if he tried going back to the former Egerland he'd be lynched. When therefore at the start of 1946 he was allowed to apply for British citizenship on the grounds of being a displaced alien, my father did not vacillate. He had spent six quite decent months working on remote fell farms, the last one being his favourite, as, while the majority of his team were herded together on the Lowndes' estate four miles down the fell from Orthwaite, Klaus himself was allowed to be sole prisoner-labourer for Jakie Baggrow, a bachelor hill farmer aged eighty-seven who dwelt two miles up the end of a track at the far end of Orthwaite pass. The Keswick postman who cycled puffing round these endless vales and heights, sensibly left Jakie's letters at the bottom of the two mile track, and one of Klaus's regular tasks was to carry his post up to the farm. Klaus also looked after his sixteen Herdwicks, the half dozen Leicester gimmer shearlings and cast tups; the ten Swaledales; the eleven Wyandottes and the one teenage rickety mangy halitotic sheepdog called Parker (after Baggrow's mother's maiden name).

My father was well on the interesting road to becoming totally unintelligible when he left Jakie's Stumpy Heights in 1946. Understand that Klaus learnt his first English from a very old man who spoke the broadest hill dialect imaginable and who, due to bad legs, short breath and eremitical satisfaction at staying put in peaceful solitude up his two mile retreat up 't'back end of buggery', had little conversation with anyone but a couple of elderly farmers and the occasional visit of the doctor. The sixty-six year-old quack was a recent arrival from Banbury, seeking premature retirement close to his Keswick sister. He could with enormous effort make some passable sense of Jakie's euphonious discourse. No matter how hard he tried though, he could make no sense whatever out of the thirty-six year old P.O.W. who affable as he was (and a fine sketcher of the landscape) talked perfect Hottentot which he touchingly imagined to be fair attempts at proper English. Dr Gissing smiled hopefully, pulled at his chin, grimaced, and finally nodded omnidirectionally whenever my father spoke his gibberish.

For example, he came one morning after Klaus had alerted the English sergeant down at the Bassenthwaite camp, who in turn had kindly rung Gissing on Baggrow's behalf. Gissing, at first, just by way of common politeness, tried to get the German to explain what it was was wrong with Jakie. An unnecessary request as it happened as Klaus was rushing to babble out his anxious concern for Baggrow's health. Meanwhile, the old man was sitting in his bed upstairs with a cruel attack of the earache, a condition he'd explained to young Asbach as follows:

'Ahf bin powkin me lyeug ryeut, Kloose! Ah powkt an powkt but ah cunt git shotten t'gimmels insite t'pliddy farmint.'

(Of which a very prosey translation would read: 'I've been poking the root of my lug, Klaus! I poked and poked but I couldn't get shot of the waddyacallit inside the bloody varmint')

Of which Klaus's faithful construction to a stunned Dr Gissing ran *'Zekky's ben pükin iss lyük ryüt'*

'Hah,' swore Gissing, 'come again?'

'Lyük ryüt!' smiled Klaus, as if it were Gissing were the greater fool.

What sort of barbarism was that? Friesian? Estonian? Letzeburgesch?

'Lyukrut?' Gissing repeated, as if to a child undergoing speech therapy.

'Yiss!'

'Licorice?' Gissing wondered.

'Naaaaawwww!' my father remonstrated tersely. 'Lyük ryüt. *Wie so! In die Ohren!*'

'Oh his *ears*! Aha! Baggrow's *ears* are bothering him?'

'Shampyan! Si thissel dün! Vanter swiller chee?'

Did Gissing want a swill of tea? Sit himself down. Champion!

RADIO ACTIVITY,
EMISSION THE SECOND.

Tommy Little resumed.

'I went along to look at their lofts myself,' Cumcatch explained to his attentive listeners. 'It was years since I've been up to Hensingham but the place really hasn't changed especially radically, has it? That long leisurely downhill into Whitehaven; the reluctant crawl uphill to grimy ghastly old Cleator Moor; straight on for Windscale, optionally turning off at West Cumberland Hospital or Egremont as you go. Hensingham is an important crossroads in more that the literal sense as it points in all the vital directions of work; health; major town; revitalised slump town which is also of course our contractor's town. I spent a few minutes looking for the smallest house in Britain, the one that used to be among those terraces leading down. Do you remember that half of a terraced house the old woman used to live in? She must have been very cramped, even on her own. It had gone. And I noticed other minor changes. There was a new hair stylist called Apollo. Well actually they spelt it Appollo but they must have meant the classical lover surely . . .' He faltered most uneasily at Glenridding's impatient scrutiny. 'I dropped Margaret off at Apollo's to have her hair done, while I went to see Mr Leatherhead and his friends. Where I was remarkably impressed by the modesty of the fanciers' proposals. The lofts they have at the moment are all quaintly cobbled together, brightly painted, charming topsy-turvy structures, almost like canal barges or gypsy caravans in their simplicity. Naturally I was delighted to be invited in to have a look at the little birds themselves. They were beautiful things, the little pigeons; such vivid eyes and innocent expressions. So wise and curious and pert like . . . almost like little children. I felt rather like a young boy myself as I entered each of the men's huts and looked at their prize pigeons. Mr Leatherhead who was very shy only wanted a few hundred pounds for the men to disassemble and transfer their lofts to the fields behind, and he seemed to be implying that even that seemed an extravagance, though a welcome one, to him.

'So when I announced that I was authorised to offer £20,000 for them not only to transfer, but to build ten brand new pigeon huts all electrically heated, and with all the most advantageous fittings, I could see they thought I was Father Christmas or something even more mythological.'

'A fairy,' Glenridding coughed with a faintly critical smile.

'Yes,' said Cumcatch uneasily.

'A magic one. You are a magic fairy, Ken.'

Blushing Cumcatch confessed that he'd anticipated a conservative reluctance on the part of the men to vacate their age old sites. But the mostly elderly fanciers had seen themselves, as it were, *chosen* to provide the prime architectural site where Whitehaven, thanks to its *alma mater(almer myatter)*, would have its own world-class international-standard luxury athletics track.

'Sport,' mused Beeston, 'is a sure fire talisman. You couldn't have touched a stronger nerve in the local body politic.'

'Yes,' Cumcatch assented, as he cast his eyes over the tabulated list of last week's donations. Grants to village football clubs in Waberthwaite, Wasdale, Santon Bridge, Ravenglass, Drigg, Eskdale. A piffling hundred for goal post repairs; club house refurbishments, new kits for the chaps. Timid little Kenneth sprinkled his kindly bounty over ten of them and timid little Ken had ten little communities ineffably bound by filial loyalty. Those ten loyalties cost Ken only a grand and a grand in macro P.R. terms in 1986 just after Chernobyl, was rather a jokey affair. Even an international athletics track was just a rather broad witticism, economically. It was still no cause for anything but huge smiles and enormous congratulation of an obscure little coastal town by itself.

'Up to a point,' Glenridding barked, addressing reporter William, as if the recorder were already in operation. 'Yet I think any disinterested spectator of the manner in which we repay our beneficent hosts . . . for allowing us to be their welcome guests . . . should note the sheer heterogeneity of our reciprocity. Sport: no one would quibble at the positive associations of health, fitness and longevity which such a connection promotes. Yet don't ignore the fact that we also promote the comely and suave in local housing – the very opposite of Ken's old Mother Hubbard in her shoe box at Hensingham. Have you seen what a once shambling old Whitehaven looks like now that we have poured funds into restoration and improvement? Or the fact that since THORP and the contractors flying in you now get wine bars, proto-trattorias no less in White-haven! I repeat in Whitehaven! (*proter-trattoriyas in bliddy Whitehebben!*) It's like saying singles bars in Riyadh or Bierfests in a mosque! I repeat, wine in Whitehaven! Kebab houses! Wine bars! Lord, I can recall the recent day when to be seen drinking wine around here would have been seen as an incautious avowal of homosexuality. Can't you remember that, Bill?'

'I . . .'

'Kebabs in Corkickle! (*coonsal oose bit ev top Whitehebben*). The cosmopolitan implications. And we have done it, no one else, Bill, we have dragged this laggard community into the cosmopolitan age. We are broadening their palates and minds as well as giving their pigeons a taste of central heating. If it hadn't been for us there'd have been none of the exotic aura of the Middle East around here. You would still have been eating Skiddaw slate and haematite with plenty of coaldust and a double helping of pneumohaemo-coniosis, please marra! Any old noxious garbage, animate or inani-mate, as long as it could be washed down by a gallon of Jennings or undredged harbour water.'

He beamed around the room after his interesting speech, firstly at his admiring trembling colleague and then at the two young radio chaps. He awaited any challenges from any of them. After enormous hesitation, Wm. Stapleton finally offered:

'They might sell kebabs round here these days, granted. But I seriously doubt whether they sell *prune tagines* or or . . . *Bahrein pearl divers' pilau*.'

Cumcatch trembled even more at this magnificently oblique thrust of Stapleton's. Glenridding twitched and stared at him and seemed to make a sudden urgent computation. Beeston guffawed and muttered something about the extraordinary statements of his whimsical apprentice. The whimsy tickled him especially as the chap was after all a local. And they all knew what locals were like! As homogeneous as well-stirred rum butter! Cumcatch however was asking politely what tagines were. Stapleton gently explained that they were Middle Eastern lamb stews flavoured with cinnamon, saffron, allspice, cumin etc. served as a rule with mountainous quantities of couscous or pilafi. Bahrein pearl divers' pilau – it had been there on the menu at Lahcen's – was a rice dish flavoured with honey, little green cardamoms and rose water.

'Perhaps,' he went on scathingly, 'the Middle Eastern affiliation you claim you are responsible for, only goes skin deep.' He was half tempted to add at this point that he'd just made his way into their perceptions, thanks to the medium of sound energy, all the way from *Tangiers*. But finally demurred. 'What I mean is, to offer kebabs is no great shakes, even if accompanied by pitta and side salad. To offer a culinary cliché is scarcely to turn the world upside down?'

Mr Glenridding initially tense at this dietary metaphor, objected victoriously. 'Hang on! Hang on! What about the *paw-paws* I saw today in a fruit and vegetable shop on Lowther Street?'

'No truly local local buys those,' Wm. said flatly. 'They lie there decorative but entirely superfluous. Certainly no Scot or Geordie contractor from Yoker or Byker would touch a paw-paw with a . . .'

'I don't accept that for a moment,' the publicity man blustered. 'Why I myself had a paw-paw for dessert, when I dined with the manager of the plutonium reprocessing last week!'

(*Willum puzzent up is fyass aw scornfell at aw this jabber aboot po-pos. Cos ee reckent there wuss neah way any true Cummerlan Cummerlan feller er body wudd ivver eet any tropkell bliddy fruit frae t' Sooth Siss*).

'Meaning,' he flung back, 'what in my mind's eye I envisage as his tiny chateau tucked away behind Wastwater? I happen to know that in most local chip shops they still continue to shovel 'curry sauce' onto their chips and then their panting customers shovel this excremental mixture into their mouths.'

Cumcatch agreed mournfully. 'They are primitive in towns like Workington. They really do do some extraordinary things up there. Do you know that the last time I drove through it, I saw two youths actually *fighting on a zebra crossing*? Can you credit that? They were holding up all the traffic as they tumbled backwards and forwards across the stripes.'

At this point Wm. interposed an absolute lie. Irritated beyond measure by their cruel denigration of his county, a denigration which sounded only with conviction when it came from local lips like his own, he thumped his fist upon Glenridding's gleaming filing cabinets and said:

'Well I happen to love Workington! Even if the haughty *Sunday Times* a quarter of a century ago, categorically declared it to be *the* dirtiest town in the whole of Britain. Whereas, as a handsome little town I would say it is second to none in the entire western hemisphere.'

'What!' chorussed the other three.

'Aside from nearby Maryport perhaps. Yes I would say that paradisaical Maryport obligingly vies with crumbling old towns like Florence, Sienna and Avignon, but at the end of the day has the definitive edge on all three.'

'Hang on!' snorted Glenridding, whose own powers of hyperbole were feeling a giddy envy at this chap in the mustard woollens.

'Let me put my cards on the table,' Wm. declared as he once more felt the clockwork mechanism winding him up to full torque. 'Let's face facts, extremely uncomfortable ones in the present context. Is it true or is it not? That I am the only *bona fide* local in this room?'

There was a grotesquely uneasy silence from his audience.

'I am,' he went on riotously, 'a local who unusually can talk in very big sentences if need be. A main clause, a predicate, verb adjuncts, adjective adjuncts, and with multiple subordinate clauses running to paragraph after paragraph if need be. I can place between two and two hundred adjectives before every substantive if I wish to. I can resort to the gerund, gerundive, subjunctive, causative, optative, desiderative, frequentative, aorist and more. I don't always choose to do so, but if I omit to do so it is *my* decision, my *choice* rather than my involuntary admission of ineloquence. Do you all agree?'

'Alright,' Glenridding admitted wearily. 'We take your point, local laddie.'

'I thought you said you weren't interested in words?' Beeston protested irritably.

'So as an *insider*,' Stapleton went on deafly, 'I can tell you more about Workington, Whitehaven and Maryport, the three compromised coastal towns that constitute all that industrial Cumbria amounts to, than any of you will ever learn in a thousand million years, the half life of Po^{238} would be a ready analogy.'

'Regarding,' he went on admonitorily, 'the putative internationalism brought about by your company settling in this locale. And especially of noble Whitehaven, birthplace of the celebrated Paul Jones, hub of the illustrious whaling . . . sorry I mean notorious slaving trade in the eighteenth century when the noble town vied only with aristocratic Liverpool as the principal British port along the north-west coast. Let us marshall your evidence cited as signs of the new attitude. Number one: proliferation of wine bars. Let us accept for the moment that the presence of one in Whitehaven or Workington or Maryport means that we remote, inbred, letterless provincials have decided to embrace the grown up ways of the world at large. Furthermore pro. tem. accepting that the ready availability of kebabs and pitta means a plutonium process worker from Mirehouse or Greenbank is now saying. "Ho! I accept the whole world and all its flavours/Just as I accept an international nuclear consortium and all its charitable favours." '

The college teacher noticed Glenridding hastily writing something down and Beeston winked at his colleague, as if to agree that the Publicity Man must have thought that bouncy couplet a neat little jingle.

'All of that being taken as true provisionally,' Stapleton concluded with a poker face of mordant scepticism. 'Then why is it the case that nearly all the good folk of my home county *continue to spit in the face of the Irish?*'

'Eh?' Glenridding gasped, a monumental disingenuousness stealing across his heavy features.

100

'You know what I'm talking about!'

'I haven't a clue,' said Cumcatch truthfully.

'I mean that lustfully penetrating programme made by Beeston's TV colleagues over in Yorkshire.'

Mr Cumcatch tetanized and sighed at its memory and even Glenridding brushed back his hair and pulled angrily at his tie. Geoff Beeston seemed very wistful as he imagined what it must be like to be working for a ground-breaking TV documentary team, instead of trumpeting about worms and hounds on this side of the Pennines.

'The programme you recall was entitled *Windscale – The Nuclear Laundry*. Apart from mentioning such lame gnostic heresy as meaninglessly-skewed clusters of childhood leukaemias (*laal kids wid lucky mes mare roont Wabthat an Byutl an Siskell an Refglass an sek like spots, says Willum wit a bustin pink fyass*) . . . it also spoke of the scale of emissions into the *Irish* Sea. As a result of which the horrified Irish government made a polite resolution to the European Parliament that it would be humbly gratified if its honourable British counterparts would very kindly close the laundry, and hand back the Cumbrian coast to the wheeling seagulls.'

'Gah!' snorted Glenridding, and then with unstoppable violence. 'The *Irish*! As if what *they* say matters a monkey's fu . . .'

William was genuinely startled by that off-the-cuff obscenity from a man in high office. He felt as if he had seen something he ought not to have seen.

'But the Irish *are* foreigners,' he insisted. 'Like it or not they are abroad. And if our *Prozessarbeiter* are ready to embrace the kebabs and the *Gewürztraminer*, then why no open-armed cosmopolitanism when it comes to Louth, Monaghan or Dalkey-by-the-Sea?'

'Ireland,' insisted Glenridding with absolute finality, 'is not foreign. They are not . . . it is not . . . it will never be foreign. They say they are foreign but they are not. They are a symbiotic . . . no a parasitic clone on our body politic. Why even the Cumbrians look down on the Irish and I always believed it was impossible for the Cumbrians to look down on anyone apart from the Blacks.'

'There are no Blacks in Cumbria,' Wm. stressed, feeling painfully as if he were back in his General Studies classes again.

'No there aren't,' the Publicity Officer agreed. 'But the locals here despise the protests of the Irish because they despise the Irish *per se* with the most sincere contempt. They despise the Irish because they have no Blacks to despise. And of course they have to despise someone in the world as everyone else despises the lowly Cumbrians.'

Stapleton looked carefully at the three men in the room and silently acknowledged that yes, even mild Cumcatch despised him because he was a local.

'But why do you despise us?' he asked, almost with tears in his eyes.

'You know the answer yourself,' Glenridding retorted contemptuously. '*Rum butter. Gurning.* The Biggest Liar in the World Competition. The most ductile tractable workforce outside of Taiwan or . . . or . . . the Channel Isles.'

'Cumberland Stew,' leered Beeston equally pitilessly. '*Mr and Mrs.* Need we go on?'

'Border Television,' chipped in Cumcatch vauntingly. 'Derek Batey. Appalling utterly unbelievable, amateur nonsense. Good Lord, everyone in the world despises you Cumbrians, I'm afraid.'

(*Styapleton clowst his eyes, shufft iss fingers inter t'lyeugs, latit them oot gay sharpish and opent t'eyes agyan*)

'I . . .' he was about to say.

BLIP BLIP BLIP BLIP BLIP

'*Ah want ter gah yam!*' Stapleton found himself repeating outside Lahcen's. As it got to ten o'clock the Rue Sanlucar was thronging with strolling couples, speeding taxis, darting youths, the occasional inconspicuous tourist. Moulay Ismail had his huge threatening nose half an inch from the Nazarene's and was interrogating him as to the purpose of this formula which he claimed William had been muttering trancelike for the past ten minutes. Si Mohammed was grinning unflappably and shouting across proudly that it was the English radio producer's game; his gimmick; it might even be his personalised signature tune, by analogy with his go-go colleague Moulay Ali who stuffed his pop programme with brilliant jingles and excellent rhymes.

'Why does he sit here with that idiotic staring expression?' Moulay Ismail demanded petulantly. 'Staring like some *mejdoub* sunk deep in contemplation and muttering *unter gahyan, unter gahyan?*'

Fatoma deigned for once to turn to the poetic eminence opposite. Maybe, she hissed scornfully, the Englishman was simply hypnotised by Moulay Ismail's far-famed eloquence. And as for vacant eyes and rhythmic gibbering – that was exactly how Moulay Ismail recited his own poetry. Wasn't that sufficient recommendation for his present behaviour?

'Goat shit!' sniffed the virile versifier. 'Listen Stapleton, what on earth is this "unter gahyan" rhapsody?'

William hestitated before sheepishly replying (*in Morkan Arrapick ev cowrse*). 'It means "I want to go home" '

'Is that all?' grunted Moulay Ismail. 'Well so do I, come to that. Come with me and follow me down to my place.'

Stapleton looked anxiously down the table and observed none of them making a move. Instead he watched Moulay Ismail presenting his car keys to Si Mohammed so that he could drive Habiba and Fatoma to their homes. There was a vague promise from the young producer that he'd be down to join them at his brother-in-law's by midnight, so that he and William could plan the structure of the guest producer's study tour. Midnight? Moulay Ismail chortled, and remarked uproariously that a true poet never sleeps, cares nothing for day and night, does not acknowledge the temporal constraints of the non-poet.

'But where are we going?' Stapleton asked as the poet seized hold of him in a playful vice and marched him off across the street.

'Home of course,' said Moulay Ismail cheerfully. 'Precisely where you said you wanted to go.'

'Where is home?'

'I live down by the sea front. We'll head through Rue Magellan and then onto the Avenue d'Espagne. Right on the corner of the Rue de la Plage opposite the railway station, there's a first class patisserie. We'll halt there and have mint tea and cakes. I presume you understand that as poet I'm obliged to eat a great many sweets and cakes?'

'I . . .'

'Don't you desire something sweet yourself? After polishing off all that prune tagine?'

'Listen when I said home,' the Englishman carefully explained, 'I meant my own home, Moulay Ismail.'

'You have rented a flat here?' the poet asked sharply. 'Or are you in one of those decaying hotels run by old English homosexuals?'

'Certainly not!' snapped Wm. indignantly. (*Cos he thowt till issel that Mooly Ismel nut owny reckent he hed neah crimmy spunk ter makk a laal bairn, but wuss a bliddy owld shucker plum ferry intil t'bargun.*)

'Good,' said the poet. 'A foreigner, a Nazarene especially, should see the inside of a Moroccan home and get to know the people and the country in that way. Come and eat some *majoun* with me and then I will recite some of my lovely immaculate verses. I gave Si Mohammed my car without protest tonight so that you and I can enjoy a walk through this beautiful city by night. Together, William Stapleton, we will enjoy its vigour, bustle and intoxicating colour. Tangiers is an unparalleled city in my view, because it combines the best of both worlds. It manifests itself in the *ville nouvelle* which we are presently passing through, as a modern cosmopolitan city. Here one can purchase the latest French and American novels; video cassettes; imported pet foots like Chum, Lassie, Bounce and Trill; imported Heinz specialities; electric dishwashers; the most costly French and German wines . . .'

Stapleton could not but assent as he gazed at the shop windows. However a germ of a query, a quite preposterous inquiry of his memory by his brain, was making itself felt. There was a seed of hope, a faint clue to the mystery of his radio voyaging. It had of course to do with the relationship between where he was and where he'd come from. He saw in his inner eye a distant image of what looked like a huge cargo ship. He saw as plain as day the rusted railway lines along the front of Whitehaven docks. Way below him, in his radio eye, he glimpsed an imposing Moroccan seafront. To his bewilderment on the extreme right of his vision in huge neon letters planted outside some sort of prison-like compound the English words *Camp Africa – Middle East Holiday Complex.*

'However the modern Tangiers is only the ghost of Tangiers,' Moulay Ismail continued severely. 'Just as for a true Muslim a Nazarene is not a true man but an empty shell or a ghost.'

The African stopped to look at the Englishman whom probably he regarded as nothing more substantial than a ghost. The Englishman who was after all here only by courtesy of the medium wave, could hardly make any contradiction.

'The real Morocco lies in the medina,' the poet declared gravely. 'In the medina you have bustle, life, fertility . . .'

'Fertility?' said Stapleton and blushed.

'Yes, the medina is the old Islamic town, the guts, the viscera, the entrails of my city. A teeming warren, a colourful maze of narrow streets, complicatedly interconnecting just like the body's conduits and apertures, do you appreciate? Here is the souk, here the best stalls, the grains, the spices, the chickpeas, the odorous olive oil, here the spirit of the place. In huge medinas such as in Fez or Marrakesh, a Nazarene will simply get lost without a guide unless he has an incredible memory.'

'Oh?' said Stapleton warily.

'Yes. Your Occidental notions of a grid system, the legacy of the French imperialists, is altogether anathema to the true Islamic heart. I, in fact, am a first class mixture of the modern and the ancient Moroccan. As a poet I am both a fervent internationalist and also a fervent Muslim who scorns all other faiths. I therefore accept the *ville nouvelle* which is to say Europe, liberal culture, Bugs Bunny, *The Rockford Files*, and educated values. Equally though as a poetic son of the medina, I am a simple child of the mazes and alleys of the souk, and I heartily repudiate all your pitiful Western notions of sexual equality, of free love, of disdain for the family, Bugs Bunny, *The Rockford Files*, of deliberate childlessness, not to speak of your cacophonous popular music.'

All at once Stapleton's glimmering ruminations fructified and gelled into a truly shattering awakening.

'Why?' he blurted out to Moulay Ismail. 'Why is bloody Tangier Street called bloody *Tangier Street*?'

'You will not,' the poet scornfully replied, 'find your fancy period hotels in the medina. There are no Cecils, Biarritzs, Ibn Batoutas up around the perimeter of the Petit Socco. In the Grand

105

Socco which is the demarcation between medina and *ville*, there are your one- and two-stars but not in the old medina proper. There in those squalid but life-rich pensions you will find no pansified flush toilets nor immaculate showers. Instead there is wholesome nay godly dirt; the occasional flea; the perfectly acceptable smell of cat piss on the sheets.'

'Listen,' Stapleton gasped. 'The street parallel with White-haven harbour is called *Tangier* Street. It's only just occurred to me. I feel such a fool awakening to that crucial fact. Surely it must have some significance mustn't it? The fact that I'm striding down here with you along the Rue Magellan in Tangiers? But what I want to know is *why*?'

'Why what?' snorted Moulay Ismail.

'Why is Tangier Street called Tangier Street?'

'The difference between East and West,' sniffed the poet contemptuously, 'is very simple indeed. You Westerners as well as plague and fever and Death and so on, have even tried to abolish your own excrement, or at any rate its outward and visible signs. In a 'Western' lavatory why there is scarcely any smell, no evidence that anyone has squatted and emptied their bowels of cheerful faeces. Likewise in a two-star shower there is no damp, coagulated body hair nor other fallings from the body. Now the body is by its nature impure, a spiritual pit, a falling away from the original glory of pure untarnished spirit. To me as a true poet it is a sign of the highest felicity that when I walk into a good Moroccan lavatory as like as not it will be choking with a smiling mass of happy *caca*. This seems to me to be merely a candid admission of what we humans are, despite our hypocritical protestations.'

But Stapleton was completely preoccupied in ransacking his memories for the Whitehaven/Tangiers connection. Hastily he was seeking enlightening parallels. Was there a Marrakesh Street in Workington; a Casablanca Street in Maryport, the other pair of once prosperous ports? Were there analogously named streets in Whitehaven itself? No, no, no, to all those questions. Were there any other foreign city names in the streets anywhere in any of those towns? Venice Vent, Hamburg Lonning, Dubrovnik Cuttings? No, but disposing of the dignified west and turning to the miserable east, were there any Mombasa Mews, Dar es Salaam Drive or

Bombay Boulevard? No, no, no. Ergo Tangier Street must not be casually so-named but must be so-called to commemorate something. And Wm. sensed deep down that he knew what it was, though hard as he strained he failed to bring the connection up to the surface. It was something to do with his schooldays was all that he could recall. Something which he had studied at the old Grammar School (*t'owld brothel on t'ill*) A musty textbook, a feeling of dismally heavy afternoon tedium. Was it Geography? – it must have been surely. No, no. Was it history then, an ancient commercial connection? No, no, the lingering smell up his nose was that of something organic, inorganic, something like bleach or Dettol mixed with starch, Dyox, the smells of hygiene and/or house improvements. His mind was working overtime to establish the connection. Science it was he was thinking of, something to do with *science*.

They had strolled down past more gleaming banks, travel agents and tourist offices and were now cutting through a residential area which sloped down onto the seafront. It was a steep descent down a series of steps upon which were randomly strewn bits of masonry, broken glass and dog excrement. Stapleton picked his way rather carefully, rather anxiously, as there was little in the way of street lighting. Around him he noticed two or three blocks of high rise flats but immediately in front a little corner shop, brightly lit, in and out of which children and mothers were going for bread, olive oil, sweets and cigarettes. An old man wearing a red fez hobbled past them with a kind of dignified exhaustion. Two young men in suits bolted past scuffling and laughing down the last flight of steps to the Avenue d'Espagne.

Once they reached the fronts they felt the sharp tangy breeze from the murmurous ocean. From the little railway station a horde of travellers disembarked from the Meknes train, the richer ones dashing across into taxis, the rest either melting into the city or heading for the ramshackle buses which were all waiting opposite. The bus conductors, mostly men in their late teens, were hustling for customers in an aggressive sometimes desperate way. For the first time tonight Stapleton awoke to see palpable poverty as he looked at the row of peanut and halva vendors bawling and imploring by the sides of the buses. (*Laal lads with dutty britches and snotty-*

107

beaks like in t'dock bits of Wukton thutty 'ear sen). The travellers getting on the buses to Chaouen, Ketama, Tetouan and Meknes were not all dressed as favourably as the poet soliloquising next to him. Some of them looked extraordinarily poor. One old man was dressed in a djellaba that was exactly like a dirty potato sack. An old, skinny, tired-looking farmer was pantingly handing up a box full of live white chickens to be put on top of the bus. Everyone and everything was yelling. Stapleton had never heard such a din of exhortation, command, indignation, reproach.

He commented to his host. 'There's certainly a lot of the colourful bustle you spoke of.'

'Gah,' Mouley Ismail concurred. 'An invigorating, picaresque, teeming, fevered tableau, Stapleton. Just the kind of scene to stir a great poet to pour it all out.'

'Some of them getting on that bus over there look very impoverished,' the Englishman said with a ripple of pity.

Moulay Ismail looked at him sharply and growled. 'Oh really? And what is that supposed to mean?'

William returned his gaze to the first old man and replied. 'I would say that it is wearing a filthy potato sack on your day out into White . . . I mean into Tangiers.'

'Gah,' said Moulay Ismail, looking indifferently at a group of three or four pathetic old men and their quiet, worried-looking wives. 'They are hopeless old rustics, Stapleton, from another age believe me. They are not so much poor as simply preposterous. Take that squinting old grandad straining there with his box of chickens. Let me tell you that when he gets to the other end at Chefchaouen or whatever mule-handlers' outpost between there and Tetouan, his little old ninety year-old wife will be standing patiently waiting and petrifying in the freezing dark. He'll stare at her as if she's worse than cholera, and then get the bus driver to toss the box of chickens down to her. She'll bow her rickety, dirty old back and take the impossible burden and stagger on behind, while he struts on smugly in front like Sultan Ahmed el Mansour.'

'That's certainly uncalled for,' William said. (*An he sez as weel that they diven't even carry on like yon in Wabthat nooadays, and yon's a laal ootpost for conniesewers of ootposts*) But really Moulay Ismail, if

anyone even in a backward area like mine went around wearing
something indistinguishable from a potato sack, he'd be arrested
for vagrancy.'

'Mm?' the poet inquired, yawning stertorously. 'So. Acknowledge the superior intelligence of the Muslim orient. We don't jail
people for being wretched. What do you think we are, tyrants who
only add insults to injury?'

The old man in the potato sack was chewing a small handful of
pistachios which he was carefully prising from their shells as
if worried he might spill some into the dust around his feet. The
poet slapped his guest's back and steered Stapleton firmly towards
a cafe table right on the corner of the Avenue d'Espagne and the
Rue de la Plage. Here he ordered a light supper of fresh orange
juice, mint tea with extra sugar, espresso coffee and four fancy
bloated pastries, all variations on *cornes de gazelles* or *kab
l-ghzal*.

'Cream horns,' mumbled William in Moroccan Arabic, as he
awkwardly shovelled it down.

'Cream my buttocks,' scoffed the burly poet. 'It is almond
paste in the middle. Isn't it yum-yum delicious? Tell me, how do
these compare with the fancy cakes they eat in your town?'

'These are far superior,' Wm. admitted, licking his caked
fingers as he once more scrutinised the rustics clambering aboard
their bus in their dirty old garments. 'Provincial English confection-
ery always makes me feel sick whereas this *kab l-ghzal* puts me in
more of a pleasantly heavy, pensive mood. Even into a curiously
enjoyable deliciously melancholy sort of state.'

'Exactly!' Moulay Ismail gurgled approvingly. 'A few of these
almond horns inside a great poet like me and I feel just the right
degree of sad compassion to help me break forth into a spontaneous
fit of combustion.'

The English traveller was nodding automatically until he
checked the movement abruptly and asked the poet to repeat that
last phrase. 'Spontaneous composition don't you mean?'

'No I don't, said Moulay Ismail petulantly. 'I mean spontaneous
ignition. The flame, the tertiary fever of creation. It consumes me
Stapleton like a conflagration does a forest. It is not a case of
composing, putting things together like some doltish plodding

bricklayer. The fire of creation works through me like a bolt of lightning and quite literally I *ignite*. Plumes of smoke come off me in the literal sense.' (*Mooly Ismel clemt that when he wuss spootin iss luffliest powtry, ee wudd litrlee start ter smyeuk and fizzel like a katrin will on Gwy Fuchs Neet*).

Stapleton looked terrified at such a fearless confluence of art and magic.

'Of course, sadness' Moulay Ismail insisted judiciously, looking approvingly at the rag-tag boarding the Ketama bus, 'is the very highest, truest, wisest, deepest, greatest of the poetic emotions. In the old Persian love poetry you know when the young poet was aching with yearning for his loved one, the ache would spread down to his kidneys, which the ancient medical practitioners of that time would assume was the seat of lachrymation. The poet would start to weep and sob and so deep was his yearning for the object of love he would weep and weep in literal streams, torrents, absolute lakes of grief. He would weep so copiously that *literally* his feet would get wet, he would create an actual flood around him.'

Wm. Stapleton began to titter helplessly. The image of such aqueous sadness was irresistibly funny. Included in his embarrassed mirth was the relief of the realisation that Moulay Ismail's talk of catching fire (his imminent meltdown) was just this mad oriental balderdash of *hyperbole*. A love so surpassingly deep it causes you literally to drown in your own tears. Hah! Everything of the order of myth, everything larger than life, greater than science, bigger than the pyramids!

'It's your poetic exaggeration,' he replied to an affronted Moulay Ismail. 'I'm sorry but it made me laugh. It sounds so amusing to an . . . to a . . .'

Then suddenly he remembered what the connection was, what had been nagging irritatingly at his mind for the last half hour! He seized hold of the poet who looked most perturbed by his touch. Moulay Ismail violently shrugged away the Englishman's excited hand.

'The connection,' Wm. cried, 'between your town and mine is nothing less than sulphuric acid. Or rather, to be more precise, is tripolyphosphate detergents!'

He went on with something of a dizzy, vainglorious gleam in

his eyes. 'The great paradox, the impossible syllogism, the defiance of all logical relations. That which is work; that which is Cumbrian; that which is *not* – can you credit it? – nuclear!'

'It sounds unlikely to me,' the poet said boredly as he tucked into a third almond horn.

'Sulphuric acid, the preparation of,' the radio enthusiast intoned in something of a rapture. 'Take a few tons of sodium phosphate rock. Fresh from Morocco, straight from Tangiers docks, just ten minutes from this cafe by the fast way cutting through by analogy *Rue d'Whitehaven*. Here the precious substrate is loaded up to go all the way to Cumbria, to the birthplace of etc. the hub of etc. etc. Once reached the noble, history-steeped English port it is unloaded, put on the Marchon lorries, carted along Tangier Street, taken up to the suburb of Greenbank, unloaded at the works, finally mixed with the sulphur dioxide and superheated steam conveniently to hand. Then . . . then SO_2 plus . . . plus $NaPO_4$ plus H_2O gives, ah, $NaHPO_3$ plus $NAOH$ plus, ah, $GBFL_3$.'

'What was that last one?'

'Greenbank filth. One mole of Greenbank, that is, to the three moles of ambient filth.'

Stapleton paused from his inorganic equations as he became aware that there was a whole row of attentive young man had massed before them clutching small quantities of extremely uninteresting manufactured goods. Cheap plastic belts; tawdry shirts; hideous wrist watches; all manner of fairground rubbish. Moulay Ismail ordered more gazelle horns and coarsely shooed away a starved young man of about thirty who was trying his best to sell the poet a thin blue anorak.

'No I don't want your camel-boy's anorak,' the celebrity said nastily. 'Can't you see by the shirt I've got on, a Pierre Cardin, that I am an inordinately discriminating individual who offers to dress with some taste?'

'Then what about the Nazarene, sir?' the vendor asked hopefully, fascinated by the garish, fashionless cardigan on the Englishman.

'Nor does he, you fool! And watch it, sonny boy, he speaks perfect Arabic even if he looks an eccentric idiot. In any case who are you to call a Nazarene a Nazarene, you unemployed gypsy?'

Stapleton blinked guiltily from his preoccupation with the tripolyphosphate detergents, which paradoxically created local filth while absterging the international variety (in Tangiers shops too he had noted packets of Surf and Tide and Daz and biological Ariel). He took in a total of twelve young, eager, thin, worried, tired little men standing in a row outside the patisserie, selling all these entirely unappetising gew-gaws at half past ten at night.

'Has anyone ever bought anything they hawk?' he asked Moulay Ismail with genuine scepticism.

'About once a week perhaps,' the poet sniffed.

'And they're all unemployed gypsies, metaphorically speaking. Desperately selling this trash at all hours just to earn some bread for their families?'

Moulay Ismail said abruptly, 'I have no patience with any of them. For one they are all far too thin and I detest thinness as a way of life, just like Julius Caesar did. And for two it is a buyer's market isn't it, William? As your own most sapient Sultana Margarita rightly says. Why don't these hustlers tout something with a bit of style instead of all this ghastly South Korean trash?'

Suddenly thoughtful, Stapleton said. 'Actually I happen to need an anorak. And let me add that nobody where I come from would turn their nose up at a solid, unpretentious garment like that one. In fact they all wear identical overcoats,' he mused as he pictured any little Cumbrian town on any winter's day, 'where I come from. What's more, Moulay Ismail, I genuinely happen to need some protective clothing *immediately*.'

The poet was vastly scornful of that naive, newly confident tone of his. 'It doesn't look like rain to me,' he grunted witheringly.

'Nor to me,' Wm. answered. 'But I'll bet my last dirham that it's bucketing down in Tangier Street. Even if it's not quite the tail end of summer.'

Slowly the poet understood that Stapleton was intending immediate departure for England. He gazed at him astounded, his mouth awash with almond crumbs and leaves of mint.

'You're not intending to take a flight at this time of night?' he challenged.

'No, I haven't enough dirhams to get a flight to Newcastle just like that. But yes, I bet I can get a phosphate boat homeward bound from down there at the quay.' He pointed into the distant darkness where the lights of numerous boats at dock were glinting. 'To take me all the way to my hometown.'

He blinked at his own ingenuity. Then he strutted across boldly to the disappointed anorak salesman and stuffed about ten pounds worth of dirhams into his hand before seizing the Korean manufactured windcheater. Amazed the other eleven vendors hastily plied him with belts, watches, electronic calculators which almost shattered as soon as Stapleton looked at them. Wm. awkwardly took the lot, poked another ten pounds worth of dirhams from his pocket and delegated the anorak seller to dish it out equitably, allowing a slim twenty two and a half per cent commission for himself.

'Stapleton!' cried Moulay Ismail, disdainful of such pointless beneficence. 'Aside from encouraging all the dregs of Tangiers to come every night pestering regulars like me till the end of time, I have another criticism to level at you!'

'Ah?' said the Englishman carelessly, stuffing all his purchases into his anorak pocket. 'Well you'd better trot beside me as you air your grievance. I'm off down to the harbour now to find the Marchon phosphate boat.'

'Gah! And what about my brother-in-law?' said Moulay Ismail angrily, reluctantly rising from his chair. 'Si Mohammed is all elevated to the heavens because you are doing this exchange business of Radios Tangier and Khambria. Now you're proposing to sail off without as much as doing one guest appearance at his management meetings.'

'I'm afraid that's all nonsense,' William snapped, paying the waiter handsomely and putting on his new anorak which he dolefully observed was seven and a half inches too short in the arm.

'You're right there,' Moulay Ismail guffawed, slapping his huge thighs with hilarity. 'You look absolutely ridiculous, Stapleton! You look more like a monkey than you do like a tourist!'

'I didn't mean my duds and spats,' William retorted calmly. 'I mean my identity, as you Tangerines perceive it, is all a nonsense. I am *not* a radio producer, do you understand? I am a Grade 1 lecturer in General/Liberal/Social Studies in a third rate provincial technical college. I teach nuclear instrument mechanics how to furnish written accounts pertaining to the screwing and unscrewing of a hinge. How to say hello and goodbye to the receiver of a telephone. How to roll on a condom the full length of the erect penis, carefully expelling the air from the teat as one does.'

'You're an impostor you mean!' the poet replied suspiciously. 'You've duped the high-ups at Rabat into arranging a phony exchange with poor old Si Mohammed?'

'Don't be absurd!' Stapleton shouted bitterly. 'If you must know, Moulay Ismail, I don't know how the hell I've got here! On Aladdin's magic carpet I think. By radio, by sound energy, by nodes and troughs and sinusoidal conformations. I was minding my own business as I always do. I happened to be listening to beautiful Fatoma on my old valve wireless back in England and I became so enraptured by her singing, her quite miraculous voice, that I literally left the attic and ended up talking to your blasted brother-in-law in the studios of Radio Tangiers.'

'Goat shit!' bellowed Moulay Ismail, slavering thickly at the lips. 'Do you take me for a superstitious country bumpkin of a fool?'

'Yes,' admitted Stapleton. 'Yes I know it sounds incredible. Though scarcely impossible surely to a poet like you who believes in his own ability to achieve self-immolation.'

'What?'

'To a man who needs a bucket of water thrown over him when he's in the fizzing phosphorescence of artistic creation.'

Moulay Ismail stared at him amazed, outraged that a gormless Nazarene wearing a yellow cardigan underneath a South Korean anorak that was half way up his arms, should cast doubt on the vertiginous dimensions of his artistic axes.

'You know what you look like?' Moulay Ismail retorted with a threatening leer. 'You look like a scraggy little mountebank.'

'You're not the first person to say that,' Wm. said pacifically.

'A Moroccan mountebank too. The type that capers and jabbers and does fool's tricks in the Djemaa el Fna in Marrakesh. And with that colloquial Arabic of yours, I might even take you for a genuine Moroccan! In fact you know what, I think you *are* a bloody Moroccan! A trickster, a confidence punter, an albino with a crazy Arabian Nights story. So what I'm going to do *right now*, is to grab hold of you and haul you off to the nearest police st . . .'

'*But az garn yam*,' bawled William, helplessly falling into childhood dialect, '*ont' fosfet bwoat till Whitehebben!*'

BLIP BLIP BLIP BLIP BLIP

The temperature dropped as if in response to the fearless impetuosity of a great impersonal force. Wm. Stapleton shuddered for that microsecond of waveband travel as it occurred to him like in a heartless dream that his wireless knob back home might this time have slipped from Radio Tangiers to Radio Bucharest, Radio Johannesburg, Radio San Salvador. The last thing he could bear at this stage was a full-blooded ideological nightmare in the form of a radio play incorporating a stroll in the vicinity of the city police cells and the unmistakable sound of some screaming prisoners. It was with frustrated relief that he found himself in a stationary C registered Ford Fiesta with a boyish impresario confidently twitching the wheel with one hand. Geoffrey Beeston turned and winked at him and with a louche smirk announced that he had passed the Advanced Driving Test when he was eighteen and a half; a baffling achievement yet consistent with the fact he'd passed the ordinary driving test on his seventeenth birthday.

'I made history in Rugeley,' he said, 'though I was only the seventh to do it in Staffs over all. The boss man in Carlisle thinks I'll certainly be in the top local radio stratum by the time I'm twenty-seven. Between ourselves,' he purred, 'I've got my eyes focused on horizons so high some of my colleagues can't even imagine the vertigo involved for weaker aspirants. Television, needless to say, not the anonymity of radio. I think my puss should adorn a screen, it's quite a handsome puss I feel. Not any old TV outfit either. Not Border, Channel, Grampian, Southern, HTV, none of those dusty parish pump houses. No, I'm either after Granada features or the BBC news room.'

Stapleton unheeding was simply obsessed with where it was they were. It certainly wasn't Carlisle this time. It was some small village as viewed from an unusual sidewise angle, from an unlikely gravelled lonning. There was an ambience of cultured size and

115

resplendence, of sleepy large white terraces and comfortable old family houses with grounds and nodding fruit trees, all to be glimpsed between two rows of far less dignified terraces facing their car. They were in the humble back rows of a very desirable Cumbrian village. A flash of mellow sandstone in the far distance below confirmed at once that this must of course be St Bees, home of the ancient eminent public school.

'Is this where you live?' William asked the producer, craning his neck. Then hurriedly, shiftily. 'If you cut up by the back road to the A595, just before the Moor Row turn off, and then drop me off at the corner there, I can walk the rest.'

'Walk?' cried Beeston. 'All the way to blasted Windscale?'

'Not at all,' Wm. whimpered. 'To my home, that's all. I don't want to go to BNFL again. God Almighty, Rhoda must be worried senseless about where I've gone and vanished.'

'Don't be damn ridiculous,' snapped Beeston. 'We're off for you to record a rehashed interview with Wilf after that wholly unprofessional vaudeville you succeeded in staging last time! In fact,' he whispered confidingly, 'it might even be advisable for you to start with some brief extenuation, as Glenridding was so terminally irritated by your absurd tactlessness.'

Stapleton asked anxiously. 'I was impolite was I?'

'Awful,' Beeston muttered. 'All this tendentious swordclanging stuff of accusation and unsubstantiated snippets. And now after you've taken Glenridding's advice and seen the Rices, you have no option but to return to the alma mater (*almer myatter*) to bow your silly head.'

Veiling his incomprehension as much as he could, William managed to tease out out of his colleague that they had just been to interview a certain Rice family of St Bees at the Publicity Officer's instigation. Number 17, the one with the bright gold knocker, was their modest little terrace. Mr Rice he learnt by playing the ingenuous comedian in need of a superfluous rehearsal, was employed by the alma mater (*almer myatter*) as a plutonium process worker (*pluttnam prossis wukker*). His wife Shirley also worked at the plant as a canteen assistant. His daughter Minnie was a trainee radioactivity monitor (*ready actyvittie monty*). His younger child Desmond aged six was not an employee of course, but Desmond's symbolic condition was proof if anything was of the staunchness of local independent-mindedness.

'A symbolic condition?' said Stapleton wonderingly. He also wondered dimly where it was he had heard or read of a Rice family in some signficant local context.

'Leukaemia!' (*Lucky me!*)

'Leukaemia?' (*Lucky me?*)

'Certainly. That's one definite constant in among all the confusion of unrelated variables. He has definitely got leukaemia (*lucky me*) rather than say meningitis or persistent flu' or diabetes.'

'The poor kid,' began Stapleton who had only the vaguest barest sensation of ever having met a small child with a fatal illness. 'And his family are presently sueing the company?' (*t'almer myatter fer compen fer lucky me*).

Beeston began to counsel his wayward apprentice firmly. 'For God's sake stop turning everything on its head will you? Rule number one for any journalist working outside of Prague or Taiwan or or . . . Tanbloodygiers. Avoid personal fantasy, wishful thinking and seeking crass outward confirmation of inner private hostilities. You are seeking investigative truth, not confirmation of partisan prejudices. Stick to the facts, Billy Stapleton! You saw how Mr and Mrs Rice and Minnie put their hands to their hearts and professed themselves all proud to work at the plant even if their little boy has got the megalurgy.'

'I did not!'

'That's what you *heard* whether it pleased your ears or not! It's on your cassette there if you need to refresh your memory as to the interview. You heard Mr Rice. He's been there twenty years and he obviously hasn't got the nanolurgy. Clearly neither has his wife or daughter.'

'But what about the child?'

'Mr Rice says he loves his boy like gold but he could have got his becquerels living anywhere. Kids he affirmed do get leukaemia in places like St Neots and Penzance. The trouble with you,' Beeston concluded with haughty disparagement, 'is that you don't listen to the hearts and minds of your own people, your own sensible kin. You got more and more hectoring and impertinent as the 'interview' with Wilf proceeded. For instance when he cited the public meeting called by the council to discuss emergency plans for a local-style Chernobyl (*A Shurnobble Cummerlan-style!*)..'

'Yes,' said Stapleton anxiously. 'What did I say?'

'Wilf was telling us how a feverish total of twelve concerned citizens turned up at the meeting, typically enough. Q.E.D. the community's complete faith in the plant to manage its own scrupulous housekeeping.'

'Housekeeping?' gasped Wm. racking his brains to recall even a glimmer of the interview. 'Did he really use *that* word?'

'You interrupted him ever so harshly and said all it showed was their disgusting blind indifference. Your adjectives and imagery generally, got more and more Gothic and rococo and intemperate. You said that they simply couldn't imagine themselves frying alive; puking up their own intestines in forty different colours. Amnesia was the word you kept using. I find that actually a laughable case of personal projection, Bill.'

Wm. stared at the amateur psychologist who was presently steering them through deserted Egremont, the town which if any, would feel the full bonus of a local-style Chernobyl (*A Shurnobble – Cummerlan style!*) They paused to let some schoolgirls cross the road and the producer squinted his boy's unblemished skin and eyes against the powerful sunlight.

'Amnesia!' he repeated challengingly. 'Of all words.'

'What's so significant about that?'

'You!' accused Beeston gravely as they stopped at the traffic lights outside Beckermet. 'You, Billy! You forget everything. You forget where you've come from. Where you're going. Who you're interviewing. Who you've interviewed. I recognised all that dumb show back there; don't take me for a naive young freelance from Rugeley! You couldn't even remember you'd been interviewing the Rice family and their dying little boy. And worse than that you have this really childish wish to be dashing off home all the time to your wife! Christ, you're like a little boy yourself who doesn't want to face the real world of difficult challenges and hard decisions, and adult maturity and so forth.'

Stapleton blushed at such unbridled personal animus. Silently stewing for some minutes, he was trying to articulate a difficult comparison. That if Beeston had found himself totally overcome by his own medium (viz. sound), incorporated into it, subsumed by it, and even whizzed around the globe as on some whiplashing fairground switchback, then Beeston too might start complaining about feelings of concussion and amnesia. For Beeston to be totally governed by his medium; to eat, sleep and drink Radio Cumbria that is; was mere innocuous metaphor at present. For Stapleton it was the paralysing truth of his experience.

'So I'm going down to apologise to Wilf, am I?' he said aggrieved, even sulky.

'Yes. And to ask him about the leak.'

'I've done that already,' snapped William defiantly.

'No, marra. The *new* leak.'

'Eh!'

'Emission the *second*, you amateur!'

'Oh my Christ!' snorted the waveband wanderer.

'Scarcely,' Beeston explained. 'This one constitutes neither a leak nor a dribble as it's been accounted for as more of a luxuriously slow seepage. Some building down there they use for decontamination of equipment has a anomalous excess of becquerels underneath it. They've put a stop to it – G. Beeston beat the local tabloid to that laal scoop, asser marra! – and Wilfie told me that it's safely confined to the tiny upper layer of soil immediately beneath the building.' (*Beeston gadger sez greet Wiff frae Winskell sez they'd pluggt t'laal wols unterneet t'shed where t'ready acty vittie protekshun gadgers ed tyan sum fancy clart apparetuss for lossin its ready acty vittie wid a laal swill doon wit tietraytit carblick or Reetgard unnerarm shite or sek like ev manyoover.*).

Unscientific Stapleton tried to picture the little quanta of radioactivity staying calmly put in the topsoil, not burrowing despoilingly down like so many esurient, edacious! (my exclamation, E. J. Asbach) (*issyurrient, iddashus, laal griddy getts of laal solwurrams!*) earthworms. Then from nowhere once again he felt that awful clockwork mechanism taking over his voice box. And the unmistakable speech rhythms of a certain strident Tangerine poet taking command of his over-emphatic speech.

'Regrettably of course the trouble with Orientals,' Wm. fluted languorously, just as if he were Mr Mercaptan in *Those Barren Leaves*, 'is that they don't try and conceal the smell of their excrement, Geoffrey.'

'No,' Beeston concurred gravely, as if at last his colleague was making intelligent general conversation. 'From about Zagreb to anywhere east of same, it's stale urine and stinking lavatories from start to finish. I had enough of that dysentery and nonsense in my student days. From then on, for me and Candy, it's been a nice little villa every August in the Valley of the Wolves.'

'You go into their lavatories,' Stapleton complained with lairdly prim disgust, 'to be assailed by the embarrassing evidence of the impure body. While here in our fastidious local towns, if anyone presumes to pass water in the street, they are smartly arraigned for unauthorised leaks.'

'Mind you,' Beeston chuckled. 'This slow seepage phenomenon is even less of a P.R. problem for old Wilfred. Because it's so slow, its effect is so gradual, uncatastrophic, undramatic. The whole thing is much more of a by-your-leave and bugger the cynics than something violent and unpredictable.'

Stapleton only caught the tail end of that last remark and felt himself quiver at the resonance of those two words.

'Unpredictable violence?' he sighed.

'Mm. Last year some Friends of the Earth (*Marras ev t'Uth*) pointed out that a sudden seismic tremor (*sezmick trimmer*) might shake Calder Hall to its foundations and give us another ghastly 1957. Except videoable in colour this time instead of in black and white. God,' he slavered parenthetically, 'think of those days, Billy, when an actual majority of people listened to the trusted wireless in preference to the spurious television.'

BNFL was approaching bigger and bigger, without embarrassment. William stared at the four cooling towers looking so beautiful under the late afternoon sparkling sunshine. He sniffed the air suspiciously, a bit like a shifty bloodhound, as if to detect the likelihood of seismic tremor.

'They had the most awful earthquake in Morocco when I was a boy in Waberthwaite,' he remarked. 'It razed Agadir of course, but from the phoenix of their ashes they've made a brand new prosperous commercial tourist city.'

'But there aren't going to be any fortuitous earthquakes round here,' Geoff guffawed, flinging his car door to so heartily that Stapleton's teeth shook and for a moment he misapprehended a tiny tremor. 'They might have had one back in 1222 but the age of portents and asterisks is dead. Don't you think so? Especially in Cumbria and especially in West Cumbria for crying out loud. Angels and demons and allegorical figures are generally a bit selective about where they do their *son-et-lumière* (*sunny lummy agh*)!'

END OF EMISSION THE SECOND

Asbach recalls his Coming of Age and The Great Purge.

ITH an absurdly deprecatory pout, Little finished Beeston's speech about the undesirability of our area from the evangelical angel's point of view. He ceased his delivery abruptly, then took across his empty glass for a refill of sweet stout and lime juice. The murmurs from his audience were this time nothing short of . . . inscrutable. A majority of the Santon Bridge audience had found itself chuckling about childhood cancers (*lucky me; lucky me?*) and the resultant jarring bray of cognitive/ethical dissonance was deafening. They weren't laughing *at* the idea of infant cancers of course; even the oldest Furness fell farmers knew that. No, they were laughing at the idea of such an evil being treated as a jest by a fantasised inner cynical voice which was possibly misrepresenting officialdom, statistics, radiological science, Sir Douglas Black etc. as dissembling, fallacious handtools of the heartless state. Theirs was rather like one's own queasy reaction to the way teenage boys ten years earlier used to make 'jokes' about spastics and metal detectors or about aborted embryos and funny-tasting sago. It was a clash of aesthetic categories, no less, and Little was perhaps at fault here in his neglect of the essential rules of composition. Assuming that the dominant moods of the oral epic or oral lyric are e.g. the Humorous, Heroic, Poignant, Horrific, Yearning, Erotic corresponding to the finished Comedy, Martial Adventure, Melodrama, Horror, Love in Separation, Love in Enjoyment, then Little here had indulged in the unsavoury tastelessness of mixing Humour, Grief and Horror in a melange that led the audience not to a beatitude of impersonal enjoyment of a truly artistic

122

tale, but to a dose of aesthetic colic. They didn't know whether to laugh or cry in short, and it did not make them happy, no it did not.

They all knew who the 'Rice' family was, as its original had been interviewed and displayed in a photogenic piece in a Sunday supplement. Likewise they were all conversant with the luxurious removal expenses of the Hensingham pigeons. The environmentalists' warning about the earthquake was of course a comedy at their, not Ibn Hafl's, expense, but even here Little's representation of his Candide-idiot Wm. Stapleton worrying the possibility into fictional fruition . . . even that was enough to make the chuckles a trifle worn and hollow.

As for Tim Boston, flesh and blood radio producer, his imputed disdain for the locals, was making him very uncomfortable. As he walked to the bar he looked weakly, defensively at a few suspicious, conceivably murderous glances. Cumbrians love to laugh at themselves (as well as at the Irish, Blacks, Nazis, Joooormans etc.) but take great exception to being mocked by others. From what I knew of Boston he had no actual disdain for his raw material. Little's barbs seemed to be more the standard post-Sixties satire upon anyone obliged to play a part in that inevitably collusive combination of media and untruth. In any case, anyone with any sense could see how coarsely biased Little's own satire was: how bending of the truth rules; how tennis-matchish and determined the dialogues between naif (Stapleton) and rogue (Glenridding, Moulay Ismail etc.) This duality in itself was evidently insufficient for Little's propaganda purposes, so of course he had to make his idiot sporadically argumentative, sardonic, hyperbolic and so on. His one triumph it seemed to me was to make his idiot self-consciously aware that he was being *manipulated*, clock-wound by someone, and again anyone with any brains could see who the clock-winder was. That Bewcastle shepherd; the nomad from non-existent Ridgerstown aka Blennerbuggery, Fuckalltown, Neewaspeshal . . .

Klaus's painting meanwhile kept staring at me, demanding that I in turn keep staring at it. From this distance it was probably Ennerdale, but I also thought it might have been Crummock from an eccentric angle. I could not help but reflect on the Candide-like folly of my own father, a William Stapleton without benefit of locomotion via undulatory energies.

He had his peaks and troughs of course, and was hurtled over the globe in random fashion as the impersonal jesters of Fate and Birth and Race and Racelessness decided to skirl him from Egerland to Reich principalities to Iowa to Jakie Baggrow's Stumpy Heights. Also while we are at this cumbersome business of comparison and character, my father failed to be a real Gulley Jimson in the most vital respects. Cary's hero you will recall would sooner have defaecated diamonds than taken any steady employment; he sponged off old working class women whom he beat with fist and indifference. Forever he was maunderingly speechifying about the lunatic, romantic, suicidal nature of artistic commitment. As I've said, Klaus did *paint* with the passion and energy of Jimson; after retirement he simply locked himself away and laboured six hours at a stretch. However despite the occasional surliness of his drunken moods he never beat my mother and very rarely chastised his son. In the most tedious fashion, a typically Cumbrian fashion, he worried himself sick about making ends meet. He went cheerfully to a succession of lowly factory jobs as if he were honoured to be given any work at all. His final totem was the wage packet rather than his art. Work like a dog, drink like a fish, paint as an impassioned but *lucrative hobby*. Perhaps his memories of being orphaned, of an unending diet of nettle soup and horse sausages in Asch in the Twenties, perhaps these were enough to keep him clocking on at biscuit, spectacle, shoe factories, until finally he settled into a job he claimed was the best of the lot. But *why* did the man bear no grudge whatever, neither actual nor speculative, against his distraction from his true talent?

I cannot remember Jimson showing anything in the way of kindness nor tenderness to anything but the romantic memory of his hero William Blake. In my teenage conformist years when I was doing my Tempo Commercial Graphics down by the docks, Klaus treated me with a remarkable paternal tenderness. Once he gave me fifty pounds for my birthday which was three times his late Sixties wage packet. It was a four foot Dunmail Raise I think, sold to a publican at the far perimeter of the county: Dufton or Penton or Bardsea perhaps, where they might only just have heard about the Whitehaven P.O.W. He took me out to a pub at Moor Row when I was underage and insisted on getting me drunk for my one and only time. Such a tender, touching, delicate little ceremony! The pub was a quiet, empty little hole, the haunt of underage kids and deaf old men, and Klaus forced seven pints of extra-fortified real ale down my sixteen year-old gullet; one for each of his two. For some reason we weren't in his Reliant, we were travelling by double-decker bus back into town. Returning home we sat upstairs, where Klaus smoked a malodorous Wee Willem and began to sing at the top of his lungs in what in my foggy liquidity I assumed was Czech. Perhaps on reflection it was some Lakeland hunting ditty he'd learnt from Jakie Baggrow (*Duster Kün Chön Pöll?*) but whatever it was it drew raucous insulting applause from a posse of young lads who were sitting some four seats behind us. From our shaky upstairs perch I noticed the lights below, the street lamps around Hensingham looking remarkably gothically misty against the terrace walls. Then they began to sway, to lurch and indeed to make weirdly motionless zooms up and down like a waterfall going both ways at once. I was tight of course, stupendously so. Klaus turned and blew a huge noseful of Wee Willem into my face and laughed his head off as I grimaced and coughed. He picked me up at our bus stop and led me to the top of the stairs. I stood there swaying, feeling frail and fat and bilious. Klaus gave me a lusty clap on the back and bawled. 'Appy Butter, Ett!' I catapulted forward with a beautifully lyrical momentum and proceeded to roll down the stairs like ten stones of Sudeten buckwheat. Klaus I noted as I spun the length of the steps was laughing uproariously. So much so that he too missed a step and therefore stumbled and shot after me, as if by rehearsed agreement. Father and son then rolled off the bus in perfect sequence, cartwheeling like Carpathian acrobats into the facing gutter. Luckily no one impeded our path for no one was wanting on at our stop. I came to a halt and proceeded to vomit in a conversational tone into the gutter. Klaus lay beside me, staring up in a daze at the stars and swearing windedly at the bus.

'Bliddy chokker!' he muttered grievedly at the conductor, who with a brisk glance confirming neither of us was dead nor injured, smirked and departed.

I think it was at this stage as a sensitive overweight teenager that I decided to be seen as little socially with my father as I could. I realised as

I hadn't done as a small boy, that my father was regarded by quotidian English standards, even Cumbrian standards, as *a bit of an idiot*. This of course was quite a bitter paradox given the local dialect tradition of exalting the fool to heroic status. Even Klaus's pals in his local seemed to keep a final protective distance from the full extent of his 'character'. Klaus was a character but rather too much of a character. Anyone who bought drinks for the entire pub at least once a month must be seriously foolish. And those fearsome gestures, that aeronautic saliva, that incalculable passion! When he was angry the steam rose from his whiskery nostrils; he made Tommy Little's Tangerine poet look like say Mr Larkin. When he was generous he gave his cloak as well as his coat. When he was sad he wept publicly. The English were appalled. And dammit, I was more appalled! A sixteen year-old fatty with no girlfriend but with a Dad who talked like a music hall Boche and worse than that had once been the enemy, a *Feind*. Ilse with some discretion, spent her evenings domestically ninety nine times out of a hundred, and watched the television or read novels. She and I had a warmly sympathetic relationship which I believe made Klaus mildly jealous or at least acerbically sarcastic if he was spoiling for a fight. In my adolescence I talked to Ilse about absolutely everything. Politics; religion; human relationships; girls; personal doubts and problems; everything. She never laughed at a single naive opinion or question of mine. I also lent her every book I'd read and insisted that she do likewise and discuss it with me. So together we waded through Thomas Mann, William Saroyan, Henry Miller, H. G. Wells, Joyce Cary and Dostoievsky. A motley and, as it were, hypermasculine bunch, what? But one thing I reflect that they have in common is that they are all as writers massively opinionated and partisan, rather like the Bewcastle shepherd but with a bit more education. Ilse and I both being naive and thirsty for nourishment were very impressed by their messages and would as equal topics discuss Wellsian socialism, the speech of Masterman say, and the speech of the Grand Inquisitor or an eloquent excursus by Miller on the Wonder of the Artist, with the same lust for watertight opinions and whimsical convictions. Ilse worked in a sweet factory until she retired at sixty, and I doubt if any of her workmates read *The Idiot* during their lunch breaks under the duress of their tubby little specky little sons. Then

126

again, although some of them had husbands who were good with their hands, skilled amateur cabinet makers or rug makers perhaps, none were as sheerly prolific nor had temperaments like fuming sulphuric acid ($H_2S_2O_7$, to use an appropriate local simile.).

Klaus's tenderness almost killed me and in more ways than one. As a demonstration of his high regard for me once I had settled into Tempo Graphics and was doggedly earning my keep, he insisted that I come home for lunch those alternate weeks when he was on the afternoon shift. He the proud Dad of a fledgling businessman (yan day, Ett, you'll be dun promoshun an nice laal pamflet for Martian an' Salatfeld; commushal grafik is big money an bliddy big profit..!) wanted to make my lunch in between his morning's painting and putting his bait up for the back shift/dead man's shift which began at three o'clock. I would have preferred to have taken sandwiches and then sat in the town library, but his offer was so eager and affectionate there was nothing to do but accept. So for a whole month I accepted his tarragon omelettes; his potato puffkes; his sauerkraut; his polony, brawn, liver, the delicious salamis from the Cockermouth delicatessen he raided every month and from which he filled up the back seat of his three-wheeler. It was indeed hearteningly touching at first to arrive home at half past twelve and for old Klaus to be standing there grinning at the cooker and welcoming me with a huge pot of tea and a four-square luncheon.

After about three weeks I noticed he was tiring of his selfless routine but was too proud and embarrassed to discontinue. I offered to spell him off and spend my lunch hour in town, but he put on his most scathingly dismissive pooh-pooh face and gave me an elephant's portion, just to convince me of his rock-solid dependability. Then distraction proper set in because, he explained, he had just received a huge valuable commission from a whole brewery chain: to provide them with a total of twenty pictorial inn signs for pubs the countywide. Proudly he enumerated the staggering total on outspread fingers.

'Ah haff to pent Plack Cock at Aspee; Maltn Shuffel at Pardsa; Flissy Ram at Klitter; Dock an Cun at Pikrikk; Neah Poot at Carlal; Oily Chonnies at Wukton, Plack Line at Merrypot; Poynter Dock at Heddeskill . . .'

'Hethersgill? The Pointer Dog?'

'Laal spot neah Carlal. Neah Langtun an sek like, Ett.'

'Oh. These polony sandwiches are very good, Klaus.'

'Gut poy. Witshiff at Brotton; Lam Kin at Brikum; Plack Pull at Cockmaut; Rumpunt Pull at Cockmaut.'

I nodded admiringly. 'You're going to be busy.'

He scratched his head. 'How am I do a plack cock, Ett? I know me lake backward, I can pent Wasswatter wit eyes shut. But a plack cock. Know anyone wit any laal cocks, son?'

I scratched my incipient whiskers and tried to think of any friends who kept cocks. None of my pals were poultry-keepers but I said to Klaus that surely some of his own in the Black Eagle were bound to be.

'I think I go to lipry, Ett. Get nice pukk on hens, nice photo ev cocks an cockrels. I got neah bliddy time fer chasin bliddy cocks run gatten or famyards.'

A week later he was so up to his eyes in Cocks, Bulls, Boots, Lions, Pointers and Shovels, that when I got home for my lunch there was a little note saying: *Edward. Diner in oven, Love Klaus. Shout if you want help Im up to me eyes. Three and six on mantelpiece is for Wee Willems, get it at tobbaconists near Bus Station because discount is worth haveing money dosnt grow on bloody trees, Ed. Love Klaus.*

On the Wednesday which was also washday Klaus had not only got my lunch of polony and chips keeping nicely warm in the oven, he'd also filled the kitchen with steaming laundry inadequately rinsed from Ilse's twin tub. I was sitting eating my polony and chips and reading the Guardian in the midst of soaking shirts and jeans which were hanging from any convenient nail and hook as well as the line over the fire. A sizeable shower of drips would land on the floor and siss on the fire; the laundry was making a little pattering concerto in our cramped little kitchen. Next door I could hear my father cursing viciously, a sure sign that he was painting at full stretch and agonising over some monumental effort of taxing verisimilitude.

'Pliddy cock!' I heard him growl. 'Pliddy cock an pliddy pull! Bliddy cocknpull story mek neah mistek!'

His p and b labials were interchangeable, of course, depending how far down his Wee Willem he'd got.

That morning I had been doing some preliminary rough-outs on a sales leaflet for a Maryport solvent works. I had been choosing typefaces, letterheads, logos, and doing some helpful little sketches of their extraction process. My desk happened to be squashed at the harbour-facing window and I had been looking enviously at the gulls and fishing boats and wishing like them I was out in the cold, tonic sunshine. With the fretful impatience of a spoiled eighteen year-old, I visualised my tubby little person crushed perpetually, indelibly against this scratched old desk, scribbling and sketching away like some bronchitic Victorian clerk; a bulbous Uriah; a dissident Richard Feverel. I envisaged the rest of my working life spent in over-varnished run-down offices, fiddling desultorily with sheets of letraset and printface manuals. My sole tame diversion to be trotting down to the printers on Tangier Street to 'liaise' with the same peevish print manager and make the same formulaic jokes and feel the same sense of spiritless stagnancy. West Cumbria I felt, *was* pure stagnancy; plus or minus hazardous industries, irrespective of 'Martian' and 'Salatfeld'. For me it was a region of outward and inward spiritual dereliction. Of course I daredn't *say* as much, not voice my antagonism publicly, or I would have been lynched for it. Certainly by my father, at any rate. Or told to go and get out, and take my foreign carcass with me. But this was why I desperately needed a mentor like thirty-year-old Bermondsey-hailing Charlie Timson, who fronted a business, but not for profit; liked unusually progressive jazz; read widely in oriental philosophy, though always Cockney tongue-in-cheek about it and mocking his own enthusiasm. If I hadn't had a guiding elder brother like Charlie, I'd have gone crazy; provincial life undiluted would have killed me.

It was this attack of lunch hour dolefulness, of ingrate's ennui, that suddenly seemed to manifest itself *physically*, in the kitchen, in an appropriately physiological sense. I stopped my chewing abruptly and thought to myself: Christ, eating this lunch I can actually *taste* my own spleen! I seem to be digesting my own bile, for God's sake, as I chew away at this polony and chips!

For I could feel the most persistently unpleasant taste there in my mouth. For a couple of seconds I sincerely believed it was the psychological counterpart of my inner *disgust*. What's more – as I chewed away, I found I was becoming more and more thirsty, as dry as a desert cactus. I always drink copiously with my meals, so wasn't at first dismayed to be polishing off three glasses of water in a row. Later though I found I was needing to trot to the tap after every two or three mouthfuls of lunch. By the time it was three quarters eaten I had disposed of a total of twelve beakers. Which meant that from my pyloric sphincter up to the nape of my gullet felt like a solid piece of plumbing, a hydraulic pillar of water, and that if I coughed too strongly a half gallon of liquid might shoot out and send our kitchen clock flying.

What on earth was this foul taste in my mouth? (I asked myself like Jessie Twentyman, after inhaling too much of the Furness dew.) Was it the polony that was off? I picked it up, sniffed it and touched it, and saw nothing amiss olfactorily or otherwise. I looked at my chips and thought yes they look a bit paler than usual. Then I seized an individual chip and smelt it. It had indeed an unusual smell. So for good measure, I thrust it a foot away from me, then whisked it back to take it by surprise, inhaling an enormous whiff to assure myself I wasn't dreaming.

'Odd!' I snorted.

I took a gingerly nibble of a second chip and really could not place that astringent, extraordinary taste. I picked up half a dozen more and carefully sniffed and sampled nibbles. They all tasted the same, which was not how they should taste, which I had for the moment forgotten! But *how* should they taste I asked myself at this point? (I also ask myself at *this* point, apropos Tommy Little's *Radio Activity*, how does a chap with 'lucky me' first *know* that he doesn't feel quite right?) Perhaps chips did always taste like this and I was simply misperceiving, my foolish senses were at fault rather than the innocuous food. Then I stole a nervous peek at the fat in which my chips were swimming, and observed that it was blood *queer-looking* stuff, wasn't it just?

Normally when food is sitting in oil, the oil betrays some viscosity, it hangs to the food to a certain extent, caresses and cloaks it rather than just being some flat indifferent medium in which food squats. My chips were *not* being hugged by their surrounding fat. I glared balefully at that fat and said aloud: Christ that fat will never coagulate in a thousand blasted years!

I was about to fetch Klaus when suddenly the rampant bull himself appeared in the kitchen. Characteristically he had lost all his irritation and was beaming at me radiantly as if his imminent factory shift did not exist and as if the recent frustration with his Black Cock was just a silly trifle.

'Ah done some bliddy good wukk!' he boasted loudly, as he helped himself to a large mug of tea from the gallon pot. 'She's a bliddy luffly cock.'

I grinned very weakly, feeling quite ill by now. 'Klaus,' I got out feebly, 'I really appreciate how you make my lunch every day.'

'Gut poy,' he tenderly grinned.

'The polony's fine.' And I hesitated long before criticising his constant kindness. 'But it's your chips I'm worried about.'

Klaus stiffened sharply, instantly sour at my ingratitude. 'Wat?'

'I . . .'

'Theyr bliddy gut tatish, Ett! They cost *ten pop* a stone from Flitt's.'

'I'm sure they did,' I apologised as I fought a shudder of woeful nausea. 'I don't doubt it. But there seems to be something wrong with the oil they're fried in.'

'Öl!' Klaus snapped. 'It's gut öl, Ett! I pie it in pulk from bliddy keshcurry place.'

'But look,' I protested, pointing at the fat on my plate. 'The oil doesn't cling! It doesn't even look like proper oil. And the chips taste very strange if you don't mash them up with the polony. They taste sort of bitter, metallic, altogether very odd.'

My father leered indignantly, then made a truculent speech about pampered children of the Sixties who hadn't known what it was to eat P.O.W sorrel soup that the French guards had first pissed or salivated in. I didn't dare tell Klaus that my chips tasted as if someone had pissed *and* spat on them. Shuddering I offered him a few of the loathsome chips which he seized on and gulped down with absurd voracity, as if he were doing a poignant TV documentary about his war experiences. He yum-yummed a good three seconds before wrinkling up his question-marked face and admitting with pained difficulty they weren't perhaps his best.

'But ah put in bran new öl,' he insisted vehemently. 'I chensh öl in ship pan cos it haff so much crocklings and rubbich in it.'

Ah! I said bitterly to him. If not murderously. He'd *changed* the oil had he? Oil from the cash n'carry place down at Distington? I experienced a sudden ghastly intuition. I thought out loud and asked Klaus, wasn't it customary to buy oil from these discount places in *large plastic containers*?

'Yis,' admitted Klaus in full innocence.

'Don't tell me,' I said enraged, 'where you keep your plastic drum of oil?'

'Why unter yon shink,' he said dimly. 'I keep it wit all plastic drums Yan fer öl. Yan fer white shpirit.'

'White spirit!' I screamed terrified. I leapt from my seat, fanning my mouth aghast. 'In that case you've gone and bloody killed me, you crazy imbecile!'

'Diven't be shtupt, Ett,' he scoffed after leisurely deliberation. 'Hoo could I mistek white shpirit for kukk öl. I'd hev to be blinnt, dumb, daft.'

'Well what other drums have you got in there?' I begged him, my heart thudding as I enjoyed my last half minute of life. 'Apart from cooking oil and white spirit?'

'Only wesh up liquids,' Klaus replied.

'Oh,' I said as immediately I felt my bowels beginning to sublime and simmer like a radioactive meltdown.

'Lemon flafer,' Klaus explained discursively. 'Gut fer skin, Ett. Yeller wash-up liquid wit sitrass dituzhent.'

'The same colour as the cooking oil,' I grimaced. 'Well thank you very much, father. And I thought you'd squeezed a lemon over my lunch for a touch of style! Now, can you ring them up at Tempo and tell them you've incapacitated your son with chips fried in citrus-flavoured *washing-up liquid*.'

'Git away!' said Klaus.

'And he's spending the afternoon on the lavatory. What a pity he's not in hospital.'

'Wat?'

'It would have been helpful if he'd been having a hospital operation. It would have been a really good lemon-flavoured purge.'

Klaus blinked, tittered, walked over and took out two yellow plastic drum drums from under the sink. They had been flanking the white spirit drum and had their labels turned away from us. He turned them round – in all fairness they looked near identical – and I saw that one was labelled vegetable oil and one as lemon detergent liquid.

My father like a great many foreigners knows how to laugh from his very depths. Comedy for him is like a luxurious full-blown fit. While he took his fit I went upstairs and surrendered myself to the stinking pyrotechnics of the 'flying shites' as old Kelly, my boss at Tempo Graphics, always called them.

RADIO ACTIVITY,
EMISSION THE THIRD.

It was a quarter past twelve in Santon Bridge and everyone in the audience, though attentive, was bleary-eyed and looking rather strained. Tommy Little cleared his throat, then energetically resumed.

STAPLETON found himself staggering through the surreal pitch darkness of Tangiers docklands, having shaken off Moulay Ismail by an embarrassingly ungentlemanly tactic. When the stout poet had seized him by the flaps of his Far Eastern anorak and threatened to whisk him off to the police, William had weighed his physique against the celebrity's and decided not to struggle whatever else he did. He had glanced hopelessly at the tubby, phlegmatic cafe proprietor who was watching this cosmopolitan uproar with interest. The street vendors alone were muttering their hoarse support for the Nazarene scarecrow and suggesting that he damage the fat poet in his legendary testicles.

William closed his eyes and prayed for inspiration, opened them smartly and then spat a great gobbet of thick saliva into the Tangerine's face. (*Willum clowst iss eyes, med a laal speech till iss Myakker, opent em faster than t'spid ev bliddy leet (discovert be a Jurman coed Yan Styan) and then went an gien a greet gobfel of slaver reet intil Mooly Ismel's slaverin fyass! He poicked that ard he va'neah droont yon bellerin Tansherin!*) The rag-tag vendors all cheered before scarpering, terrified by the roaring bull of a poet. Blinded, Moulay Ismail released his grip and Stapleton fled like a hare before a lurcher. He raced not quite blindly in the welcoming direction of the sea and the darkness, past the bus and railway stations, puffing and squeaking as he went. Anyone, even an unemployed Moroccan, could have seen William was in an urgent hurry, but despite this various alert young males in their early twenties attempted to block his path and cried out to him in confident English:

'Wonn change money?'

'Halloooooooaaaa, my friend! Good hash, baby!'

'Welcome to Morocco! I have at your dispersal a perfect one star pension, my friend!'

'Welcome! Welcome to Morocco! I bid you welcome to my country! Sir, I have an excellent uncle who runs a quite fascinating carpet museum.'

'Do you?' puffed Wm. sarcastically in Arabic.

'And sells artesanal crafts. Historic carpets! Berber jewellery! Daggers! My uncle is himself personally a Berber. I too am a Berber, personally. I invite you now with Berber hospitality, to come and have some Berber mint tea with my Berber uncle and me.'

'Thank you, but at half past ten, no,' snapped Stapleton in terse slum Arabic.

Ultimately demented by their relentless pestering, their persistent following his flight down the street, he shrieked. '*Imshee! Imshee!*' (*Arrapick fer buck off an boonce*).

'I will *not imshee!*' a fearless, captious young tout informed him in slick American English. 'Why on earth should I *imshee*? It is my country. I can go where I bloody well like! Tell me, my friend, are you simply a pig of a racist? No? Well why don't you want to stop and talk to me, then? Is it simply because I am black, an African? Well, I have a heart like you do, let me tell you, and it can feel rejection just like yours can.'

'Oh bugger off!' William shrieked at him, as the young hustler mercilessly refused to let him continue, actually clinging to his skimpy anorak like an officious policeman.

'And you fuck off too!' the tout bawled back, relinquishing his hold but laughing sardonically. He then recited musically in Yankee English. 'Fuck you! Fuck the sky! Fuck the whole world, my English fucking friend! There is no such thing as being *alone* in Morocco, do you know that? You neurotic First World overlords want to come over here and be left to pig yourselves and have nothing to do with the real Moroccans. Well we are a hospitable people and we refuse to let you be all alone on your own. You should learn how to mix my friend! You could start by dressing less obnoxiously; less like a Harry Carshnow, Ringo Jagger type.'

This speech followed *diminuendo* as William sped on into darker and darker alleys, into an incredibly diffuse maze of warehouses, wharfs and feebly-lit offices. Of course he did not know where the hell he was, other than in what seemed to be a vast and fearsome Red Light area. He saw a couple of young French-speaking sailors linked arm in arm, very drunk. He stopped and secreted himself round the side of a rotting building. He was tempted to speak to them but feared some sort of defensive attack, especially dressed the way he was. He presumed he might look like an albino Moroccan transvestite. His only consolation at the moment was that Moulay Ismail had obviously given the chase up long since. The poet who could crush lesser tarsals, but was hopeless when it came to competitive athletics.

'By the skin of my teeth,' William muttered to himself in Arabic. Then realising he was quite alone he repeated the same thing in English, and at once his native tongue sounded barbarous, incomprehensible and quite abnormal.

'Christ!' he gasped in guttural Arabic. 'What on earth am I to do? Rhoda will be white with worry! I wonder – am I still sitting there in the attic in three dimensions in front of my wireless? In a staring trance, like some West Cumbrian Dervish? Is Rhoda trying right at this minute to wake me? Has she gone for the doctor in desperation? Is . . .'

He went on twittering in this pointless vein for a few minutes. Then he spied what looked like he must be a dockhand sauntering past the warehouses.

The man under the weak wharf lighting appeared a sober enough, unassuming, unworrying enough individual in his early fifties. Night shift cargo-loader Sidi Rahal turned round with a start and shrieked in great terror when he saw what seemed like a white-faced *mejdoub*, all quilted blue and hideous yellow and staring-eyed.

'Don't be put out!' Stapleton comforted him, reassuringly patting him on the back. 'I'm an English tourist, that's all.'

'A tourist!' gaped Sidi Rahal.

'No. No, I'm not. I'm, ah, an English industrial *chemist* who is studying the mode and the effectiveness of the mode of the cargo boat transport of phosphate rock between Tangiers, Morocco and Whitehaven, Cumbria, over in England.'

'*Hamdullah!*' squeaked Sidi Rahal. 'And I thought you were a holy madman.'

'Holy? My wife once dabbled in anthroposophy,' Stapleton explained patiently. 'But she gave all that up once we got our dog. I'm a free-thinker if I'm anything at all.'

'*Bismillah* – why are you wandering on your own here at the dead of night?' Sidi Rahal asked in a worried voice. 'English scientists maybe dress like that in England. Down here though, you're bound to be taken for a homosexual prostitute.'

'Really?' shuddered Stapleton disingenuously.

'You can bet your life.' the dock hand answered. 'I could almost fancy you myself. Especially speaking horrible gypsy Arabic the way you do.'

'The point is,' Stapleton hissed awkwardly, 'I went for a stroll up into town this evening, just for a change from my tape measure, my hygrometer and my graphs. I was sitting up on Rue Sanlucar stuffing myself with first class tagine and beer. Then I had a few excellent almond horns in that fancy bistro place off Rue de la Plage. Then I set off back to the docks here and confound it but I can't find my damn boat! Can you credit that? They all look the same to me in the dark, those ones anchored over there. There are absolutely dozens and dozens aren't there?'

'Ah,' said Sidi Rahal considerately, patting the poor foreigner on the back. 'Nowa problemm!' he added in his two proud words of English. 'Just tell me your boat's name and I'll tell you where it is.' He scratched his dirty old cap reflectively. 'Not that I've ever known any *phosphate* boats to leave from Tangiers.'

'Haven't you?' Stapleton flashed incredulously. 'But you must have. We have a local factory makes detergent phosphates and imports Moroccan substrate. Furthermore, Whitehaven has a major artery called Tangier Street. Now why else would it be called that if it wasn't the connection?'

'You have me there,' shrugged Sidi Rahal earnestly. 'But what was the name of your boat?'

William pulled guiltily at the sleeves of his anorak which refused to become any longer and thus hide his ochre woollens.

'Christ, I've forgotten!' he stammered. 'I've no memory, I really haven't. A very gifted Moroccan poet was telling me just that tonight. And look – there I go again! No, it wasn't Moulay Ismail said that. It was that precocious producer Geoff Beeston back in St Bees.'

'Sint Piz?' repeated Sidi Rahal, fascinated.

'Isn't there a harbour master round here?' Stapleton said. 'Surely he would know where my boat is docked?'

'Abd el Krim,' Sidi Rahal confided importantly, 'is on the late shift. He's got his office down in that direction. I'll take you down to see Abd el Krim. He's a very educated chap, no doubt of that. By the way, have you got a foreign cigarette for me?'

'I'm afraid not,' Stapleton sighed, pulling a cheap pen from out of his cardigan. 'This biro's all I've got in my pockets.'

'My wages are pitiful,' Sidi Rahal scowled, pocketing the biro unabashed. 'I usually smoke the cheapest Moroccan cigarettes, but now and again I get my paws on some good English and American fags. For instance, *Señor Sivas*. Do you know them?'

'I don't smoke,' said Wm. 'But my father used to favour Passing Clouds.'

'M'bssi!Kp'stan! Gul Flq!Kp'stan Ful Strnt! Those are all excellent cigarettes. By the way would you like to buy some kif? I have plenty of contacts. My brother-in-law lives in Al Hoceima.'

Abd el Krim, a handsome, approachable sort of man of about forty, was sitting in a poky little office containing an old fashioned very cumbrous typewriter, a couple of worn old desks, a great collection of reinforced heavy boxes in which some dusty elementary filing system prevailed. He had his small transistor radio on and was half listening to some dull magazine programme while puffing a pensive Marlboro. He looked transiently startled at the sight of a pale, blinking, sheepish Nazarene wearing a most outlandish gear with very foreshortened arms. He thought perhaps Sidi Rahal had captured some drug addict or thief but soon acknowledged that whatever sort of bird this yellow and blue one was, it was most definitely rare.

'I found this man lost round the back of the warehouses back there,' Sidi Rahal explained momentously. 'He's an English expert doing a study of the Moroccan cargo boats carrying fertiliser. He's working on one between here and what was it?'

'Whitehaven,' said Wm. 'A port in Cum – '

'In *Cumbria*?' Abd el Krim asked, as if that area mysteriously meant an enormous amount to him. Equally mysteriously, he spoke with a mixture of eager intelligence and awkward puzzlement. 'Sidi Rahal, fetch the poor gentleman some mint tea! And don't take all night over it, either! Make it with a great deal of extra sugar while you're at it. Why look at him, he seems absolutely exhausted. As if he's been running for his life in fact.'

The dock hand grunted then disappeared for a few minutes, during which Abd el Krim listened with extreme attentiveness to the pale stranger.

'Thank God you've heard of Cumbria,' William said with dazed relief. 'So you at any rate must know of our connection.'

'I know of a connection certainly,' Abd el Krim said kindly, if slightly warily. With gentle ceremony he then offered Wm. Stapleton one of his smuggled Marlboros.

'Marchon,' William breathed with a sigh of relief. He even accepted the cigarette, he felt so direly in need of something soothing. 'Known these days as Allbright and . . .'

'Wilson,' Abd el Krim finished for him, smiling warmly. 'World famous detergents, fatty acids, polymers, solvents, a fantastic chemical cornucopia! Of course I know all about those prodigies!'

'*Hamdullah!*' gurgled Stapleton. 'And fancy meeting someone as up to date as yourself so far from home.'

'And you're a remarkable linguist,' said the harbour master, returning the praises. 'But, forgive me for saying so, for a chemist or sales personnel or whatever it is your field, you look rather ah . . .'

Stapleton blushed and explained that he'd bought this absurd garment in a fit of compassion for some hungry-looking street salesmen. Only after he'd purchased it, had he realised how monstrous a fit it was. Abd el Krim smiled with an expression of partial relief. As if hesitantly to acknowledge that there is always a reasonable explanation for everything if one is patient enough for the mystery to unfold.

'Are you an actual chemist?' he said with an unnervingly candid gaze. 'Or are you conversely some sort of industrial accountant doing an exhaustive study of cost effectiveness?'

Cautious Stapleton, with gaping mouth, would have plumped for the latter. Unfortunately Sidi Rahal returned at that moment and informed Abd el Krim that the stranger had claimed to be a bona-fide chemist.

'That's excellent!' Abd el Krim congratulated him warmly, as if relinquishing all puzzling doubts for the moment. 'A real European scientist, the first I've ever met! You know I hesitate to say it but I'm something of an amateur self-taught myself. I take a dilettantish interest in all sorts of subjects outside navigation and marine transport. I'm especially interested in the entire range of the natural sciences, from woodland ecology via quantitative psychopathology all the way to nuclear spectroscopy.'

'Aha,' Wm. returned with a waxy expression.

'I'd have liked to be a research chemist or physicist myself,' Abd el Krim confided sadly. 'But my parents did not have sufficient means to push me through Rabat University. Instead I have become a humble maritime bureaucrat on a rather static salary. But with sufficient light duties in the small hours of the night to let me read and study all the recent developments. On the quiet that is,' he said hastily, as Sidi Rahal began to smirk. He pointed to a couple of old Scientific Americans which were sitting underneath a heap of figure-strewn papers. 'I read in that one, sir, that our physiological sense of taste might seriously be related to hydrogen-bonding around the surface of the tongue.'

'Aha!' Stapleton got out, with glassy wonderment.

'Allow me to congratulate your wonderful firm immediately!'

'Thank you very much,' sighed Stapleton.

'Your new extraction process is quite remarkable Mr . . .'

'William Stapleton!'

'Your brilliant ketonic purification process, Mr Stapleton!'

'Call me William,' the radio traveller insisted.

'Which you developed yourselves, you artful analytic rogues!'

'You must call me William!'

'To produce very pure, very highly refined phosphoric acid, later to be employed in the demanding British food industry. Instead, of course, of the necessarily crude version you use day to day for the synthesis of your tripolyphosphate detergents.'

'Oh, *do* call me William!'

'Weel-yam,' said Sidi Rahal with difficulty.

'$Ca_3(PO_4)_2$ plus $3H_2SO_4$ . . .' began Abd el Krim with a self-deprecating smile at his amateur's enthusiasm. 'You see,' he grinned, 'how I can balance my valances, Mr Stapleton?'

'Like a Marrakesh juggler,' applauded William, and the apt simile had popped into his head as if by magic.

'Please complete the equation!' Abd el Krim invited the expert warmly.

'Wheel-yum!' repeated Sidi Rahal determinedly.

'Call me William!' Stapleton urged Abd el Krim.

Abd el Krim finished the equation himself with a gesture of benign assent at the expert's incredible largesse. 'Yields $3CaSO_4$ plus $2H_3PO_4$!'

'It is rather neat,' Stapleton purred.

'This clever fellow,' the harbour master explained excitedly to Sidi Rahal, 'attacks our Moroccan substrate with his conc. sulphuric! Thereby yielding him his initially crude phosophoric.'

Sidi Rahal looked admiringly at the clever attacker, whom mentally he saw as the equivalent of a European football star or boxer.

'What's more I believe you find it more convenient to synthesise your own reagent?' Abd el Krim added with a laudatory moue of the lips.

'As a rule,' blurted Wm. 'And up to a point, we try to do just that.'

'Whereas formerly you synthesised your own concentrated sulphuric acid using indigenous English anhydrite mined locally at what was the name of the place?'

William was just about to babble Cogra Moss when Abd el Krim flicked his fingers and answered. 'Sint Piz was the name of the town?'

'St Bees,' chortled Stapleton frothily. 'Of course. Of course we did formerly, Abd el Krim!'

'Sint Piz,' echoed Sidi Rahal proudly. 'He's told me that already.'

'But now,' Abd el Krim concluded with most possessive warmth, 'you import your own liquid sulphur dioxide and synthesise fuming sulphuric acid through the illustrious contact process using platinized asbestos as your favourite catalyst!'

'Our firm choice,' Stapleton admitted. 'We've no time for anything less!' And,' he burbled hastily, 'having established all that and with panegyrics of sincerely-felt laudation on both sides, I'd be very very grateful if you'd tell me where the deuce my boat is. I'm such a scatterbrain, *bismillah*. I've lost my bearings, or my navigational moorings I would say is a truer metaphor! I have to be back in Whitehaven as soon as possible, Abd el Krim.'

'Believe me,' said Abd el Krim, looking most concerned, 'I would point you there personally if I could.'

'What?' said William anxiously. 'No, just draw me a little map and that'll be enough.'

'You wouldn't by any chance be suffering from amnesia,' the harbour master asked him with a tender anxiety, 'or having some kind of reaction to intense overwork?'

'His memory is a bit weak,' Sidi Rahal interrupted proprietorially. 'He was saying to me before people are always complaining he has a mind like a burst water bladder.'

'No I did not!' Wm. protested indignantly. 'What on earth do you mean about amnesia, Abd el Krim? I tell you our firm imports its phosphate rock from your country.'

'Yes,' said Abd el Krim, lifting his shoulders embarrassedly. 'That is certainly true.'

'And my town commemorates the connection by calling one of its incomparable main streets – containing *two* Indian restaurants and the principal bus station – *Tangier* Street,' Stapleton urged with an emphatic shake of his anorak toggle (*t'laal t'wassacomie fer pullen t'hud teet ower t'eed*).

'I believe you if that's the case,' said Abd el Krim politely.

'It is true I tell you!'

'Yes, I accept your statement as scientifically true.'

'Good! So why on earth can't you just direct me to my phosphate boat?'

Abd el Krim sighed as he gingerly responded. 'All I can do is suggest you catch the next train down there?'

'What on earth are you talking about?'

'But if as you say your cargo boat is really moored in Tangiers, I'm afraid I'm completely mystified.'

'A train?' snapped Wm. outraged. 'A train to Whitehaven from Tangiers? Submarine I suppose for the bit across to Spain?'

'To Casablanca,' said Abd el Krim. 'To *Casablanca*, Mr Stapleton.'

'You what?'

'Your firm of worldwide repute imports phosphate rock from *Casablanca*.' Abd el Krim explained patiently and with obvious truthfulness. 'Not from Tangiers, I'm afraid.'

Sidi Rahal added. 'Are you sure you haven't gone and lost your memory, Wheeeeeel-yooooooom?'

BLIP BLIP BLIP BLIP

Stapleton shuddered and shot forward, clutching precariously at Beeston's right arm. Unfortunately his interviewer's tape recorder went flying out of his left hand and it was only the lithe gymnastic lunge from the boy producer which managed to save it from crashing and smashing on the immaculate but rock-hard tiles. Blushing guiltily William saw that they were progressing along an extremely long corridor with many office doors and numerous neatly-fashioned designations on those doors. It reminded Stapleton of the science block of a university or of a London office block devoted to credit, assurances and mercantilism! (My exclamation, E. J. Asbach) (*kridit, shoorns an muck anty lissom*).

'This recorder cost us over two hundred pounds,' Beeston bellowed angrily. 'And you go playing pell-mell and hoopla with it!'

William finally could not help himself. He fumed! At being continuously insulted and demeaned! He was so fed up that he almost shrieked at Beeston he'd just panned in from Africa at breakneck speed! Hence the disorienting tidal motion still apparent under his feet. Not to speak of the quite extraordinary slippiness of these polished tiles along the corridor.

'What's more,' Beeston complained acidly, 'I do think you

might have spruced yourself up a bit more respectably for your next interview. Why in hell are you wearing your disgusting primary school anorak over that diarrhoea cardigan you always sport? Is it some sort of puerile gesture, some talisman of protest? As if to say, I dress topsy-turvy to express my contempt for all this scientific order and technological good-housekeeping?'

William snorted. He stopped short, *spat*, and immediately doffed his coat. He spat again, then stood there energetically ripping the quilted Third World embarrassment to shreds, muttering to his colleague that that was the last time he was going to give in to redundant gestures of kind-heartedness.

'It's not how you are underneath the trappings and vestments,' he announced to the astonished producer. 'It's how you *dress*, how you appear on the surface that impresses the world; Third *and* First Worlds that is. You never spoke truer for once.'

Stapleton hardly needed to be told that they were back inside the alma mater (*almer myatter*) at BNFL. Vague as his recollection of the geography of the last visit was, he realised they were in an entirely different part of the complex, apparently heading towards some sort of recreational area. For they had passed numerous swing doors indicating a succession of canteens, social club offices, and the rooms where countless BNFL sports teams held their committee meetings.

'Lord knows why we have to meet Cumcatch and Wilfred in the *gymnasium*,' Beeston was grumbling with irritable impatience. 'I wasn't aware that either of them went in for vaulting or wall-bars before today.'

William shrugged. He looked rather gloomy as he suggested that Glenridding was wanting this apology made over a game of squash. It was the way they did it in snappy contemporary films, wasn't it? he added dispiritedly. Cut from, *par exemple*, bedroom scene, to two men aggressively pounding a squash court and planning some heist or sting or import of ten million pounds worth of untreated heroin. Focus on squash ball belting against wall, then pan to sweating entrepreneurs burbling in smug confabulation. It was not what you said but how you said it, he went on indignantly; not what you filmed but how you filmed it. Geoff, he wearily added, would know all the equivalent tricks in sound broadcasting.

Start with a gothic canine howling that might have been a radio drama about the Hound of the Baskervilles, but then explain that this is a prize Senior Maiden live before a trail from Spadeadam, Cumbria, where the strategic rockets used to be built.

'Very original that discursive philosophising of yours, 'Beeston murmured sarcastically. 'But once again, you're out of sync., my old local.'

'Oh no I'm not,' his trainee replied testily. 'If anything needs put in sync., it's the tuning knob on my wireless. Which keeps insisting on shifting focus and returning to the same old drivel on local radio.'

'Oh?' said the producer indignantly. 'Returning from what? Penderecki and Ponce on Radio 3?'

'No! Arabic love laments! Broadcast on an African station, as it happens.'

Beeston tushed this arrogant highbrow bent, as he termed it. All too typical also was William's wish to work for an organisation that he at bottom despised; he wasn't the only local radio employee who played that game, ho no! And, he added with profound disapproval, Stapleton was also playing the bloody topsy-turvy idiot once more, talking about tendering apologies when they had already been made last week.

'Did I?' said William with sudden meekness. He trembled once more to infer that he had an unknown past as well as a disturbing present inside this radio time warp.

'An apology so impertinent that Glenridding started shouting at your negative manner and lack of correspondence to the local type. He concluded you weren't really a local, or you wouldn't be so fractious and fond of big words. Then he chuckled and said he'd never met a genuine Cumbrian who knew a single big word unless it was "marmalade" or "paracetamol". Wilf laughed his head off at that and I did too, I thought it was quite a good joke. You took him literally of course, you have no sense of latitude or metaphor. When I saw you turning purple with pique I butted in to say that I know at least three Cumbrians who do know some big words. The other day a Workington lass in the Whitehaven studios said "disorientate". An old Wigton chap in the Carlisle studios said "negotiation". And a bright sixteen year-old clerk we talked to in

Maryport social security offices said "consanguinity" correctly after only three attempts.'

Stapleton interrupted impatiently. 'And now I've come to make Glenridding a second apology, have I?'

'No you haven't,' Beeston spluttered, throwing up his arms. 'And frankly I'm extremely bored by this obsessive game of reminding you what it is you have to do next. And even more bizarre, filling you in on what you've already done!'

Stapleton blushed at the awful, paralysing inadequacy of his radio-memory. Yet a glimmer of angry, proud defiance asserted itself as he retorted: 'I'm surprised, I really am.'

'By what?'

'Because I just happen to recall a recent Pot-Pourri show which interrupted my attentive listening to Fatoma. It was fronted by you, Geoffrey Beeston, of all people.'

'Ah?' said Beeston, moderately sheepishly.

'Just as she was singing most movingly about a lake of her tears so vast that it threatened to drown the whole world like Noah's flood, I was interrupted by *you*, of all people. You then told me ten times in ten minutes that it was respectively 8.20; 8.21; 8.22 . . . all the way through to 8.29. You also told me five times in ten minutes that there was fog on the A66, as if, had I been driving along the same road, I would have failed to notice an outer nebulosity without your pertinacious emphasis. *And you have the gall to talk to me about repetition and faulty memory!*'

'Stapleton,' riposted Beeston pompously. 'We save lives, it's a proven fact. We cheer up moody motorists and urge them to be considerate and cooperative instead of competitive egotists. A cheerful wireless show like mine unites all objectively isolated listeners as a cheerful group with socially cohesive and cheerful aims. And who but a sneering misanthrope like *you* would pass water on that?'

When Stapleton nervously enquired the purpose of this third visit then, he had already guessed the answer. There had been a third emission of radio-activity in the plant, Beeston responded absently. Or rather, what had happened was a quantity of imported Cumbrian radio-plutonium had gone *missing* up at Dounreay, Scotland. Though not in the literal sense Beeston had instantly affirmed.

It was simply a case of banal accountancy; of crass housekeeping; of investigating the kitchen cupboard and reaffirming that yes we actually bought a bit less margarine than we thought we had bought.

'As in a fit of amnesia?' asked Wm. impertinently.

'Up to a point,' Beeston sniffed.

They had reached the very end of the corridor and the door before them was marked Gymnasium. Beeston pushed it open.

They saw what at first sight looked like preparations for a small scale ballet. Of the dancers themselves, there were but three. Of music or other ornamentation, precisely none. As for colourful costumes? There were two familiar managers attired in their workaday hundred pound Burton suits. A third character was sporting oily denims and a waterproof green cloak of the kind worn by rock climbers and fishermen. Fittingly this weather-tanned man who was in his early sixties, had brilliantly white hair, vivid ultramarine eyes and a black peaked cap that could only have been worn by a retired mariner or a jaunty angler. He looked, William decided, almost exactly like that leery old salt who advertises a proprietorial brand of fish fingers on the television.

The ballet was potent in its bluff simplicity. It consisted of Mr Glenridding standing at the near end of the gym, his back to Stapleton and Beeston, facing at the far end the stern scrutiny of the mariner. In between them (*like a laal marra lakin 'pick in t' middle' wit hiss nut seah laal pals*) was little Mr Cumcatch. Cumcatch was apparently suffering a bizarre kind of torment in the form of a perpetual tossing to and fro between the two much bigger dancers. Stapleton watched amazed as Wilfred Glenridding seized hold of Kenneth Cumcatch by the scruff of his pants and neck and then flung him the whole length of the shiny gym (*wit t'laal pins gahin elterskilter as he scuttert an fleed hiss way doon t'chimneysyam*). Kenneth of course went flying with an absurdly pattering haste. Then as soon as the terrified little P.R. man reached the opposite end, he was roughly seized on by the old fisherman who spun him round, grabbed his neck and backside, and tossed him back up the floor to his smirking colleague.

'What on earth is this?' Stapleton asked bemused. 'Is it some sort of anthropological ritual do you think?'

'Mm?' sniffed Beeston.

'This repeated flinging of the P.R. man along the gymnasium floor? I'd gathered that the contractors had their own autochthonous fertility cults: the flinging of the car keys outside the Working Mens Clubs on Wife Swapping Night so I was told. But I'd never have guessed the *managers* went in for all these modish rites and rituals.'

'I doubt it,' purred Beeston wisely. 'I doubt that this is casebook Lévi-Strauss . . .'

'Well it isn't something *erotic* is it?' wondered William blushing. 'I mean we aren't intruding on anything intended for lurid private consumption, are we? It isn't going to get any hotter or bluer or alpha-beta-gamma-fissile-fusive if you follow me?'

'Not that either,' grinned young Beeston. 'Though as a matter of gospel I did once witness Glenridding giving Cumcatch a punitive thrashing on his trousers.'

'You didn't?' mumbled Wm.

'Aha. Wilf once mercilessly paddled Ken after he'd announced off the cuff that he had a few residual worries about some hazard or other. He hauled him off to one side and put him across his knee, while I was there supposedly investigating a recent leak. He told me to switch my machine off and consoled Ken as he trounced him that this was the only effective medicine he knew for a professional man's doubts.'

'What doubts were they exactly?'

'I never learnt directly. I don't think poor Cumcatch could articulate them properly. Hence Wilf's contemptuous belabouring.'

'Poor little wretch! And who on earth is that funny old man who looks like Captain Cat's granda?'

'A Cumbrian fisherman of course. Don't say you don't recognise that square, archetypal fizzog of his?'

'Not immediately I don't.'

'You don't recognise Lars Olufsen?'

'Olufsen? A Swede you mean?'

'He was born in Copenhagen but has lived here, a naturalised local, since 1947. Christ, your town is full of Scandinavians, haven't you noticed the splendid Danish consulate down near the docks? Don't you envy him his motley provenance, however. Ever since that Yorkshire exposé of 1983, Lars's sales of fresh fish and plump cockles caught by the mouth of the outflow pipe have plummeted disastrously. While the quantity of his potential catches, for some reason or other, has been growing exponentially. The irony of that would drive many a weaker Dane to suicide. The poor man even went and ate a jug of his best Sellafield cockles before the TV cameras, cheerfully attesting to their wholesomeness and elixiric quality. 'Løk!' he exclaimed in his mellifluous Scando-Cumbrian to ten million gagging viewers. 'De køkøls *int blody pøson!*'

They were obliged to hush at this point. Because, as if by prior agreement, Wilf and Lars had decided to turn their speechless nuclear ballet into a noisy radio-opera. While Cumcatch was busy wailing and catapulting the distance between his colleague and the fiery Nordic salt, Glenridding burst out into a cavernous, beseeching yet indignant recitatif.

'Ask. And ye shall be given
Which of ye asking for bread would
Haveafathersoinexpressiblyperversewouldofferapiece
Oflakelandgranitetoeat?
*Eh?*Basta!*Yield!*
Como se chiama?
Whose natural radio . . .
Activity tivity tivitytivitytivity TEE VEE TEE
Our criticsverminscumfilthexcrementalpissoirs . . .
But why should I go on? I repeat, why should I go on? I repeat . . .

Then Cumcatch shrieked out from the opposite end of the gym:

'Silt! Silt! Silt!
Sisisisisisisisisisisisllllllllllllltttttttt!

It was not, Stapleton concluded, that Cumcatch was taunting or contradicting Wilf Glenridding, but that something, a libretto writer for example, was forcing him to make this susurrating retort to his colleague's mellow baritone.

'I'm confused,' Stapleton whispered to Beeston. 'What's that fine snakelike mantra issuing from Cumcatch?'

Beeston was enjoying this radio-musical enormously and took some considerable time to respond. 'Oh that? That's a case of these opera characters being stuckfast in something of a profound time warp.'

William raised his eyebrows but felt queerly reassured to learn he wasn't the only one present suffering an insensitive treatment from Old Father Time (*crool Owd Fadder Tim*).

'Lars for example,' Beeston explained, 'has never got beyond 1983 as far as one can gather. He was sixty-three then and apparently he's still sixty-three in 1986, instead of being a hale old sixty-six. Before 1983 he could sell his Ravenglass fish, push it through several national retailers, even export a bit and make a passable living. Now he can sell only to a few steadfast locals straight from his wee boatie. These days pregnant housewives like my Candy Beeston ask where the catch has come from in the wet fish shops, and tend to cheer at responses like 'up Scotland way' in preference to 'down Revglass, lass'. Poor old Ravenglass (*puir owd Revglass!*) Poor old Lars Olufsen. Ken Cumcatch is trilling away about silt because that was another precious commodity crashed on the Stock Exchange in 1983. After that Job Breaking Documentary of Horrid Memory in the same year I mean. Gorgeous little Maryport having these vast disused *silted*-up docks . . .'

Wm. nodded sardonically at being lectured in such a stilted documentary manner about his home county. The significance of that noun 'silt' was slowly coming back to him. He recalled how the Gem of the Solway had intended to dredge its docks of its phenomenal quantities of first class silt-sluther. How this sluther-operation would so to speak pay for itself, as it was marketable to certain construction companies as a quality foundation material for road building. How the pitiless Yorkshire exposé had taken a sample of the silt some twenty five miles upland and upwind of Ibn Hafl, and exposed it to a rather literal-minded Geiger counter. How, as a Radio Eireann producer had phrased it, the demented trilling of the little darling had indicated a broth of a nanoREM. How some of the exquisitely peerless Maryport silt (*a Prezunt ter Lunnon frae Marypot, a makk ev Marypot Rumm Buttur!*) had been dumped by literal-minded environmentalists outside the Houses of Parliament where by law and medical decree it had to be cordoned off by some gingerly bobbies (*A Prezunt frae Cummerlan!*) How therefore the Gem of the Solway had subsequently wished to sue the entrails out of its alma mater (*almer myatter*) lying twenty five miles down the coast.

'A tarnished Gem of the Solway,' Wm. sighed reflectively.

'Poor old Maryport. They've even closed down its bus station, its sole civic possession. It has over thirty per cent unemployment, like Londonderry but without the bombs and excitement.'

He stopped talking as Cumcatch piped in a peevish counter-tenor.

'*When will you two stop flinging me about?*'

Then, as if in obedience to some paradoxical brainwave, Kenneth Cumcatch stopped dead. He slammed the brakes upon his imposed acceleration and stayed stock still in the middle of the gym. Glenridding, as if in rehearsed sequence, flung up his own beefy arms, but instead of freezing into the tableau suggested by his co-musicians, he turned round with upraised hands to face the media.

'Ah, the *media* . . .' he greeted the two young chaps, a little awkwardly.

BLIP BLIP BLIP

END OF EMISSION THE THIRD

Klaus has farcical dealings with policemen both honest and corrupt.

B Y the end of the third emission and by two in the morning the audience was no longer confused. Instead it was noisily awoken to the insult of Little's accusation of its total childlike *ignorance*! Its supposed lack of anything but a fairytale knowledge of the reality of its environment, which is to say, of *itself*! For of course many of these citizens here ate 'outflow pipe' fish with the same devil-may-care gusto as 'Lars Olufsen' from whose non-fairytale prototype they mostly purchased it. I, with gingerly circumspection, consumed only Scotland-imported fish, but in other respects I was twice as ignorant as the naivest old farmer here tonight. For example I, Edward Julius Asbach, was seven years old when the Calder Hall radio-iodine fire took place less than twelve miles from my home. The sole therapeutic instruction offered to my pals and me at the time was to refrain from wearing *Mickey Mouse wristwatches* fitted with luminous (hence radioactive) dials. Conceive to yourselves, I urge you, how Klaus and Ilse and their Cumbrian counterparts got *hold of* this gem of Mickey Mouse preventative medicine, when the rivers, streams, lakes, milk etc were guilty of Lord knows how much unfigurable potence . . .

My own faith in my personal ignorance was virtually limitless until I reached the age of nineteen. It took in not only the delicate state of my environment but also the embarrassing historical allegiances of my immigrant family. I was well into my late teens before I began even to think to ask Klaus about his own personal loyalties before and during the Second World War. As I said, throughout the Fifties and Sixties both he

152

and I were mocked by the local children as Nasties! I was nearly twenty before I began to press my father with some persistence and with numerous rephrasings and repeated articulations of the same awkward questions. Before that time I knew hardly anything about how it actually was for him as a naive young apprentice of racially-mixed parentage.

For instance I was made aware of something as ironical as the inaccuracy of the designation 'Sudetenland'. In much the same way as Wm. Stapleton marvelled at the identificatory indeterminacy of BNFI/ Calder Hall/Windscale/Sellafield, so I learnt that the Sudetenland was never a realisable, pinpointable area of post-Versailles Czechoslovakia. After the Treaty, formerly Austrian Bohemia and Moravia were ceded with their three million German-speaking 'Austrians' to the new Czech republic. These pan-Germanic patriots lived diffusely scattered along the ancient Czech frontiers, yet to speak of their homeland as the Sudetenland was originally at any rate entirely fictional, as the Sudeten mountain range was far away to the east near Troppau.

Nor were Klaus's Sudetens, who were of course the leading actors in the Munich agreement and the excuse for the ultimate invasion of all of Czechoslovakia, always without their understandable human grievances. When in the Twenties Europe was hit by the slump, the Sudetens, mostly engaged in vulnerable light industries like textiles and glass, had almost all their foreign markets destroyed. The Sudeten German population, including of course my father, became hideously impoverished, while to a certain degree the rest of Czechoslovakia was cushioned by a more pragmatic balance of industry and agriculture.

More eye-opening as Klaus cautiously found his Germano-Cumbrian to express it, was the fact that before and between the wars; sovereignty; nationhood; autonomy within Europe; all those very British concepts of a fixed and free nation, were just as fictional as our local autonomy before industrial giants like Little's Ibn Hafl! For when the Austro-Hungarian empire was shuffled and reassorted after 1919, not only were some Austrian Germans 'given away' but the Magyars were flung hither and thither and parcelled into Rumania, Czechoslovakia and Yugoslavia. For-merly Hungarian Slovaks were likewise 'given' to Masaryk's new republic where they could experience themselves as inferior easterners to the westernised Czechs. Both the Slovaks and Sudetens could ultimately, fatefully align themselves with Adolf Hitler against their superior co-nation . . .

I have no wish to treat my readers to a history lesson of interest only to Klaus and son. All I am saying is that at the age of twenty my eyes were opened to the fact that nations, communities, autonomies, and sometimes for that matter, individuals, only exist in brokered power relations to each other. And that the divine sacredness of uni-fied nationhood only exists for the large and the greedy ones. The small and subjugated can be chopped, parcelled, annulled and reinvented at whim.

This seems to me most significant in the light of Tommy Little's satire on the illusory independence, the proud defiance of our humble county. To me at any rate the Bewcastle shepherd seems to be saying that the *alma mater*, Ibn Hafl, only seems a wondrous cure-all for the grief of our gigantic lost estates (eighteenth century Whitehaven; Bessemer's Workington; the Victorian coal industry's Maryport whose silted up docks were big enough once to hold half the world's shipping . . .) In reality, says Little, this generous gift which provides most of the substan-tive work around was placed here by the cunning of absent mandarins, all safely dwelling three hundred and fifty miles to the south.

One fantasises two sample civil service examination questions placed before these promising young mandarins, somewhere around the middle of this century. 1. Where in the United Kingdom are there i) more than credible reserves of fresh water in proximity to limitless unpeopled coastal outlets and ii) sufficient geographical and cultural obscurity – a convenient pair of encircling mountain ranges for example – to allow a possibly controversial industry to be developed on the templates of a related and even more controversial yet strategically imperative industry and iii) which unique community would also have suffered a particularly lengthy period of painful economic decline so that iv) it would accept with open arms any sort of work even up to and including the manufacture of say nerve gas and/or cottage industry anthrax production (not as yet even hypothetically envisaged) and furthermore v) because of the same industrial decline has an exceptionally serene workforce of striking non-militancy and vi) starts with the letter C and ends with the letter D? (remember, this was 1950).

2. Identify the hypothetical proposed industry and give five thousand reasons why by 1986 it will be irreversibly imperative for the nation's welfare?

Nation? Nation phooey, protests Tommy Little!

Our industrial monoliths, our Ibn Hafls, the Bewcastle bard is insinuating, like Northern Ireland or like East and West Pakistan, should never have been invented. As stories they might be tall, but are also fairytale malign. They are impossible of safe resolution by safe alternative structures, because they were designed with the logic of malignant hierophants, by cunning *idiots* with an incalculable capacity to *lie*! All dwelling a million miles away from their gothic fabrications, the last word being interpreted strictly paronomastically . . .

Harum! To return to Klaus stripped of his history, his non-nation-hood and his sociology, but comfily ensconced in his Reliant three-wheeler. The year is 1978:

The history of Klaus's transport: From French horseback; to pedestrian 999 Command; to 1947 Royal Enfield; to AJS and side car of early married years; to the three-wheelers of his maturity. By 1982 he owned his fifth or sixth Reliant which was only about fourth hand, barely twenty years old. Its registration I recall was 883 NNN. Klaus had a mechanic friend Musgrave who in exchange for silk cameos of Talkin and Floutern Tarns and on one occasion a tear-in-eye portrait of his infant son Dennis, would do any amount of maintenance on my father's cars. Twenty years earlier he had provided Klaus with a Fifties Reliant, a painfully new model that is, but with the interesting modification of a 750cc motorbike engine fitted in the front. Thus Klaus's first ever Reliant car had to be *kickstarted*, as it was both bike and car, and my father was remarkably proud of this ambiguous specimen . . .

It happened one late summer evening, eight years ago almost to the very day, the very hour, I note, as I look at the pub clock. Klaus arrived home beaming at about twenty past two to inform us – Ilse and I had been sitting up late happily listening to John McLaughlin and Ornette Coleman – he had just had one of the pleasantest hours of his life with two of the very pleasantest chaps you could meet. Tom and Henry these acquaintances were called, and they had made him a plateful of ham sandwiches and given him numerous mugs of good quality tea. The sandwiches also contained real ham, good thick stuff with 'neah bliddy shlimechelly', and the bread had been smeared with good unsalted butter instead of cheap margarine. It was the fact it was unsalted appealed strongly to my father – it reminded him of Europe proper. Klaus was only half tight and neither Ilse nor I were suprised to hear about his small hours social call at the home of two chaps with names not immediately recognisable. They could have been inebriated art patrons; they might even have been undiscovered anglicised P.O.W.s who wanted to reminisce about incarceration from a parallel if not complementary point of view to Klaus.

'Tom an Henry?' Ilse asked benignly. 'Where they live at? In Workington? Where you gah wit them, Klaus?'

(I do not misrepresent my mother's speech by making it less Teutonic than my father's. She genuinely did talk less like a foreigner, if only because she spoke slower, less expectorantly, and without the wish to prove a dogmatic point every three seconds.)

Klaus did not know *that*, he admitted mysteriously, with an explosive hiccup and an implosive giggle. Probably a Mirehouse or a Woodhouse council house in the suburbs; they had strong 'asser marra' accents that was for sure (incredibly my father always sneered at over-strong local accents, tush-tushed mercilessly at those who spoke 'ower brod'). Nee, he had no idea where they lived, the conversation had not got round to that precise degree of confidence. Klaus had had to tell them where *he* lived however, and it was proof of what affable, thoroughly decent fellows they were, that he had urged them to drop in at his house any time they were passing for a Douwe Egbert and a bite of Hungarian salami.

It took me nearly ten seconds to guess the riddle of Tom and Henry. What had puzzled me was that Klaus had told us earlier he was off to visit his old pal Schachtel through at Workington. Wolfgang Schachtel was another Cumbrian P.O.W., a huge, humorous, though brittle-tempered old man who had worked in the Bessemer plant of the steelworks ever since 1948. Schachtel, originally of Mönchen Gladbach, was famous for the extraordinary speech he had made at Klaus's stag party in 1947, to the uxorious Sudetner and ten young Cumbrian males. What he said in all beaming ignorance was : *'When I fust came to Cummerlan — aboot Englan I knowed fuck-notting. But now I glad to say I know fuck-all!'*

'Would Tom and Henry have happened to wear uniforms?' I asked Klaus brusquely.

My mother looked aghast and flashed at me accusingly for even daring to think such a thought.

'Yis,' Klaus chuckled, sinking into his armchair and igniting his Wee Willem.

'No,' gasped Ilse, quivering with alarm.

'And I tell you wat,' my father purred smugly. 'If lats like Tom an Henry is lookin efter us, we haff nowt ter be flate off! I can walk the Witfen streets at neet an nut botter aboot mukker, rape or tief. I tell you, Ett, the ham was *that* thick! Haff an bliddy inch!'

'Shut up!' my mother shrieked, 'aboot bloody ham!'

'Hah!' laughed my father.

'You was in bloody police steshn? For what was that?'

Klaus waved his hand loftily at her old womanish anxiety. Then he cleared his throat and began. Or rather he did not. He began to talk about unsalted butter. Then he saw his wife's pallid horror turning into blazing irritation. He left off an analysis of the relative merits of saving money by buying 'Anka at Copp' or walking up to 'Finn Farr ter buy Luppek at sixsie tree pee a paket'. He told us instead about Schachtel's new retirement bungalow out at Stainburn, Workington's most delectable suburb. Prosperous Schachtel now had an ornamental mock carriage gas lamp hanging on his carved pine name plate. His beautiful bungalow with concise accuracy was called 'Chankry Laaaa'. They had three of Klaus's silk miniatures hanging above their Skiddaw slate fireplace (Walla Crag, Dove Cottage and 'Krett Kebble'). Wolfgang and Minnie had it a 'byütiful laal palast', no doubt of that. They had a five hundred pound video, five hundred pounds worth of stereo equipment for Wolfgang's superb collection of Nat King Cole, Box Car Willie, Klaus Wunderlich and 'Mass Piegriff' LPs. Their eldest lad Simon was an important manager down at a brand name chocolate firm in 'Shlow' near London. Disclosing which Klaus looked disdainfully at his own offspring, me, who was just at that period negotiating a double mortgage to allow the purchase of the new pottery.

My father and Schachtel had had a first class night of it. Minnie Schachtel had gone out to Clifton W.I. where the competition that week was for 'Best Three Ginger Snaps'. She had cheated in getting Wolfgang, a brilliant amateur cook, to make the gingers to an old Mönchen Gladbach recipe using 'mess an allspiss' instead of just ginger and nutmeg. So, the wife out of the way, Wolfgang had got out some expensive malt whisky, Cardhu, which had been given to him for his birthday the previous week. As well as the Cardhu the old chums had polished off a dozen cans of 'Calspock Speshal'. They had talked of their families as fathers do, Klaus informed me with a look of solemn solicitous gravity. Then about the war, wartime politics, the 'Basstwat' camp, Jakie Baggrow, for whom Klaus now shed a voluminous tear. Poor old Jakie Baggrow of Orthwaite who had counted his sheep by the old fell numeration. *Yan-tyan-teddera-meddera-pimp-sethera-lethera-hovera-dovera -dik*. Klaus in 1946 had counted *yünchüntüdramüdrapompsitralitrahofradofratik*. 'Bumfit' meaning fifteen, he had pronounced 'bümft'. He and Schachtel had chortled and wept about their first pitiful mistakes in the new tongue of the 'Feind'. Schachtel inventing 'fuck-notting' as the antonym of 'fuck-all'! Christ, how they'd roared the pair of them! How they'd laughed like two old Englishmen would not have known how. Till they might have taken myocardial infarctions.

At a half past twelve Klaus had had to be steered and pushed towards his three-wheeler. Earlier, on his way there, he had stopped at an extended hours supermarket to buy a pound of sausages for tomorrow's breakfast. He had also been clutching the envelope with Ilse's competition entry for the TV Times Free Trip to Florida which he had promised to post en route. He was still clutching the letter as well as the bangers when he'd staggered out with Schachtel to his Reliant, still killing himself about the time he'd thought the English for twenty-five was pomperchükt (pimp-a-jigget) just because that was how Jakie Baggrow has counted his gimmer shearlings.

Tottering towards the three-wheeler the two old Germans had passed a large English post box. With loud relief Klaus posted his sausages and continued to clutch Ilse's Florida entry to his tender breast. Laughing now he handed over the envelope upon which obvious signs of unsalted butter were smeared. Ilse scowled and swore at his complacent merriment. Klaus now paused to cachinnate lengthily over the lost sausages, the fine old 'gifthoss' for the Workington postman in four hours time.

Wolfgang had had laudable doubts about letting him drive off so drunk but Klaus had insisted that he could not leave Ilse unprotected in the house these days with all this 'mukkinfendls an sek like'. He told Schachtel that Eddie his son was visiting for the evening but he never stayed overnight these days, always bolting back obsessively to his mouse-ridden house and pottery.

Ilse and I nodded and gaped at each other. So, it was *our* fault that Klaus had had to drink-drive home, instead of sensibly taking the spare bed at Schachtel's Shangrila . . .

Klaus had not been rash though, not a bit of it. He'd reasoned as he waggled down deserted Ramsay Brow (right in the middle of the road admittedly) that he would have to take an inconspicuous back way home. If he went on the Distington road he'd be so much more exposed to public scrutiny, especially as the police cars liked to sit there in the lay-bys spying like 'bliddy camp garts at Basstwat'.

He had calculated that there were two possible devious back routes into Whitehaven. One was to take the main road nearly as far as the Westlands, then up through that C road maze around Gilgarran and Pica, then sidewise back towards Walkmill near Moresby, then down past Rosehill Theatre whereupon you were almost home. It was an ox-bow route adding on about ten miles, yet feasible in its extreme obscurity. The other, the one he finally took, was to snake his way up Washington Street and then follow the Harrington route through some of the choicest of Workington back streets; Annie Pit; the steelworks, past Westfield, etc. Then when you reach Harrington, cut off and take the deserted Lowca road, in the direction of the civic refuse tip. Once reached lovely Lowca and pretty Parton, nip through to the main road, by now two-thirds sobered, and again you are almost *zu Hause*.

It would scarcely have occurred to the soberest or the most cynical that Tom Minto and Henry Mumberson would have used the identical logic. That a nice quiet night might be had by driving their Panda down past Lowca, parking up by the refuse tip for an hour or two. One farm lorry an hour if you were lucky, and time to sit and think and grumble repetitively about their respective problems. They were both aged twenty-six, both married six and a half years, both had three very badly-behaved children and both felt, what was the word? *tied*. Later in the police station they had disclosed some of these personal problems to fatherly Klaus, both young officers fascinated to hear about his artistic talent and sadly rueing the fact they had to apply the same laws of the land to a great painter as they had to a BNFL contractor.

Klaus had waggled his way towards Harrington, clinging painstakingly to the middle of the road. He was so drunk he could not strictly speaking distinguish right from left, so decided to take the median. Miraculously there was no traffic other than pedestrian, the kind that hoots at three-wheelers bestriding the entire carriageway. Klaus had no time to acknowledge their cheers. Once onto the Lowca turn off he accelerated to sixty and soon hit something which had the outline of a sheep. He was tempted to stop and scoop it up into the Reliant as he knew someone who knew someone who rustled mutton off the fells and had contacts with criminal butchers. But the wish to get home to protect Ilse was too powerful, so instead of halting Klaus accelerated to a capacity sixty-eight.

It was at this stage he passed Mumberson and Minto who were dreaming by the rubbish tip. They awoke to see a roaring, farting three-wheeler with illegally half-a-candle-power lights and a cruising speed of what seemed aeronautic. They weren't sure, as they rubbed their lids, if it were a car or an old strategic rocket from North Cumbria. Dazed with hot excitement, Mumberson clumsily reversed into the tall wire gates outside the rubbish tip, scratched the car paintwork badly, then shot off in pursuit. He set off their screaming siren and confidently anticipated the ridiculous vehicle ahead of them coming to an immediate halt.

But Klaus Asbach, like Wm. Stapleton, kept on travelling. It took him at least a minute to accept that it must be a police car saying *Police – Stop*, not the ambulance service having a joke between calls nor the fire brigade ditto. Then another two minutes where he argued with himself that perhaps he could go *faster* than the police, that in any case it was suicidal of them to go at such dangerous speeds on such awkward roads as this one. The bliddy crucks, he gasped to himself indignantly, look at them! they were no better than he was, and at least he had the excuse of being tight on Cardhu and Carlsberg . . .

Klaus evaded pursuit for a whole five minutes, as he waited for a *deus ex machina*. Initially diverted by the comedy of hurtling after this unimpressive quarry, eventually Mumberson was piqued by Minto's sneering at his pansy driving. Henry put his big boot down to eighty-five and on a long and relatively straight stretch cut conclusively in front of the lunatic, my father.

Klaus had to stop of course. He pulled in, halted, waited. He did not tell us as much but I construed that now as he waited for the policemen to walk back and apprehend him, he was seized by an awful unparalleled reminiscence. Of the dreadful hour or so while he had waited to be arrested for his negligence during the sabotage of the bridge by the naquis. Henry Mumberson with his lumbering, threatening gait under a sickle moon just outside Lowca, perhaps put him in mind of fanatical Tischbein who had arrested him for deserting 999 Command. After Mumberson came Minto – there were two of them to interrogate him! They both looked angry! Perhaps they would now beat him up for his recklessness and impudence.

What happened next had never done so in all of Mumberson's experience. He had never even read of such a thing in the manuals, never mind observed it on the plains of Lowca. The squinting old man in the Reliant, at first frozen rigid at his approach, suddenly started up his car! Then, like a Bronson or a Bond, he revved his feeble engine till it screamed, pulled away and shot off up the road regardless!

Now of course they really did want to beat him; anyone would have, even his son or his wife. They galloped back to their ticking patrol car, puffing and swearing unpleasantly. This time Mumberson accelerated to a vengeful ninety while hurtling past the snoring citizens of Parton. The two lawmen had to repeat to themselves that they were being given the slip by a *three-wheeler* in the control of a senile lunatic. Luckily, just as

Parton ended, so did my father's fit of madness. He had not the con-noisseur's madness to lead the law onto the main road. Naturally his sense of guilt was multiplied fifty-fold as he pulled in and surrendered again. At once he noted stony Minto standing squat in the middle of the road, daring him to hit and run a policeman. Mumberson, a big, powerful man about a third of my father's age, ran over and leaned by the Reliant window panting. My father rolled it down and murmured politely:

'Yon's kwit a nice mun.'

Mumberson panted painfully. Ignoring the moon, he asked my father what under say *the sun* he thought he was playing at? Klaus swallowed his saliva, discovered he was temporarily stone sober and earnestly retorted:

'Ah ponickt!'

'Did what?'

'*Ponick*, son! Ah was fillt wit ponick!'

A few months later Klaus was banned from driving for two years. After his trial he always took the works bus and ordered interested art patrons to visit him at his Whitehaven studios. Here as well as accepting initial commissions, he could act as eloquent curator of his entire saleable oeuvre and sometimes make a killing. When he desperately needed new brushes or specialist materials he would ring me at my new pottery and get me to take him through to Carlisle the following day. Of course in a town as big as Carlisle there were a good dozen elderly 'Nasties' and these little outings had to be converted into day long excursions. I would do business in the covered market or visit a couple of city gift shops, then pick up my puddled father from Denton Holme or Botcherby or whichever suburb housed Kupner, Winckelmann, Kästner or – from Stanwix – a delicatessen proprietor called, to everyone's gratification, Theodor Maximilian Scheidt.

The very last outing my father took was in the summer of 1984. This was a harsh year in various respects. My business seemed on the brink of terminal bankruptcy; I had just been embroiled in a painful adulterous affair with one of my nightclass students (her outraged husband, aged twenty-eight and a hai-ki-do virtuoso, as well as threatening me with a javelin through the pottery window, also called me a 'Jurman forren Nazi' and added that the Italians, Belgians, Spanish and French were all

162

just as treacherous, bad, oily and dirty and *fat*.) Klaus of course was very ill by now but was doing his best to keep up appearances, painting during the mornings at least, and determinedly continuing his social visits. He was remarkably grey around the gills, hopelessly emaciated, when I drove him through to the Grey Goat at the hamlet on the Penrith-Alston road and left him there for the afternoon. While he supped with his old publican friend Storey, whose new inn sign he had just completed with slightly less promptitude than formerly, I continued through to Alston and to my astonishment sold three dozen plates to a brand new tourist shop. I was cheered by my own determination and this entrepreneurial flair which presumably I must have inherited from Klaus at the last minute, as it were. Optimistic about acquiring a mortgage on a mortgage on a mortgage, I returned speedily to the Grey Goat at about four o'clock. The hamlet was so remote I expected to see them swilling away fearlessly at the bar. Later though I learnt that George had been raided by plain clothes detectives the year before, whereafter his persistent after hours boozers had been taken into the private parlour.

I had to knock on the back door when there was no reply from the bolted front. Inside, through a side-window, I could see my old father, still ashy-faced, but gaily laughing his head off as he held aloft his pint. He was three quarters tight and was muttering something about 'shut'. Next to him, to my surprise, I saw a fat elderly policeman in uniform, also sipping a pint of lager, also laughing uproariously. I could see two other runty, red-jawed little men who I presumed were regulars. They too, busy on shorts of rum, were also guffawing fit to burst. The presence of the policeman was not outstandingly mystifying; he was obviously the local bobby – not the C.I.D – enjoying an illicit drink or two. Moreover this was the notorious back road from Penrith to The End of the World, and a lone policeman in particular has to have some sort of social life . . .

One thing I noticed about one of the two shrunken locals was that his hands seemed remarkably grubby, as if he had just finished first, back and night shifts on a coal lorry. I tried to peer further into the Storey's parlour but could only catch the knee of someone, probably George, and oddly motionless it looked from this angle. I hammered for half a minute on the window until eventually, after a deal of nervous confabulation and the tubby policeman dodging back and forth into the kitchen, my father came to the window and deigned to recognise his son.

'It's Ett!' I heard him twittering affectionately through the window. He had one of the sunniest faces I'd seen for months, just as if he'd cured himself of his illness. 'It's my laal latt! It's my laal Ettie!'

He unbolted the back door, then throwing down his pint, seized and tenderly kissed me. One of the little chaps followed suit and benignly dealt me a squelchy kiss. I flushed, smiled as best I could, then entered the parlour proper to encounter what looked like the set of a village hall murder drama.

George Storey was sitting slumped on his fireside chair, eyes closed, centre stage. Insensate that is with drunkness rather than death, for he was snoring with that heavy chainsaw sound one associates with beer drunk by the gallon. Above George on a pulley and rope system was suspended Cissie Storey's drying linen, as it had been drizzling all that summer's day. There were six towels, two sheets and even a pair of floral bibs belonging to a visiting grandchild. (Cissie, I later learnt, was out shopping in distant Carlisle with her grandson.)

Klaus, the copper Claude Espersyke, and seedy hamleteers Frank and Sidney resumed their roaring at George on his fireside stool. This was because George was smeared all around his brow, cheeks, chin, temples and the entirety of his bald head with something very like coal dust. He looked like a dead negro minstrel, a slain pierrot of a country publican. The immaculate washing above his head was also plentifully smeared and soiled with blacking of some kind. Then I looked at Sidney's hands again and asked:

'Have you been playing charades together?'

Klaus answered. 'No, wis been playin wit shut!'

Then he explained how George had fallen asleep at half past two while the others were still game for another four or five hours drinking. Espersyke had kindly volunteered to fill up all their glasses from the bar, but as well as proferring no payment to George's till, had tsk tsked disapprovingly at his having to do another man's job, at old George's miserable staying power. He was getting old, Claude lamented (Claude himself was a mere adolescent of sixty-one) and if he or Cissie for that matter carried on as feebly as this they would soon end up sedated in the Old Folks Home at Brampton. Consequently he suggested to Sidney that he might wake him up with say a glass of cold water down the inside front of his trousers, just to fool the old lad that he'd pissed himself disgracefully. Klaus too thought that was 'a bliddy gut gamm' but quiet philosophic Frank had suggested something a great deal more vivid and imaginatively theatrical.

'Powk thee hand up t'chimley, Sidney,' he advised slyly through his rum. 'Powk it up an git thisel a greet hantful of *syeut*.'

Sidney frowned, scowled, then nodded admiringly. He rose, downed his ninth Jamaica rum, rolled up his jacket sleeve and shirt and delved up the chimney like a taciturn vet about to deliver a calf. He scraped away industriously until he had a huge fistful of soot. Then at Frank's discretion he pasted the top of the publican's completely nude skull. Claude Espersyke returning with the pints and rums congratulated him warmly and decided that old Geordie looked like a 'bliddy owld Hindoo Rappie'. Sidney thought that was enough for the time being but the policeman ordered him to rake his hand up the chimney again and do a bit more make-up for their parlour play. Then he asked Klaus if as an artist of county-wide repute, he thought old Geordie had had enough embellishment. Klaus scowled his grey face, shook his head vehemently and said no, '*niffer* in this *wult*', George could easily stand two or three fistfuls more . . .

So Sidney pasted his temples, cheeks and chin, and then Espersyke said it was a shame to leave his neck so clean at back and front. Sidney pasted that too and then looking round asked Klaus if he knew where Geordie and Cissie kept their dusters and 'floor cloots', so that he could clean his hands. Espersyke phlegmatically replied that it was a pity to scratch around for those when Cissie's washing was conveniently dangling above. Sidney took his advice and wiped his hands thoroughly on Mrs Storey's lovely linen. Then they all sat down to congratulate themselves upon their unrepeatable handiwork, these hee-hawing Jackson Pollocks from Blennerbuggery. Then I had come to the window and even Claude had become a little agitated in case it was someone had spotted his police car and wanted him on urgent business.

I looked at old George in his innocent beatitude, his sooty gorgeousness, and began to laugh myself. Which meant that five sane adults were all bursting their guts at this overgrown Water Baby before his first baptism. My father exchanged wild chortles with me his only son, and to judge by his extreme hilarity you wouldn't have guessed he had only months to live. He was screaming with comedy, this unusual homeless foreigner who'd known more hardship and irreconcilables than I could even conceive of. As for Espersyke, those of you my age might recall a curious record played repetitively on the Light Programme for British soldiers posted abroad to Aden, Malaysia and Germany. It was called 'The Laughing Policeman' and it was simply that, the ditty of a supposedly corpulent English policeman who roared and hee-hawed until he and his listeners wept. Espersyke sounded as if he'd spent half his life listening to that 78 record in his police bungalow, patiently perfecting his plagiarism! But at what precisely were we laughing? Whence comes this urge to simple-minded buffoonery? Is it universal, is it twentieth century, is it strictly Cumbrian? I felt as if I were witness to a Cummerlan tyal, as if it had been scripted and rehearsed by outside hands for my benefit. Our laughter grew more and more terrific and even a little terrifying. Our guts ached so and our jaws were so fatigued. I thought if I kept on laughing like this I might go mad, all five of us might end up in Carlisle's Garlands. What pained us most was the fact that old Geordie slept on perfectly regardless, that the object of our mirth knew nothing whatever about it . . .

Circus clowns stopped amusing me by the time I was four, whereas unwitting clowns will make us all screech until we enjoy our death rattles. G. B. Shaw once asked – how do you know that you are not a fool? To be sure at that moment I did not know if I was a fool or not. My father thought I was of course. He was seemingly ignorant of the fact that many people judged *him* to be just that. I knew I was fat and fatness usually makes people laugh, perhaps because it reminds them of the rotundity and placidity of their own chubby babyhood, an idyll of uninterrupted innocent chuckles.

I laughed until anxiety overtook me. It occurred to me that when Cissie returned to this mayhem she would certainly strangle us all. She might be old but she was a huge woman with big wrists and even bigger fists. I had once seen her punish an insolent local – a pretentious self-employed carpenter who'd been grumbling offensively about some lack of 'facilities' in her bar – by seizing him round his neck and mockingly tearing off his toupé! Cissie had waved the horrible hairpiece victoriously aloft while restraining the enraged carpenter with her free hand along the humiliating egg of his pate.

I dragged my father away and watched as Claude and Frank and Sidney dragged themselves drunkenly in our wake. Espersyke became as grave as could be as he entered the fresh air. He announced that he fully intended strolling down here again at six to give Cissie Storey a stern warning. She shouldn't let her greedy husband lead the foolish public into her back parlour for illegal drinking. Why, he pointed out, it was criminal, and he laughed uncontrollably like the laughing policeman. Why she had already been caught by Penrith C.I.D last year hadn't she? She wouldn't have a leg to stand on. Nor would Geordie. He'd likely have two black eyes off Cissie, poor George.

RADIO ACTIVITY,
EMISSION THE FOURTH.

Little resumed.

BLIP BLIP BLIP BLIP!

WHEN Abd el Krim told Stapleton that he'd have to catch a train down to Casablanca, William felt himself blushing with the embarrassment of an impersonator lost in a maze of deceptions. William was not much of a dissimulator in ordinary life and he was not keen on telling untruths to a man as gentle and frank as the one before him. However the disclosure of the truth of his situation to Abd el Krim was just as hazardous as the loophole he'd been given, of claiming amnesia due to being hit – this was Sidi Rahal's perfectly serious suggestion – by a swinging crane. If he told the truth he'd be taken for a lunatic (*if he tellt wat wass reet he'd be tyan fer a hunnert psent preuf immersal*). Even if Abd el Krim were to believe his story about trans-global travel via the radio waves, William would still be no better off as Abd el Krim himself was part of the same untrustworthy time warp (*let's fyass it, Willum wuss fyass ter fyass wit a solpsizm!*) (My exclamation, E. J. Asbach). Abd el Krim could scarcely save him from whatever nonsensical encounters were in store for him either in Tangiers, Casablanca or Ibn Hafl. For instance he might set off now to catch the train down to Casablanca but end up being shunted in the wrong direction towards Ceuta, just at the whim of his radio. In truth the whole thing was a sonic nightmare and the only possible thing to do in a nightmare was to scream, to make some *sound* himself!

Stapleton gave a little scream which sounded more like a

168

soprano cough. Abd el Krim looked at him with pitying concern and asked if he had a cold, now that he had discarded his anorak. Sidi Rahal sententiously murmured that it was bad policy for a foreigner to skimp on overcoats when African nights could be so atrociously cold.

'The irony is,' William mused aloud, 'that I'm so desperately anxious to get home to England. Rhoda would be the first to tell you how I can't stand an unending diet of life in the English provinces. She often suggests a cottage holiday in Devon or Dorset but I insist we go abroad every year to get out of England, away from its appalling unendurable reality, the seven years of biblical famine since spring 1979 when Sultana Margarita came to power (*Willum nidless ter add, felt yon owd clockwukk gadger winin im up agyan!*). Yet once I'm pulled away from the place without my consent, I can't bear it. It would really be best for me in the present circumstances if I could just relax and treat this Moroccan experience as an unexpected vacation. After all, I'm bound by mathematical probability alone, to find my bearings sooner or later.'

Sidi Rahal took the chair that Wm. had vacated and said wryly. 'They can say what they like. But home is where a man's heart is. Weeel-yaaarm.'

'In England,' replied Stapleton, 'that would simply be taken as a sentimental adage, but in your mouth in simple Arabic, Sidi Rahal, it sounds like the most numinous truth.'

'Home,' Abd el Krim said softly, with vatic certainty, 'is an apt metaphor for a person's intimate private reality I do believe.'

Wm. started and looked at him gravely. The word 'reality' had special salutary pregancy for him at the moment.

Abd el Krim went on with the concentrated poetry of a concentrated poet. He certainly did not feel that anyone was winding him up in clockwork fashion. With his lush moustache and in his mild handsomeness he might have been taken for an older brother of Kahlil Gibran.

'Reality is where the heart is, Mr Stapleton! It is not where the head is, Sidi Rahal!'

Sidi Rahal sucked his cheap Moroccan cigarette and disdainfully muttered. 'I lived in Germany for three years, Weel-yam. As a *Gastarbeiter* you know. *Gast* in German means 'guest', the law of opposite meanings in their case. Even the worst Arab knows how to extend some sort of hospitality to a stranger, it is the law of the land. But these lunatics in Germany think that if they don't spit at you, don't ridicule you, and above all don't talk to you, that is the ultimate in hospitality. For those three years in Stuttgart I did not feel like a man, Weel-yam. I did not even feel like the person I am, Sidi Rahal. I felt rather like you the English scientist here looks. Sort of plucked up from the soil, cast about, thrown to the winds and lost his bloody memory into the bargain. Thrown together in a motley mess, like a jumble of rags on a beggar, just like you! In Stuttgart you know I even felt as if my memory were deceiving me, that I had never known what it was to walk around feeling at ease and happy and glad to be alive. Imagine it working and living for three years and for all that time not once really feeling glad to walk down the street whistling and scratching your backside.'

Stapleton who was colouring at being epitomised as a jumbled-up rag-bag of a person, listened painfully attentively to this discursive dockhand.

'I'm confident they're not like that in England,' Abd el Krim interrupted, to spare the foreign chemist's feelings. 'The Germans are a stern officious people and the enemies of the English for two great wars. Undoubtedly they are the temperamental opposites of the English too. I'm confident you would have been kindly treated by all peoples and classes over in England, Sidi Rahal.'

Wm. smiled glassily, thinking of his apprentices and their fearless horror of all things to the east, the west, the north, the south.

BLIP BLIP BLIP BLIP

'We sent it up to Dounreay,' Glenridding rehearsed to an imaginary radio audience, before he would allow Stapleton to switch on his tape-recorder. 'As it was fairly important it was sent Red Star by three fast trains instead of the firm's Honda courier up the A74 and beyond. I saw it despatched myself at the local railway station, in a neat little Jiffy bag, the tiniest one you can buy. It said *Please Handle. Specialist Artwork*. That was to fox potential terrorists, lunatic nationalists like The Manly Sons of Duncan Ban for example. I gave it to the old guard chap Dimmock and he passed it on to his oppo'

Tommy Thwaites at Carlisle and then Tommy passed it on to railwayman Bull McCorquodaile at Glasgow and then it went by the Caithness express courtesy of B.R. employee Tam Dean MhicThomais who lives in a *folie à deux* with his stepsister in a ground floor bedsit in Tomintoul, or so he told Bull who told Thwaites who told Dimmock who told Cumcatch, didn't he Ken?'

'Ye . . .'

'So, Bill, not pronounced Bull, Stapleton. If those amateur Caledonian analysts up there at Dounreay are a few grammes short, then it seems to me we have four feasible hypotheses, from a convenient bird's eye perspective. I incline on balance, hee hee, to opt for either b) or d):

a) Our weighing scales at this end are faulty. (*Oor skyals at Winskell is wrang*).

b) Their weighing scales at their end are wrong. (*Their Dunry skyals up theer is wrang*).

c) Both their and our weighing scales are wrong, but not in invisibly complementary fashion. (*Yah skyal's a bit oot an so is t'uther laal bugger, but twa bliddy wrangs dusn't mek a bliddy reet!*).

d) Either Dimmock, Tommy, Bull or convention-flouting Tam Dean MhicThomais or possibly an alliance (they might just all be covert emigrant members of The Manly Sons of Duncan Ban) are milking off the odd pebble of Po_{238} and selling it to the Mancunian guard Ted Golightly who goes as far as London from Carlisle. Golightly then sells it to ONCF employee Alphonse Schouette who travels the overnight express to Paris. Then it goes with the Kraut guard Ruprecht Castorp as far as Munich. Austroguardperson Trude Brotkrume then lugs the priceless pebble as far as Wien. Then Alihodja Mutavelic by express Jugotrain as far as Skopje. Then Apollo Skiberras as far as Thessalonika. Then Nazim Evren as far as Istanbul. Thence they secretly fly it to Tripoli with Libyan air hostess called what was it, Kenneth?'

'Myrtle,' said Cumcatch with a quiet pride in the efficiency of his memory.

'Eh?' said Glenridding sharply. 'Is that her proper Arabic name?'

'No,' Cumcatch clarified, 'but her father is a Benghazi ecologist who did joint honours at Brunel was it? no, at the New University of Ulster. He christened his first daughter Bog Myrtle Keck Bugloss Hafiq but she chooses to fly by Myrtle.'

'How on earth can you possibly know all these names and connections as far as Libya?' Wm. asked in astonishment.

'That is an official secret,' Wilfred glinted with unstoppable personal pride, as if such a secret and its possession gave him a sense of true and potent hierophancy. 'But, listen, young fellow. Just you make sure that tape recorder of yours is switched off, and I'll tell you now ten mixed, assorted vital state secrets; five strategic and five non-strategic. They'll make your choroid layer pop out of your retina which in turn will pop out of your aqueous humour which should by sympathetic vibration come jumping out of the eyes in your head. By the way I've told all of this to Geoffrey here when I've been in my cups in Beckermet, but he claims none of the local listeners would give a damn either way. But here, just for a taster, listen to this, apprentice producer! Did you know that our much respected Sir To . . .?'

BLIP BLIP BLIP BLIP

Abd el Krim was listening in his office with evident pain as Stapleton assured him that Sidi Rahal would probably get no kinder overall treatment as a guest worker in London than he would in Stuttgart. Why even in the remote northern provinces where there was not even a *theoretical* basis for being a filthy racist, yet the filth remained. Sidi Rahal was nodding shrewdly and remarking that he for his part would have forecast as much.

'If a man isn't white, which is to say off-white, he isn't white,' the little dockhand said firmly. 'Let him throw away his best djellaba and wear a London suit instead. He still isn't the right kind of off white white, Wee-lyarm. Nothing will make him truly a hundred per cent acceptable. Nothing at all. Not even if he's a millionaire. The white skivvies and flunkies will still laugh behind his back and say "aha, rick black cunt".'

'Or rich black fucker,' said Stapleton in choicest gutter Arabic.

'Or rich black get,' sighed Abd el Krim with a deep spiritual sadness in his eyes. (*T'Morkan Arrapick fer 'get' Willum obsurvt wuss syam as Morkan Arrapick fer 'bastud'*).

'And if you're a poor black cuntfuckerget,' concluded Sidi

Rahal, 'you honestly needn't waste your existence. It's better not to exist, when you're walking down the main streets of Stuttgart.'

Then Abd el Krim stirred himself from these pessimistic reflections on the unalterable brutishness of much of human nature, to comment. 'Despite the vinegar of human unkindness's ubiquity (*aw ower t' shop aw at syam time is wat yubikwittie himplies*), the milk of human kindness will remain uncurdled I do believe.'

Wm. looked wistfully into the harbour master's eyes and thought to himself, what I should like to do is the following: Tell this generous-hearted and trustworthy man how I *really* come to be here filling his office with these totally spurious stories about industrial accountancy.

'*Bismillah*, I've been lying to you both!' Stapleton got out at last with a terrible struggle. 'Because I'm not really a peripatetic chemical accountant after all.'

'Oh?' grunted Sidi Rahal, without a huge quantity of deep surprise.

'This will blow you both down with a feather,' Wm. declared with a blush. 'But my actual profession is, listen to this, the teaching of liberal humane attitudes to a large quantity of hopelessly illiberal young Englishmen.'

Sidi Rahal took in that declaration with incredulous sympathy. 'You poor bastard! Is that really how they force you to earn a crust over in England?'

'Oh Mr Stapleton!' gasped Abd el Krim with the tenderest fraternal concern. He actually rose to his feet to salute the depth of William's awful suffering. 'You mean you have a so-called job that is actually a waking nightmare?'

'Yes,' said William sadly. 'You sum it up perfectly.'

'One of those positions where your task is completely imposs-ible and yet you have no option but impotently to perform it year after year?'

'Exactly' said Wm. warmly, for there were not many in this world, sonic or non-sonic, who understood him like Abd el Krim. 'That's *exactly* how it is.'

'Oh poor Weelyarm!' petted Sidi Rahal, patting his back consolingly. 'No wonder you suffer from brainstorms and walk about like a ragtag talking ragtag Arabic! No wonder you lost your bearings in Casablanca docks.'

'I tell them to try and like you Blacks,' spluttered Stapleton in a great fountain of frustration, 'and they throw it in my face! I mention the economics of the Third World and they say they want to discuss *pornography* instead. In fact there are only ever two things they do want to talk about. Pornography and the supernatural! So when I've run out of facts about mesmerism and chiromancy, I lecture them on the difference between objective reasoning and hearsay. They *are* supposed to be scientists after all, the little bastards, they are supposed to know the difference between logical argument and gobshit! Instead of which they raise themselves from their listlessness and bellow out, *exactly*, our country is being overrun by bloody niggers, Will, because my Uncle Eric in Newcastle says he's got two of the animals living in his street!'

'You poor white bastard,' sighed Sidi Rahal. 'But tell me this, Weelyarm, have you ever – let me just fling this in the air as a wild suggestion – have you ever contemplated going self-employed?'

BLIP BLIP BLIP

END OF EMISSION THE FOURTH

Klaus dies of an extremely rare cancer while gasping for a Wee Willem.

I was misled on the question of life expectancy, partly through the vagueness and variance of the experts and partly through the deafness of my father. When I learnt through Ilse that he had 'suddenly' contracted leukaemia, I was already prepared for the worst. A rampant old bull doesn't turn grey as a wintry sky and wretchedly emaciated without good cause. It could scarcely have been alcohol and old age alone.

He was in his hospital bed for six weeks, continuously losing weight and turning from ash grey to snow white to sky grey. It would have been pleasing to say that his spirit remained lively and alert till the last, but it did not. Not that he turned to weeping or terror, but his medication about whose exact nature I was never informed, had the habit of making him dozy, dazed and finally all but comatose. Assured that the very nice lady specialist was doing all she or anyone else could, I turned, as many of us do in crisis, to the public library. There were about twenty suitable works to choose from, as well as general articles in half a dozen sets of encyclopaedias. I pored through the lot – even making *notes* like some dizzy amnesiac who temporarily believed he was studying for an O level – until my head was spinning. I was beset at once with a profusion of colourless acronyms: ALL, CLL, AGL, CGL. Acute and chronic lymphatic and granulolytic leukaemias. All but one of the books explained that the acute forms, most common in small children, proceed very quickly, almost untreatably. In children between the ages of two and fifteen, an American professor declared, leukaemia is the leading cause of death from disease.

Only one of the articles offered any hope, via chemotherapy, to these infants. I consulted the dates of publication and noted that the more recent books had the greater information, but were still divided on the questions of optimism and expectancies.

Klaus, I decided, must be suffering from CLL, or possibly CGL, or there was too a myeloid version. A number of authorities were surprisingly optimistic about the chronic forms. When these arrive in later life, they stated, they needn't directly reduce the life span, when in fact the greatest risk to the patient is from secondary infection. Decreased production of erythrocytes and platelets, owing to swamping by the leucocytes, can result in anaemic weakness, internal bleeding and severe infections. Enlarging of the spleen and lymph nodes can result in the patient presenting himself initially with abdominal pain. Treatment is by chemotherapy or radiotherapy occasionally, including the administration of radioactive substances such as radiophosphorus (I almost wrote Radio Phosphorus). Blood in the urine; nose bleeds; purple patches under the skin? Had Klaus had any of these before they took him into hospital I numbly asked Ilse. A very purple nose yes, she replied quite tearfully. But she like he like me could not swear that wasn't a consequence of his fifty-year affair with alcohol.

And he was, after all, seventy-four years old. He was not a child of seven. And as I've said, some of the authorities believed that CLL and CGL could leave a man virtually unscathed, while others forecast an average expectancy of three to five years.

Klaus vanished into nothing within months. All the experts are agreed that the cause of leukaemia is entirely unknown. All that can safely be said is that there are certain feasible viral models being constructed and that exposure to Radio Activity (I mean radioactivity) can increase the risk of acquiring the disease.

Only once did Ilse and I go together to the hospital. We found that we inhibited each other and even in some way inhibited Klaus. We knew that we had more in common with each other as mother and son than my parents did as husband and wife. We felt his imagined jealousy and loneliness and felt quite helplessly embarrassed. When we visited him separately it was much more satisfactory. The fissile dynamics of my unstable family – the fact our cosmopolitan threesome did not really work – could finally be forgotten.

I did not lecture him overmuch about his last employer. Oh yes, Klaus admitted, the first thing they asked him when he saw the lady specialist was about his place of employment. And then, which part of the plant in particular. Yes, a process worker, and for how long? Aha, Mr Asbach, yes, I see.

'Ah tell t'wumman,' Klaus murmured weakly, 'hoo bliddy appy ah wass at Salatfeld, Ett. Gut money, gut pal, gut clean chop. And t'trink in wukk's klub ony fotty-tree pee a bliddy pint. (In Martian, Ett, is fotty-bliddy-six.)'

'Clean?' I said dazedly.

Of course a *Prozessarbeiter*'s job is a great deal cleaner than the dirty factory shifts he'd known before it. And the money in comparison was lordly. And the continental shifts pleased a man whose own temporal rhythms were adaptable to any shift of day or night. Klaus was continental, diurnal and cataphatic, just like Tommy Little's *Radio Activity*. Klaus had been right there in the thick of it, the radiation. He had been decontaminated four times in the last three years after four avowedly minor accidents.

I didn't bother to argue the question of cause and blame with Klaus. What possible point? He was obviously dying very quickly and was seventy-four years-old and he wouldn't hear a word said against the plant. He knew his reality by *experience*. He knew hardship, hunger, desperation, fear of execution, and to die at seventy-four of leukaemia was virtually 'fuck-notting' if not inescapably 'fuck-all'.

The day before he died he surfaced from his coma and stayed more or less alert for one entire hour. They had moved him into a room of his own full of flowers and a faintly playing Radio 2, the chance of hearing Schachtel's 'Mass Piegriff' or Klaus Wunderlich (a nickname Klaus himself never achieved) being enough to make him request that particular station. He looked through his skin and bone severity at me who was sitting there embarrassedly holding his hand. He watched me with a strange, half-amused look, as if to ask himself something on the lines of, *who* is this fat little thirty-five year-old? Who is he to be so fat and alive while I am so thin and nearly dead?

'Ett,' he managed at last.

I was looking down at his hand as I was far too afraid to look him in his victorious eye, to suffer his ironical scrutiny.

'Ett!'

'Yes!'

'Ett! Lookamee . . .'

I could not. I could not raise my head to look at him! I stared at his other hand, while squeezing his skeletal left paw even harder.

'Ett! Lookamee . . .'

With immense effort I moved my neck inch by inch until I was looking my father full in the face. There I saw my own embarrassment, my own sense of private failure, writ large. I could not, I could never, offer to imitate my father! Who could imitate an original, for God's sake? I couldn't look him in the eye because he was fearless, pig-headed, without doubts, had known the limits and the extremes of survival. While I was fat, shy and unsure and, at the end of the day, a struggling provincial shopkeeper.

'Ett! Lookamee . . .!'

I frowned at him, suddenly irritable. 'I am looking at you!' I said defiantly. Just to let him know that I wasn't really afraid of him, no matter how much he hoped I was!

'Naw!' my father croaked. 'Naw! *Lookamee! Lookme! Krebs, um Gottes Willen!*'

Even I understood that much German. He was talking about leukaemia, not asking me to look at him.

'Lookamee,' he went on quietly, 'is neah bliddy choke, Ett.'

'No,' I agreed hoarsely. 'No it isn't, Klaus.'

Then he turned to me with the fullest, most yearning, most affecting of his faces. Just then it seemed to me he was going to disclose to me a great secret revelation, of repressed paternal tenderness perhaps. He was going to tell me with the first honest candour that he was sad that as father and son we had ceased to connect once I'd changed my short trousers for long ones. That despite me going my own daft way towards pottery and indigence, that he respected me. That notwithstanding the fact I was in my mid-thirties, unmarried, and that he would sadly die 'grunbarnlos', he did not see me as an oddity, or a freak. I was his son, he loved, respected, was proud of me.

'Ett!'

'Yes, Dad!'

'Ett, lookamee . . . lookamee is neah choke! An know why?'

'No,' I sighed with the disappointment of cruel anticlimax. (Yet still, at bottom, hopeful of a final tender admission, a kind goodbye from my dying father. He would get round to a moving, beneficent speech before he died, surely he would.)

'Is coss they won't let me smyeuk me bliddy Wee Willems, Ett! *An az bustin fer a bliddy smook!*'

I turned to him with nothing short of murder in my eyes! He did not see it, thank God!

'Ett! Luckme!'

I stared obstinately at the coverlet, the hospital linen. I was damned if I would hear any more about the cruelty of his cancer so . . . so prosaically stated.

'Ett!' he barked at me indignantly. 'Bliddy luckme! *Schau mich an!*'

I started and looked up at him. So this time it really was an imperative! *Schau doch!*

'An stop squizzin me bliddy hand so hart!' he complained. 'Me hand all shkin, bone, and you squizz an it *hutt!* Look me! Luck! Go out here, Ett, an doon till laal pepper chop at bottom theer! They sell Wee Willem nice an ship wit discont . . .'

Doomed to die in ten hours, Klaus wanted to save twopence on his Wee Willems . . .

And on his death certificate it did not read CLL nor CGL nor chronic myeloid leukaemia nor anything remotely similar. It was a very long, very Hellenic medical word which remarkably I've forgotten. It was a kind of *Blutkrebs*, a very rare one, a very rare blood cancer indeed. But then my father was a very rare bird, a Sudetner-Cumbrian, the only one in the whole world! And when I went to the very kind specialist for clarification she insisted that she had told my father exactly what type of cancer he had. She smiled sympathetically, reflectively, then suggested that as she had listed the similarities between this disease and certain *acute* leukaemias, my father might have misheard and assumed it was straightforward leukaemia after all.

She also told me that the only known cause of Klaus's very rare cancer was ionising radiation. And after a year they gave Ilse some compensation in an out-of-court settlement involving no admission whatever of their culpability. But it was less than what the pigeons got. And as birds, surely pigeons are not that rare.

RADIO ACTIVITY,
EMISSION THE FIFTH.

By a quarter to four a.m., Tommy Little was preparing for the climax of his story. I had less than half an inch of my last C90 left! I was fighting sleep, like all the rest of us awestruck listeners. Still, we were awaiting a great climax, something like a 'sezmick trimmer' from the Bewcastle shepherd, even if only in the safe metaphorical sense. He resumed.

'. . . and had been involved in the child prostitution ring,' Glenridding whispered grimly, 'but had managed to escape MI5's surveillance and hence prosecution, because of an interesting concatenation of diplomatic embarrassments. Strange how *embarrassment* in the form of embarrassing secrets connects things up, what; things which otherwise would remain quite randomly unintelligible. You see, Stapleton, if Sir T. had been exposed that would in turn have implicated distinguished former statesman Sir D. whose first cousin Angela is related to Lady P. of Dalquhidder, who as we all know while maintaining international Fascist connections during the Second World War and exchanging coded Lesbian *billet doux* with Hitler's Bayerische cousin Brigitte, was intimately related to the then Lord . . .'

BLIP BLIP BLIP!

'. . . absolutely everything in the world is structurally related,' amateur scientist Abd el Krim was explaining to professional ignoramus Sidi Rahal who stood with open mouth, while his superior tried to explain about the Nature of Gases as a helpful logical model for understanding absolutely everything in the universe. 'You see, Sidi Rahal, when you have a gas contained in a jar – this was discovered by a genius of a Cumbrian scientist called John Dalton – the gas is composed of discrete molecules (*diskrit mollykells*). Nonetheless, when we use the word "discrete", we are in a sense telling lies.'

'Lies?' frowned Sidi Rahal. 'Like Weelyarm here about his job?'

Abd el Krim ignored that analogy. 'No. Lies in the scientific, empirical sense. The point is, Sidi Rahal, that the molecules are not really independent. It is impossible to separate one and say that it makes any sense in isolation, that it has any identity, any scientific or even existential reality.'

'Re-al-ity,' echoed Sidi Rahal, impressed by his own total incomprehension. 'Very good!'

'Each molecule, Sidi Rahal, only exists in terms of its relations to the others. (*Yah mollykell owny meks any sense in tumms ev hoo it gits on wit t'uther bliddy mollykells!*) In terms of mutual attraction and repulsion, of magnetic forces between them. Each molecule is therefore strictly determined by contingency and contiguity. By being related to the others in the first place! No molecule and hence no man is an island! We may take by analogy the Hindu caste system, Sidi Rahal, as I took it yesterday when I came across a twelve year-old copy of the *International Sociological Review* poking out of the dustbins of the local high school. No Hindu, apparently, is of any importance in isolation but only in terms of his place, his sociological complementarity.'

'Exactly,' sniffed Sidi Rahal, with his thumbs on his hips.

'How he fits in the whole. His caste relations with others are his prime reality. No Hindu is an island, Sidi Rahal. Away at one sweep with the lunatic modern (*they wuss diffrent in t'owd days, asser!*) Western notion of bourgeois individuality. We Orientals know the difference. We are a happily structural body, we are not an aggregate of loners. We respect our relations, sanctified by religious authority and moral law. And even science proves us right. Take any isolated problem, any isolated problematic phenomenon of anywhere in the world, past or present, Sidi Rahal.'

'O.K.,' said Sidi Rahal. 'Nowa problem, Abd el Krim.'

'Then extrapolate, resolve like a force diagram, into the several components which are the extrapolated relations of the problem. An isolated poet with his environment. A limbless beggar in the market place of his town. A fine new hygienic nuclear power station within its dirty depressed community. Become a bird, become a pigeon Sidi Rahal, and stare down at the magnetic forces, the lines of attraction and repulsion.'

'Nowwa problemm,' said Sidi Rahal, beaming.

(*But Siddy Rattle wuss leein! Coss he dint unnerstan a bliddy wurrd that Abdul Cream had sed for t'past ten minnits!*)

BLIP BLIP BLIP!

Then William was blinded and simultaneously felt a great whirring in his ears accompanied by a tumult of voices speaking in about thirty thousand different languages. For what felt like a solid half hour he experienced something on the lines of a shamanistic trance (*like yan ev them triepol gadgers swayin an mutterin in a laal fit, an ev cworse chunterin away wit iss gods while iss dyurn it*). He noted in among the primeval babel several Amerindian dialects where they not only had the singular and plural but verb forms for the dual; two warriors and a roan stallion; two youths and a piebald mare; one brave and his dog, and so on. But no, he didn't really want to end up in the studios of Sioux Reservation Community Radio, not even if they spoke perfect American English at will. Weaving through the Amerindian he also heard strains of quite intelligible modern Bulgarian. It was a news bulletin giving trenchant details of unparalleled domestic steel production for 1985, coupled with a historico-statistical survey of same since 1949. As well as wanting to steer clear of metallurgical misapprehensions in Sofia, Wm. also was made anxious by the thought that Radios Sofia and Sioux were surely *short wave* transmissions, weren't they? And if they were, then that seemed to indicate that not only was his tuning knob defective but that the wave band selector, that corrugated object on the side of his wireless on which he regularly sprained his thumb whenever he changed bands, was also possibly moving to and fro! Which seemed to him impossible. If it needed his twelve stones weight expressed through right thumb and forefinger to achieve a wave change, then it was impossible that it would spontaneously be doing so. All he could imagine was that Rhoda, on entering the vacant attic and wishing to turn the radio off, had seized upon the wrong knob.

He was freed from these frantic ratiocinations (*rashysinasians; hammerin away at thee brain wit yah bit ev reasunin, an than anuther laal bit ev pondrus spekylashun*) by the shamanistic possession suddenly exhausting itself completely. William emitted a screech of a particularly arcane sonic wavelength known only as a rule to Kirghiz shamans. He screeched in the radio-ether (*he went an skrarked in t'ready either*) and felt himself dissolving in a puff of smoke. Then he screeched again and opened his eyes wide.

The first object he saw when emerging from his trance was Papcastle. Papcastle who was observing this re-emergence in the attic den without extravagant emotion. He cocked his ears mildly (*they reckun mungrels hess a mottycombe ev suppernetcheral pooer, but yon Papkassl wuss mare like a piss-fyasst Recker-bite, if owt*). He looked with a shudder from his dog to his table upon which sat his erstwhile favourite toy. His radio was still going and lo and behold it was Geoff Beeston chattering cheerily about roadworks on the A5086 at Mockerkin Tarn! And yes, even better than Beeston's vapid cheeriness, was the fact that Beeston existed solely inside the radio, it was activity *inside* the radio, not inside/adjacent/subtending/engulfing/assuming hitherto separate/discrete/independent/self-contained listener William Stapleton . . .

Wm. looked at the clock. It was exactly the time it had been when he'd last been listening to Fatoma. Not a minute, probably not even a second had elapsed while he'd been on his radio peregrinations! Still, even in his incandescent relief at being safely back home again, he soon found Beeston's grating voice unbearable and stepped towards his wireless to retune it back to Radio Tangiers, and presumably heart-rending Fatoma.

He was just about to seize on that defective little knob, when he thought better of it. The fantasy of cyclical repetition, of a sonic nightmare without end, was just too much to contemplate. Instead he walked towards his attic window, pushed it open, and gazed down to make sure no intruder nor animal should be standing in the back yard below. Then he walked back and picked up his two-stones transmitter and lugged it gasping back to the open window.

Then he heaved it out with something of a tear in his sentimental breast. Wm.'s wireless descended with uniform acceleration at thirty two feet per second per second and then made the most hideous crash imaginable. Stapleton looked down and saw a grave and garish vandalism. There below him lay a heap of splinters and a mess of shattered valves. It ought to have brought Rhoda running up to the attic but then her husband recalled that she was out doing a WEA class on Cowper and Crabbe. Or was it 'Castle and Cross'? What a tale he would have to tell her! Yet it was so fantastic, he decided there and then it needed some careful rehearsal, a little forethought, editing, structuring, some elementary literary treatment to prevent it sounding like the ravings of a strictly local lunatic.

He decided to rehearse his story in front of Papcastle, in garbled unedited form. He took hold of Papcastle's front paws, sat him on his haunches and then related non-stop for twenty-five minutes. He did not spare the dog the intimate existential details of his traveller's panic, estrangement, deracination, ear-stopping (and unplugging) and vertigo. They were so to speak the ontological substratum (*leuk at Jack Poll Sarty's byeuk aboot bean summat an then aboot bean nowt at aw*) upon which the radio drama had been pinned. As for the Glenriddings and the Cumcatches you'd never exclude beggars like that from your nightmares, they were all strictly functional (for he'd been listening hard to Abd el Krim) and structural, a needful bit part in a ready-established drama. Likewise the braggadocio of Moulay Ismail. They were as common as muck in nightmares, these boastful, violent, swaggering, insincere, over-virile, sophistic bullies. But at least they were open about their nastiness, naive and to that extent theoretically forgivable. The only characters he had liked at all in his radio drama had been Fatoma, Abd el Krim and Sidi Rahal. A singer, a harbour master and a Tangiers dockhand. All of them locals, but only if you were born and bred in Tangiers. But what a singer! What an Al-Biruni of an autodidact, who could balance his valences like a Marrakesh juggler! What a sane, down to earth dockhand who'd decided it was better to be a penniless *Heimatlandarbeiter* than a rich *Gastarbeiter* in Stuttgart!

Stapleton slowly replaced Papcastle's paws on the ground. His radio epic was finished. And that had been a most valuable rehearsal; his tale would be so much more cogent and gripping and credible when he declaimed it to Rhoda after her 'Cowper and Crabbe' or her 'Castle and Cross'.

As Papcastle's feet touched the ground the mongrel dog yawned with an expression of supercilious boredom. Then he leant back on his haunches, produced and lit a menthol cigarette stolen from Rhoda's packet, and said sneeringly to his master:

'Let me give you some advice, should I, boss? I happened to be reading a concise edition of Aesop's fables last month. Passably diverted by it, last week I surreptitiously borrowed Rhoda's copy of La Fontaine, and I have to break it to you, Willy, that as a fabulist, you have a remarkably long way to go! You know squire, chief, master, the problem with all you frustrated Technical college teachers is that you all seem to fancy yourselves as something on the lines of potentially great writers, painter, sculptors, or whatever. I repeat, or *whatever*! Instead of just accepting that you're frustrated second rate provincial pedagogues who'd be far better off going to Hai-Ki-Do classes when your wives trot off to do their Hatha Yoga. Look at me! Look at me and you might learn *something*, William! I'm a mongrel and that's all I am, thank God. My other half is kept strictly under wraps. Yet I happen to read moderately taxing literature on the quiet and . . .'

William kicked old Papcastle. Papcastle yelped, dropped his menthol cigarette, and then relapsed into meek canine fawning. Stapleton told his dog that if ever he started talking and worse smoking again like a human, he'd get the same treatment as his old valve wireless. Then he walked downstairs to watch an inconclusive documentary about Chernobyl upon the television.

END OF EMISSION THE FIFTH

END OF TOMMY LITTLE'S RADIO ACTIVITY

EPILOGUE.

Asbach revealed as a fantastic liar; John Murray as a colossal dupe.

AFTER our rendezvous in Tognarelli's, Asbach spent another six months polishing up his *Radio Activity*, before returning it to me, his unsalaried agent, at my address here near the Roman Wall. He had looked somewhat askance when I disclosed my intended move, and indeed asked me what I had against my birthplace the industrial west. I told him it was more or less the same as William Stapleton had against it, though I tended not to broadcast – no pun intended – it. Then he asked me was it possibly intended to get away from proximity to Ibn Hafl, to which I replied that that was only true in very small part.

'Good,' he smiled. 'Because up there you're nice and handy for its little brother, Chapel Cross. Small but not beautiful, to contradict Schumacher.'

This hadn't previously occurred to me, nor that I would be living quite close to innocently ecclesiastic Bewcastle Cross, the home area of the bardic shepherd Tommy Little.

We kept sporadically in touch by telephone after that, until on ringing him at both home and pottery during the late summer of 1988 I discovered that both his phones had become disconnected. They remained so for day after day. I wrote to him after a fortnight or so of this, but received no reply. At last I rang up British Telecom and learnt that Asbach had left both his shop and domestic premises and had given his forwarding address c/o Poste Restante in an extraordinarily famous town in West

187

Germany. At which point the rashly garrulous telephonist swallowed and absolutely refused to disclose its name. So I thought eventually of ringing up his mother Ilse (who was after all an Austrian) but soon discovered that she was unlisted in the telephone directory.

I was contemplating the drive through to see her, when one August afternoon I happened to bump into a journalist acquaintance in the middle of Carlisle. He was through from the west to do some shorthand and wordprocessing studies in the county seat, and suggested that we go into the Lanes and have a cup of coffee in the mock-Dickensian tea shop.

There I mentioned my problem about locating the West Cumbrian potter Asbach and the fact that evidently he had moved abroad without notice.

'Ah,' said my old acquaintance, whose offices were about a quarter of a mile from Asbach's shop. 'I know all about that. His shop's been closed for the past six weeks. There's a For Sale notice in the window. And the window of his warehouse next door has all been whited over.'

'As it happened, I'm doing him a good turn regarding a book he wants to have published. So I'm wondering why the hell he's buggered off to Germany without telling me.'

'Didn't you know about Asbach?' the journalist said. With great pleasure what was more, at disclosing a startling revelation. 'It was all over last week's edition of my rag. He's presently locked up in a top security jail in Prague.'

'He's *what*?'

'Aha. The poor bastard must have had a fantastic brainstorm of some sort. The whole episode reads like twenty year old Len Deighton, you'd hardly think it was possible in 1988. Too good to be true after hound trails and Sella-bloody-field. But hang on. It has been on the national television, never mind in the local eye. Don't you ever watch the TV news for Christ's sake?'

'Only when I'm ill,' I said stunned.

'Well what about *The Guardian?*'

'Every day. But I've not seen anything about a local potter being jailed in communist Czechoslovakia.'

'Mm. Well if you'd read every inch of the foreign news you'd have learnt that West Cumbrian potter Asbach secretly packed his bags, settled his affairs, and travelled abroad to take up residence in a downbeat hotel in would you believe it, Bayreuth?'

'Oh my God,' I said, with a sudden dreadful inkling.

'Yes indeed. Whereupon, having secured a holiday visa for Czechoslovakia he checked out of his hotel and hired a car. With this car he drove past the German checkpoint, up as far as the booth of the Czech officials. There he leapt out and in a feverish voice demanded immediate political asylum.'

'The crazy idiot!'

'With the most amazing cock and bull story – according to the German press agency – about wanting to settle down as a potter cum cobbler cum radio and TV repairs shop proprietor. In a very specific Czech town near the German border. Before the war it was called something or other I've forgotten.'

'Probably Asch. Which was in the former Egerland. In the former Nazi Sudetenland that is.'

'I thought you said you hadn't read the papers?'

'No, but this has some bearing on this book of his. For which I'm acting now as I suppose executor. I guessed the bit about Asch from reading his book.' (And I thought to myself, Good God, talk about trying to appease the father he could never manage to get to accept him heart and soul.)

'Really?' said the newspaperman. 'Well you should sell it to the nationals. They would probably give you an absolute fortune.'

'But what happened after that?' I said anxiously. 'After his request to become self-employed in rural Czechoslovakia?'

'Well they hauled E. J. straight off to Prague for interrogation of course. They thought he was mad. As does the F.O. here and anyone else who has had recent dealings with him. He's been there about a month and they're talking about repatriating him in exchange for some Czech we have down at Wormwood Scrubs.'

'Meaning who?' I said angrily. 'Who thinks Edward Asbach is crazy? I've had dealings with him and he's as sane as . . . as . . .'

I went on to outline the details of his *Radio Activity*. The journalist showed a strong interest in the colourful bits about his father Klaus – confirming the factual truth about his pub paintings and his legendary character – but when I got to describing the Santon Bridge competition of two years previous, I saw him begin to chuckle with what seemed in the context quite an extravagant mirth.

'It's not that funny,' I said balefully. 'Not what I've just said.'

'Ah but yes it bloody is! You should enter the competition yourself, you really should! Biggest Liar In The World Competition, 1986! The year of Chernobyl indeed!'

'Well, 1986 was the year of Chernobyl!'

'Listen, *I* was at the Biggest Liar In The World Competition in 1986! I wrote it up for my bloody old paper as I have been doing for the past ten years!'

'Oh?' I said, feeling incipiently, stickily foolish. 'Oh did you?'

'Yes. I was there! I saw and suffered it all from start to finish. Do you, an intelligent man, seriously believe that there was some sort of hippy shepherd, some allegorical Hermann Hesse figure burbling away for seven hours to a riveted bunch of asser marra process workers and farm yakkers? About Sellafield? Why they'd have lynched him after seven minutes never mind seven hours. And about Tangiers? (Where's that marra, is it just ower t'fells next till Mungrisdale?). I was there from start to finish. It lasted one and a half hours in total. There was no Tommy Little I can assure you! I wish the hell there had been your Mr Weston and his Cummerlan Tyal. But no, it was as transcendentally tedious as it is every year.'

'Was it?' I said weakly. 'And what about Harrison Beatty and Fidler Armstrong and Tucker Hodgson?'

'Them? Oh yes they were there. They're there every damn year. That's part if not all of the problem.'

'Oh thank God for that,' I said with inane relief. 'Talking about igglywiggly worms; piles up the backside and, what was it: Fiery Jack scalding the ballocks?'

My acquaintance screwed up his face. 'Yes. Quite possibly. Yes I believe the old buggers were talking about that kind of thing.'

'But no Tommy Little. No *Radio Activity*?'

'What do you think?' asked my acquaintance.

> *John Murray,*
> *near the Roman Wall,*
> *Cumbria.*

Brief addendum with regard to cataclysmic changes in East Europe since 1989.

Asbach stayed immured in his Prague jail until the peaceful Czech revolution freed him and allowed him to go home. He chose instead to settle in former Asch, just as he had originally intended. Ilse his mother visits him out there at least once a year.

As for the question of Good Housekeeping at all the remaining 'Shurnobbles', not to speak of Klaus's 'Salatfeld', nothing whatever has changed he tells me in his regular letters.

> *John Murray,*
> *near the same Roman Wall,*
> *Cumbria.*